CORRUPT

ELENA M. REYES

SUMMARY:

♠

Corruption is the key to success, and I'm the collector of all debts.

The first time I laid eyes on my little flower, she was dressed up—a beautiful temptation wrapped in perfection that I wanted to own. Possess. To take away from the pseudo perfect life that reeks of the narcissistic chains—the demands—holding her down.

She's a pawn.

The daughter of my enemy.

Solimar Quintero is the future Mrs. Alejandro Lucas and doesn't even know it. She isn't aware that the man she smiles at—taunts to come closer—is a criminal. A wanted man. A nightmare for his enemies and her future.

I always get what I want.

CORRUPT
(Beautiful Sinner Series) Spin-Off
was written by Elena M. Reyes
Copyright 2020 ©Elena M. Reyes

Cover design by: T.E. Black Designs
Editor: Marti Lynch

Publication Date: August 12th, 2020

Genre: FICTION/Romance/Erotica Suspense/New Adult

ACKNOWLEDGMENTS

Before we get to the book and its yumminess, I'd like to thank each and every one of you that's messaged, sent positive thoughts, and wished for a speedy recover after my emergency gallbladder surgery back in July. I know this book took longer than what we all wanted, but you guys have been amazing, and all but demanded that I rest and recoup. It's been a rough month, I won't deny that, but I do feel so much better today than on my last E.R. visit.

Your kind words, dear readers, have made me smile and pushed me to write this book, even if it was a little at a time. Your outpouring of love and tips for dealing with a life without a gallbladder have been amazing. From the bottom of this crazy Latina's heart, THANK YOU SO MUCH. For your patience. For your support. For letting me continue to live my dream.

I love you.

Elena XoXo

Glossary of Spanish and Colombian Slang:

Guaro/Aguardiente = Anise Flavored Liqueur Made from Sugarcane
This Is Mostly Consumed Neat or Over Ice.

Güevon = Asshole

Berraco = You're A Legend or Amazing

Culicagado = Shit head

Parce = Friend

Listo = Ready, Okay, or Cool

Tombo = Cops

Sicario = Hitman

Billete or Platica = Money

Q'hubo = What's Up

Fresco = Chilled or Relaxed

Hagale = Okay or Let's Do It.

Patron = Boss

Hijueputa = Son of A Bitch

Coma Mierda = Eat Shit

Preciosa = Precious

Bailarina = Dancer

Coqueta = Coquette

Callese = Shut Up

Mijo/Mija = Son/Daughter

CONTENTS

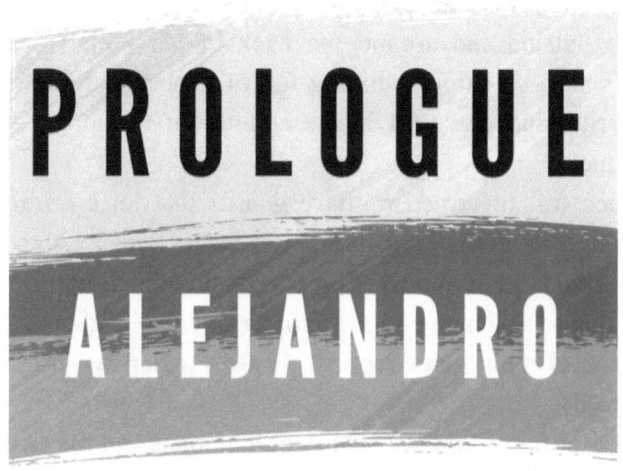

PROLOGUE
ALEJANDRO

HER SKIN IS soft beneath my roughened fingertips—yielding—almost melting against me as I pull her in closer. Chest to chest. Lips hovering. She's like the finest of silks: a motherfucking delicacy that's been awaiting my arrival and only yearns to please her owner.

Because she's given herself to me.

Every sigh. Every moan. Every inch of her has always been meant for this brute of a man.

Solimar Quintero is my prize. A reward and coveted possession.

"Please, Alejandro. I need you." Those beautifully hooded, light grey eyes are on my cognac-colored ones, and in them I see the same emotions reflected back at me. Hunger. Anticipation. A nearly knee-buckling yearning that makes me throb against her midsection.

"Say it, Solimar." My voice is rough, the grip on her right thigh tightening—fingers digging in as I place one leg over my hip and then the other; I have her right where she should always be...

In my arms, her heat against my cock.

We're outside and around the back of her home for the time being. It's an ostentatious building full of history and memories that only the rich and powerful in the country of Columbia remember with fondness.

A place full of armed military guards that let a criminal walk right through its door for a little extra cash. Because they need it. Because giving your family a good life in this country is pricey. Because they'd rather live to see another day than end up as an anecdote on the evening news reporting on my extensive list of crimes and misdeeds.

The beautiful girl pinned by my body moans and the sweet sound settles on the tip of my cock, causing me to flex against her heat. It also pulls a hiss from me, my teeth gritting as I look down and take in how the short, white cotton summer dress has shimmied up and over her hips. Those supple thighs tremble and my fingers on her right one dig in deeper, harder as I enjoy the sinful view.

Matching panties in the same color as her dress.

Goose bumps all along her skin.

Soft satin clinging to the top of her mound.

Indecent perfection.

I shift my upper body back, just enough to get a better look.

She's wet; the evidence makes the almost translucent material completely see-through.

My eyes snap up when a needy whimper passes through her lips. "Answer me," I hiss out, my lip curling up at the corner in a barely-contained snarl. The hunger in my tone is palpable, and so is the need to mark her. To leave bruises behind that'll remind her of me every time she looks in the mirror over the next few days.

Of my touch. Of the pleasure only I can give her.

My inhale is her soft exhale as she shifts a little closer. Just a tiny bit. Her small hands cling to my shirt as her hips gyrate, back arching against the large wall behind her so she can feel every hard inch of me against her core. All that stands between me and her pussy is two thin layers of clothing, and I remove the first without a second thought.

Without giving a fuck about whose house I'm at.

Without giving a fuck about who could see us.

Skimming my fingers to her hip, I grip the thin ribbon there and pull, tearing the delicate satin bow before doing the same to the other side. The material slips down over her mound, exposing the very top of her clit, but gets trapped between us.

A breath gets caught in her chest and her eyes close. "Papi, I... *please!*"

"Answer me, Preciosa." Lower, my hand encounters her round and firm asscheek. I palm the flesh—squeeze hard enough to make her mewl before gripping the tattered remnants of her panties and tugging them off.

A single pull and she hisses, shaking in my hold when the delicate material rubs harshly over her sex. My little Solimar bites down on her bottom lip, withholding the moans that want to slip free so we —I—don't get caught, and I find the action sweet. Endearing.

Pointless, since I'm here to end it all tonight. To collect on a fifteen-year-old debt.

Eyes on hers, I toss them aside and return to her flesh. Two fingers follow the path down to her back entrance, and I add just enough pressure to cause her legs to shake. For her breathing to stutter. For a motherfucking rush of wetness to coat her inner thighs, and then I brush my fingers a little lower to collect the sweet drips.

There's no resistance from her as I return and slip the tip of my middle finger inside. None when I go a little deeper to my knuckle; pumping it in and out a few times before adding a second.

Solimar's lips part, but no words come out. Instead, her arms wrap around my neck and pull us closer together. She's baiting me with the subtle rubbing of those tight little pebbled nipples over my pecs, and I bite back the groan that threatens to escape.

It's a silent plea from her with a hint of *please* that makes my mouth water. *My little flower always begs so prettily.* Quietly or on a scream, she's stunning when offering:

Her life. Her love. Her loyalty.

A commitment without an expiration date. A future that removes her past and those who reside in it. Those who will become nothing more than a faint memory.

Because I'm her future. Her only.

"Say. It." The need to bury myself deep within her is near maddening, and more so when her tight little asshole flutters around my fingers. It's the only place I haven't taken her. The last bit of her body left for me to claim, and it will happen before the end of the night.

"I belong to you, Alejandro. Only you," she moans out, lips parting just enough to see the tip of her tongue peek out. I follow how she slides it over the very edge of her Cupid's bow. How her cheeks flush and perspiration beads over her neck. "I love you."

At those words, my eyes close and I breathe in deeply. A unique scent—her sweet, sugary decadence surrounds me, and I groan. I feel her heat. Her wetness as it seeps through and caresses my cock through my slacks sans underwear.

I'm hard for her.

I'm throbbing.

I'm hers.

My hips snap forward and my dick rubs against the juncture of her thighs, finger slipping a bit deeper inside her puckered hole. There are a few *por favor* and *mas,* but I don't give in. Not yet.

Not here.

We'll be leaving soon enough.

That thought sobers me at once and after another pump, I slip from inside her tightness. My forehead falls to hers and my eyes snap open just as she whines, her pretty mouth set in a pout. "None of that."

"But Alejandro—"

I silence her with a quick and harsh kiss. "I love you, too."

Her grey eyes sparkle, bottom lip trembling. "Baby, I—"

The click of a single gun interrupts our moment, and I shift my head minutely to catch the sight of the asshole responsible. It's a man I loathe. Someone whose history with my family brought us full circle and to this moment.

"You're a dead man, Lucas," he says, and my smirk only deepens.

"Good evening, Señor Presidente."

1

ALEJANDRO

F *ifteen years ago...*

I AWAKE WITH A START.

I'm sweating. In a daze. Unable to comprehend the sudden ambush of loud noises surrounding me and look toward the alarm clock on my nightstand. It reads twenty past eight in the morning, and I try to remember if there's anything to warrant such a rude upstart—a project starting on the grounds or equipment arriving—but come up empty.

There's too much racket to pinpoint. Too much commotion to discern what it is, but it confuses me, and everything seems off—

almost eerie until the loud sound of what I think is a truck meeting a wall forces me out of my bed.

My house shakes and I stumble, fighting to find my equilibrium as more shouting comes from the opposite side of our family home. This large, Spanish-style house with over a hundred acres surrounding the two-story, eight-bedroom structure has several large cultivating fields whose product is known worldwide. And, because of its size, it should be nearly impossible for me to hear what sounds like a war zone outside this bedroom.

None of these noises are familiar in the everyday life of a rancher. None of what they're shouting makes sense.

"What the fuck is going on?" I mutter, grabbing on to the door's handle and pulling it open. Another loud boom reverberates, and the corridor feels as though it's trembling, the picture frames— photographs of my siblings and me from over the years—meeting their demise against the terrazzo floor. *Are we having an earthquake? Fuck, my family!* Shards of glass fly across the floor and as I rush toward the stairs to head down, I cut the bottom of my foot on a rather large piece.

It digs deep, slicing through flesh that now gapes and bleeds all over the floor. Rivulets rush to the surface, staining the stone flooring and my pajama bottoms, but I don't stop to inspect.

Ignoring the sting, I hiss with each step I take, leaving bloody footprints behind. My eyes shift from side to side the closer to the landing I get, noises becoming more defined, and I grip the handrail hard as a barrage of bullets sound as though they're being fired close by. Too close.

The voices are louder now, and male. The gunfire is clearer, and it's heavy artillery.

One of the few things you learn while helping your father out in the fields is how to protect yourself from various dangers. Shooting a gun is something I do well, my aim better than my old man's, and it's because he took the time to teach us to respect the weapon and not fear it.

There are thieves, wild animals—drug smugglers—and sometimes tough decisions have to be made.

Diosito, please don't let that be here. Please protect us.

I search for my family and come up empty. No one is around, and after turning the corner that leads toward the kitchen and back entrance, I come to a dead stop. Heart clenching. Stomach churning.

My mother is on the floor and on her knees, clinging to my five-year-old sister in her arms. Her eyes are on mine, though, and yet she looks a hundred miles away.

Her face is a pallid color. Her fear is palpable.

Choking me.

And it's the motherfucking pain in her expression that makes me fall to my knees and crawl across to where she sits completely still. I want to hug her, shake her, but instead take a moment to slow my breathing and erratic heartbeat. Freaking out could lead from a bad decision to a stupid mistake.

"Mamita?" I call out after a minute or two but get no response. Nothing. Just blankness. If it weren't for the rise and fall of her chest, I'd think she was dead. "Ma, what's going on? Where's Dad?" Nada, and as I take her in fully, I notice the blood on her right arm and the rapidly forming bruise on her cheek. "Who did this? What the hell happened?"

My sister, Lourdes, cries, unable to focus on me or help, and her wails are so loud they hurt. However, she's okay from what I can see, but my mother isn't. Blood seeps from her arm, the rivulets pooling on the floor beneath us as the trickles become a puddle.

I check her, lifting the short sleeve of her top, and find only one bullet wound and it's a graze. Deep, but not with an actual entry, and everywhere else she seems physically okay. *She's in shock.*

"Mamita, quien?" I try again, softer, my eyes darting past us where the firing of bullets has ceased. "Please, at the very least get up and hide. I'll find the others."

Her lips part but no sound comes out. Instead, she whimpers, and

9

it's the most agony-filled sound I've ever heard. It's also at that moment that multiple heavy footsteps enter our home.

I don't know how many. I don't know why these people are here or where my father and older brother are.

We're not criminals. We're law-abiding citizens. Our family is successful: the owners of one of the largest coffee plantations in the country.

Then, there are my father's political ambitions and ideals, something that isn't a secret. He's a respected member of the community, and with the backing of the middle and lower class of the country, a front runner as a presidential candidate in this year's elections.

However, from the look of the men inside our home, none of that matters...

Colombia's military is inside our house and armed to the teeth; their faces are expressionless as they surround us between the living room and the corridor that leads to our kitchen. Their rifles are pointed at us, their fingers on the trigger.

For a few minutes, no one speaks. They don't so much as blink.

It's a waiting game.

To see if we do anything that will justify the shooting.

Something that becomes apparent a few seconds later as the general walks in with my father and brother behind him. Both of them are being dragged, their bruised bodies nearly passed out.

My reaction is instant. Not even my mother's sudden yell to stop makes me pause.

The bastard closest to me and to the right doesn't have time to react as I ram his legs with my shoulder, knocking him off balance. And as he stumbles, the gun slips from his hold and I grab it while dodging a lazy punch. His reaction time is slow, almost unskilled and unprepared as I take possession of the weapon.

A bullet to his hand also stops him from trying to grapple with me and save face.

It's quiet now as I look up, turning with the rifle high so that I'm between my mother and these assholes. They'd have to kill me to hurt her, and in that same spirit, I point the barrel toward the general.

There's a bit of surprise on his face, maybe even a touch of respect as he holds his hands up to stop his men from shooting me where I kneel.

"Put the gun down, Alejandro. Let's not be messy," he says, taking a step closer but stopping when I pull the trigger again. This time, I lodge a bullet into the shoulder of the man holding my father's battered body. He lets him go, staggering back as my dad's chest hits the floor.

He's not getting up but is breathing, and that brings a bit of relief to me. Not that I show it; if anything, I'm more focused now.

"Get out of my home. Now."

"Disrespect me again, culicagado..." the smirk on his face as he takes a puff from his cigar pisses me off "...and I'll personally kill your mother."

"Threaten her ever again, and the next bullet goes between your eyes." My response makes him laugh, but I fire again. This time, to his left and hitting the soldier holding my brother by the hair in his chest. He drops Emiliano who is less hurt, just a split lip and swollen eye, falling back and onto his ass. My brother moves too, crawling toward me at a slow pace and with the now dead soldier's weapon. "Mamita, leave."

"She stays—"

"I didn't ask you, General. She leaves."

"You insolent güevon," he sneers, looking toward my father's banged up form and then back at me. The dislike in his expression can't be missed, and yet, I don't know this man. Other than the ranking badge on his uniform, he's a stranger to me. To us. "You're pushing your luck."

"And you, my patience." From behind me, I sense movement and tilt my head just enough to see my mother exit with my sister in her arms. Our nation's military doesn't stop her or complain, which I'm thankful for, and I only hope she leaves through the underground bunker on the other side of the house. It's a passageway my grandfather installed when he sat at the head of Cafe' Paisa and the Finca was raided by thieves looking for money and jewelry. "Why are you here?"

"We're here to take possession of this plantation and all assets within, by decree of President Almendra after Jose Quintero brought forth evidence of your father's misdeed. Your family's cartel operations are finished, Alejandro."

"What the hell did you just say?" I hiss out, confusion coloring my tone as the gun slips a bit in my hold. Before it falls, though, I tighten my grip. "Are you crazy? Cartel? We're coffee growers."

"Not according to the Colombian government, Alejandro. As the order signed by the current president with the help of the future leader of the republic states, we are to destroy your family's operations and apprehend your father, exposing him for the low-life criminal he is."

2
ALEJANDRO

F *our months ago...*

"PATRON, WE'RE HERE," Geronimo says from behind the wheel of my armored SUV as he parks in front of a popular club in Bogota. The capital city is alive tonight, busy with an idiot or five laughing—celebrating the end of a long, grueling workweek.

It's the Friday-night ritual that every country has: get paid and get drunk.

To forget. To live. To fucking breathe.

In and out like a revolving door, they slip inside of restaurants and bars like tired sheep in this busy intersection at the heart of our colorful capital. Many of them look my convoy's way. Many of them wonder who's inside and if I'm famous.

Moreover, being curious is a stupid habit. A manageable trait if a person applies itself.

Because the curiosity that humans must feed at all costs—even if it ends with their fearful gaze staring at the barrel of a gun—is avoidable.

Many of them ignore that we're born with two very dominating responses to danger, though. They pay no mind to their fight or flight instincts; to that nagging little voice inside their heads screaming—blaring signals to run and hide.

It's there for a fucking reason.

It's there to warn. To save you.

Because true evil doesn't hide. It doesn't cower. A killer will expose himself without a second thought or remorse because he knows most will never pick up on the cues. They understand how a soft smile and pleasant demeanor are far greater weapons than any knife could ever be.

And I am the definition of the wrong person to cross. The monster that plays from the shadows and rules in the light.

"Thank you." My eyes shift to his in the rearview mirror, and I hold back a chuckle when his gaze drops immediately. But then again, he's always been a very respectful man who takes his job seriously. It's the reason why he's been around almost as long as my second-in-command. "Please have all vehicles moved to my private parking area for the evening, and then join me inside."

"Si, señor," he responds immediately, and I nod before opening the car door. Tonight he's my right hand while Chiquito, the owner of that title, travels to Barranquilla on a retrieval assignment.

Exiting, I stretch my neck from side to side while adjusting the weapon hidden beneath my suit blazer. It's nestled within a custom leather holster, a favorite within my collection for a very particular reason. This Cabot 1911 Sacromonte is a beautiful piece with a story to match, but more than being a one-of-a-kind gun, its accuracy and handle make it my favorite go-to weapon.

I'm not one to waste bullets, and this makes me what I consider to be a *conscious* killer.

Good for the environment as each bullet within its magazine equals a body.

Doors open and close following my lead as I look up at the marquee. *Codicia* is a large building—unavoidable as it sits at the center of this busy intersection.

It's an upscale establishment. Ostentatious and seductive. An undercover whore house without *technically* serving women to the lowlifes that frequent this restaurant/bar. It's the owner's business plan to draw out those with lower morals and deep pockets, a smart move in most instances by the son of a foreign leader—an ally of Colombia—that resides here instead of his native Venezuela.

Signio Cortez has immunity to play, and play he does with members of both sexes.

It's also common knowledge that the young and corruptible go out in droves each weekend after studying all week. Those that attend prestigious universities with never-ending cash flows are his favorite clientele, especially if you're a beautiful woman.

It's his draw. The lure for most men.

Because you only get into a place like this via two options: personal invitation or blackmail.

The clientele here is sexually liberated. Ambiguous. Depraved. And more importantly, they love to host the corrupt of this nation for a fee under the protection of the owner's political attachments.

It's the product of one hand washing the other as the two pompous presidents hope for a union between children.

Blind eyes are turned. No questions asked.

Walking up the steps, I'm greeted by a large man holding the door open for my group. He's tall, bald, and full of homemade tattoos that remind me of the jailhouse style many convicts get while serving time.

"Buenas noches, Mr. Lucas," he says, but I don't reply. Instead, I nod and head for the lobby, pausing at the podium where a voluptuous woman in a carnival-themed outfit stands. Her tanned body is on full display, her curves accentuated by the shiny fabric of her sequined bralette and minuscule skirt.

"Good to see you again, *Guapo*." Her voice is meant to be sultry, a seduction to all that enter, and I find myself giving her nothing more than a blank stare. "Room three is ready, and your guests are seated."

"Gracias."

"Do you need an escort?" she simpers. The implication is there, and it's not to walk me toward my reserved seating. At my nonresponse and lack of interest, she arches her back a bit so the barely-there fabric of her top stretches across each tit, exposing the very edge of her areola. "I'd be more than willing to take on any role you wish tonight."

"No." It's a cut-and-dried response, one she doesn't seem to like by the slight narrowing of her eyes, and as I turn to walk through the main floor's main entrance, her arm shoots out. Those long, fake nails grip my arm. A *no-no*, and I make it a point of setting my gaze on her hand, then her. "Watch it."

"Don't be so grumpy." She giggles as if this is a game while cocking her hip to the right. An act to draw my attention but is useless on me. One of my soldiers, though, releases a low whistle behind me, causing her smile to widen before I hold a hand up to silence him. I don't care who of the four made the unwise decision; they'll all suffer if it happens again. I also don't need to look back to know the point has been made. "Those men can wait a moment or two. There's no need to rush in, *Patron*."

The bottom half of her outfit is nothing more than a band across her hips to cover the split between her thighs. And more importantly —a fact she's missing in her forwardness—it does nothing for me. *She* does nothing for me, not so much as a cock twitch, and I smirk when her attempt at a coquettish smile drops.

It's also not lost on me that she called me boss.

Like her, many have tried, and all have failed. I'm not a relationship kind of man.

I do not need sentimental attachments.

"Señorita, I suggest you keep those hands to yourself. Understood?"

"I'm just being—"

"A holdup," I finish for her, taking her hand off my arm none too gently and letting it drop at her side. "Hagale, and open the door.

"Alejandro, I..." she trails off then, lips snapping shut when I part my jacket to show her my personal escorts. Her face drains of all color. Her fear becomes palpable and I breathe in deeply, enjoying her terror.

I let her see a glimpse of the demon that resides within.

An enemy she should never meet.

"I'm going to pretend the last few minutes never happened..." my voice is low, but in the calm lies the threat "...that you never took liberties that aren't yours to take. Don't do it again." The woman has gone mute, eyes wide and with a slight shake. "Do you understand? Nod your head if you do." She does, and I snap my fingers; one of the men traveling with me walks past us and opens the door leading to the dining room's main floor. "Now, have yourself a pleasant evening."

My men follow as I walk down a dimly lit hallway that leads to a large circular space at the center of the building with five doors. This locale has three floors; each one pays homage to a different kind of need, from fine dining to themes. From music to age. There is a segregation of tastes, but one thing doesn't wane...

Sex is a unifying factor. A mutual appreciation.

There's no shame within these walls.

No moral code.

It's the perfect place for the meeting about to take place; a good amount of space between each private dining room that secures privacy. No one comes in without you requesting their service unless you're a guest.

The one I've reserved for the night is the largest.

No noise can be heard. Not even the servers can be seen.

And more importantly, it has a private exit.

Coming to a stop in front of the third door, I tap the card reader with the key and the light blinks green, letting me push the large wooden structure open. The room's lighting is dim, but my eyes take in the three faces sitting in my direct line of sight.

Three men. Two strangers. And all sitting silently on one side of the long table at the center of the large room.

They are here for me.

Because my poppy and marijuana plantations across four countries dominate several markets across the globe, from pharmaceutical companies to large cartel organizations south of the United States border. From morphine and codeine production to the harsher and illegal forms, I control ninety percent of the world's supply.

I'm a privatized general with a personal army to match, but more importantly, the citizens of Colombia are loyal to those that feed and take care of their own.

I do both, and fairly. I reward their devotion.

Something the government hates me for, but will not rise against an armed enemy.

An asshole with no remorse and his own militia. An anti-establishment movement whose sole purpose is to bring forth the demise of the Quintero family's reign and corruption. Two generations have served as president—served themselves to the country's riches—and while I'll never be a saint, I do plan to destroy them.

"Is the Jurado ready to deliver their verdict?" the judge asks the jurors sitting to the left of him. There are not many here. Just five people: three women and two men, and they're each older than dirt.

I also don't like the way they look at us.

At my father.

As if we're scum. Criminals.

There's judgment in their eyes—it's been there since before the opening statements were heard. Not that Dad's pro-bono lawyer did much to help him. The guy had no witnesses, no proof of this being a setup, or much of a defense. Nothing.

The malparido didn't even let my father take the stand to defend himself.

The slightly younger of the grandpas stands. His frail frame shakes a bit as he clears his throat. "On the charges brought forth by the country of Colombia for the production, sale, and trafficking of cocaine..." my mother grips my hand hard, fingernails breaking the skin there while my older brother sits forward to grip my dad's shoulder "...we find the defendant to be guilty."

There's a wail from beside me. It's gut-wrenching and breaks my heart, but more than that, it cements the hate that's been brewing within. My veins turn ice-cold with each hurt-filled cry my mother releases. With the way my father's shoulders drop and he shudders with his anguish.

At that moment, I vow to kill every person who had a hand in this.

"On the charges of blackmail and attempted murder of President Quintero, we find the defendant...guilty."

"Oh God," Mom whimpers, and it's taking everything in me to stay right where I am. To not jump over the short divider they have in place to separate the attorneys and defendant from their family and break each of their necks.

"Mamita, controlece. Dad needs us to be strong," I whisper low, taking my hand from hers so I can wrap my arm around her shoulders, pulling her tightly against my side. "We'll fight this. Do whatever needs to be done, but he will come home."

She nods, choking back her pain. "Okay."

That *okay* has been my driving force since that day. It's the reason why there's a bullet in my house for each male member of the Quintero family and a mass grave where they can rot. A death sentence Jose Quintero himself brought down upon his family's head the moment he stole and destroyed mine.

That hijueputa will be the last to die. He'll watch his son and brother take their last breaths.

"Q'hubo, Lucas? Where have you been hiding?" Daniel says the moment I fully step inside, and my guards take their place in front of each closed entrance and exit. He stands from his seat after placing his drink down on the table where there are a few bottles of rum, vodka, and Aguardiente open, the latter being my first drink of choice to start my evening. "Where's your shadow?"

The *shadow* would be my general, Chiquito Salazar; an ex-military operative for the state that's been under my employ for a decade working his way up the ranks, and also married his cousin, Mariana, without the family's knowledge. He's forty-five to her twenty-four, something that didn't sit well with Daniel, especially since they met through him when she moved back from Tampa less than nineteen months ago.

Since he knows Chiquito's been a womanizer in the past and this is his third marriage due to infidelities.

And while I trust both men, they know better than to bring discord to my operations. Those familial arguments are best saved for holidays and reunions.

"On his way back from picking up a new business partner."

"Are you taking them out for a game of soccer?" The asshole smirks, understanding the meaning behind the words, and extends his hand out while those sitting to his left await my response. To show their amusement or run. Because while I don't know them personally; they know me. Know of my no-patience reputation.

Of my cruelty. Of my shoot-first policy.

I keep my expression neutral. "Something like that."

"By the way, the kiddo's been asking about his uncle *Nando*."

Taking my time, I leave him hanging while pulling my two 1911s out and place them down atop the table, the barrels facing Daniel. He doesn't flinch. My guests don't so much as breathe.

"Tell him patience is a virtue."

"You try telling that to a spoiled five-year-old." He laughs, and I let out a chuckle of my own before taking the offered hand. One tug, and I pull him half over the glass tabletop and slap his shoulder. I've known him since primary school, and when my family fell from grace and my father was arrested, his parents took us in without a second thought.

No questions asked. No rebukes.

It's why I brought him along with me after establishing my business. It's why he can joke with me, and I'd never kill the fucker for it. I'd shoot him, but never end his life.

Daniel Armando is the head of my transport division in Cali and is loyal. A brother.

"You're just jealous he thinks I'm the coolest person alive."

He pulls back, the grin on his face letting me know he's about to say something stupid. "That little shit has bad taste and doesn't know any better, güevon."

The men at this table don't know our past. They're here because I need someone with their specific skill to do a job for me, and it's comical how their eyes widen. How they move back in their seats, their chairs scraping against the floor roughly, screeching as they do.

"Relax." One word and they ease up, the tension in their bodies less prominent. "We're all friends here tonight."

Taking my seat opposite of Daniel, I pour myself a drink while giving Geronimo a barely perceptible nod as he enters a minute later. He takes his place a few feet behind me, hand on his gun.

There's a beat of silence that follows. They look at me while I wait. Their body language is nervous while they find the courage to ask me the one question that's been bothering them since Daniel extended my invitation.

And it's the pudgier of the two that sits forward a bit after a few minutes, sweat beading at his brow. "Mr. Lucas, why are we here? How can we be of assistance?"

"You're here because I need a hacker."

3

ALEJANDRO

"**N**OTHING IS OFF-LIMITS for the right price," the same fucker answers quickly, and it's clear he's the more vocal of the two. He's intrigued, curious, while his friend's posture becomes falsely more relaxed.

Another mistake.

They shouldn't trust me. Not even for a split second.

The two culicagados sitting in front of me are no older than twenty, but with a reputation that precedes them.

They're not natives to my country. They're not from this continent. The two fugitives are American citizens hiding in Colombia while evading what other nations call justice.

Jason Thorn and Shawn Bosdell are wanted men in both the US and Europe for high-profile cybercrimes. For selling confidential information on the black market belonging to the clientele of Fortune 500 companies spanning the globe.

From L.A. to Shanghai.

From London to Mexico.

It's cost each company trying to right these wrongs millions. It's also made their governments scared. And they should be…

Secrets never stay hidden for long.

Moreover, they did this multiple times—raking in millions, which they stupidly spent back home somewhere in the Midwest. From farm boys to crashing Ferraris and buying anything and everything they could get their hands on.

They broke the golden rule to never draw attention. To not let superficial garbage define you.

"What and when?" Jason surprises me by opening his mouth for the first time since my arrival. He's not looking at me. His eyes are on his phone as he taps away at the screen. "Any specific date you —" I clear my throat and his eyes snap up to mine, the expression on my face making him flip the device in his hand around quickly. In the background, I hear his low *sorry* but I'm reading the notes being made on the notation app; the breakdown of what could be needed and timeframes where certain networks are dormant and can be bypassed. *Smart kid, but still mierda for etiquette.*

"I need five bank accounts emptied, leaving behind only a single penny in each." At my words, they look at each other for a brief moment—just a quick flick of the eyes—and then nod in acceptance. "There's also the matter of an encrypted message I'd like left behind for the owner when he attempts to log in."

"Anything."

"Done," they say in unison, Jason being the latter. He's still adding to his notes, fingers a blur over the screen. "Can we ask *whom* and *what*?"

Second mistake.

Never ask questions. Wait until the information is provided.

"No. You can't."

"Sir, we mean—"

"How do you feel about corrupt governments in general?" I interject, cutting him off instead. Bringing the drink to my lips, I take a sip and then another, downing the shot and placing the glass atop the table. The anise taste is crisp, settling into a slow burn as it spreads, and I let the question hang in the air between us for a full minute.

The immediate disdain on their faces is enough of a tell.

Shawn speaks up first, his expression full of unresolved ire. "I'm an anarchist, Mr. Lucas. Fuck them all."

Jason nods in acquiescence, first-bumping his friend before placing his phone screen up beside his glass of water. "While my views aren't as extreme, I agree with how much greed and corruption have taken control of governments across the globe. Politicians no longer work for the people who vote them into office, but for millionaire donors and their private agendas."

Right answer.

"Then you'll have no problem playing the role of Robin Hood for me." At my words, Daniel snickers across from me, but quickly hides it behind a sip or two of liquor. "Take from the rich to feed the poor."

"None whatsoever." Again in unison. They remind me of two bumbling idiots I once knew and are dead now.

"Good. Then you start tomorrow." They look like they want more information, better instructions, but I snap my fingers and Geronimo comes right over with a nondescript folder in his hand. Shawn and Jason shrink back as he towers over the table but are smart enough to take the file without prompting. "Everything you need is in there, gentlemen. I expect to see progress by the end of the week."

"Sir, I'm—"

"Bosdell, this is your cue to leave. Take it and don't push your luck." At my words, they stand and after giving me a pussy-looking bow, leave the room.

Moreover, if it weren't for how good they are at what they do, they'd be dead already. There is more to their moronic antics than they think I know. Like the fact that each stole three hundred grand from an associate in Cali.

Money that was ultimately mine.

My eyes shift to one of my men standing next to Geronimo, and he leaves after my nod. He'll be watching them. They're not allowed out of his sight.

"Well, that was entertaining, to say the least," Daniel says, leaning over to grab the bottle of Aguardiente this time to pour us each another shot. He's forgoing his usual drink, so I know the man is right at the cusp of lit and hungry. Could out eat anyone I know when drunk. "The skinny one almost shit himself. Another glare from you and he would've had an accident."

"That's disgusting." I take the offered drink and let the clear liquid swish lightly around the edge of the glass before taking another sip. "And the truth. No backbone or self-preservation on either of them."

Because fear doesn't equate to awareness, not when the person you're making a deal with is someone you owe money to.

I own Cali. Barranquilla. Medellin. Every single inch of this country works for me, something that the pieces of shit holding the presidential office will learn soon enough.

It's taken me years to get where I am, and not by luck. Blood. Sweat. Death.

After my father's sentencing, things changed for us. Our lives were turned upside down, and working became my number one priority. To maintain my family and bounce back. To be able to afford a one-bedroom home in one of the poorest neighborhoods of the country while simultaneously sending whatever we could to our father in jail.

For food.

For protection.

For the rights to a simple visit, and that fee was imposed by the tombos at the jailhouse.

And while my mother cried at night, I worked harder. Smarter. Made the right connections with a man that I'd kill near the end of Quintero's second term and overtake his illicit throne.

The day I took possession, I personally sent Quintero a gift via a car bomb outside of the presidential palace. Just one car. The exact replica of his. The message was loud and clear on my behalf, but if by any chance he still didn't understand, I called him. My phone call didn't last long, just a few seconds, but I made sure that he heard the one word.

My name and the date of my father's arrest.

That's it.

Jose Quintero became president off the back of false accusations toward his honest opponent. Off a man that refused to play dirty. A man that served six years for a crime he didn't commit, and after a visit from myself to the newly appointed leader, I persuaded him to see things my way in exchange for a financial contribution to the national debt.

And while Quintero fled the country with his entire family, I bided my time. To this day he hasn't come back, but I know where he is. Where he hides beneath a pile of rocks like the snake he's always been.

Guatemala isn't far enough.

"Now, back to something a bit more important..."

"What's he asking for this year?"

"You hungry?" he asks instead, standing with a bottle in his hand when I shake my head. "Then let's head upstairs. There's someone I want you to meet."

"You sure you don't want to eat?"

"After my surprise."

With a brow raised, I wave a hand in the air. "Lead the way."

The moment I rise from my chair while taking my guns, the soldiers with me move toward the entrance and open the door. Two walk outside with their weapons drawn, while the others stand between me and the hallway. A quick search finds everything clear and they step aside to make room for my exit.

We go back the way we came in but stop midway where a hidden panel resides behind a painting. With a flash of my keycard across the oil medium the wall parts, exposing a vintage elevator shaft with exposed metal and a manual door you push aside to open—and secure it closed with a hard pull and a latch. It fits three people, and I signal Geronimo to head inside while looking over at the others.

"Take the stairs across from us and meet me on the rooftop."

"Yes, Patron." They're gone before I fully turn around, and the sound of a door opening meets my ears while Geronimo stands waiting to close the metal entrance and then pull the lever.

Three floors separate the clientele here, and while the first floor is quieter and more reserved, the next two are festive—open-bar settings with small dining tables littering the floor, and the kind of music playing is a little more *Criolla*. From old school to top hits. From vallenato to cumbia.

The elevator passes and stops. This one is for the younger crowd.

The rowdier hipsters of the country, and the music reflects that.

Urban Latino blares from the speakers of this rooftop club for a throbbing sea of bodies. Men and women all blur into each other, their bodies grinding—moving to the beat of reggaeton as one at the center of the room. It's a depraved gyration that catches the eye of every person within as hands wander beneath short skirts. As heads are thrown back in bliss and the smiles on glossed lips are one of dirty satisfaction.

No hiding. No pretending.

And while the lighting is minimal beneath the cool night sky, I stride across the room toward a small VIP section toward the back. There are two private seating areas and my men are already there on the left, standing guard as a waitress places a few bottles of liquor atop a table between the arranged seating.

A few people try to get my attention: women and men for similar reasons. To talk shop or offer me easy access to pussy. I'm interested in neither and at the sight of my glare, they step back.

Not tonight. This isn't the time to try to make a deal.

I'm the first to take a seat. The oversized red gothic chair between sofas gives me a view of the entire floor, from the large bar, the DJ's station, and the dance floor where now a woman is on her knees with a cock down her throat, bobbing her head as those around her cheer the petite woman on.

"Are you keeping with the same drink or...?"

"Rum."

"Good choice." Daniel pours us each a drink, and I look back at Geronimo who stands again just behind me. I tilt my head and he gets the hint, taking a seat to my right and opposite Daniel who's looking at him. "And you, parce? What's your poison?"

"I'm driving. I'll stick with water—"

"Join me in one," I say, and he nods without another protest. Geronimo's a good man. A good soldier and always on guard. "Poor him a double. We're celebrating tonight."

"Thank you, Patron."

"Hagale and relax." Looking back at Daniel, I raise my glass and the two men follow. "To the beginning of the end. To the death of many." They nod, and so do the other men surrounding my area. "To the mercy of God finding a home in my country, because until that family is six feet under, every street will run red in supplication."

"Your word is the law, Patron."

"Those hijueputas don't deserve to live." The latter comes from Daniel.

"Your loyalty is appreciated, gentlemen. Salud," I say, throwing back my drink and then sitting forward, grabbing the bottle to pour another round. For tonight, though, I won't discuss my plans any further. Not with so many ears around. Not with a few familiar faces trying to subtly get close. "So, what does my favorite kiddo want for his birthday?"

Daniel doesn't miss a beat and snorts. "The pony you promised."

"Is he taking riding lessons yet?"

"Yeah, but the wife isn't..." he's talking, animatedly waving his hand between us, but I've stopped listening. There's a sudden prickling sensation—an undercurrent that travels through my body as a giggle meets my ears—and my cock swells at the sound. It's feminine and arousing, and I can't stop myself from looking over at the private section across from mine.

A group of women, in their early twenties at the most, arrive and take their places around the center table where their drinks of choice await. At once, I'm picking apart their faces, trying to decipher which family in the capital they belong to. None seem familiar, though.

They're laughing.

Shooting shots of clear liquid.

All except one.

Motherfucking Preciosa. I can't take my eyes off the one to the far right and how she moves her hips sensually to the rhythm of reggaeton. She's mouthwatering, and my heart beats like the stampede of a thousand wild beasts. My muscles tighten. My jaw ticks.

The sounds around us dim and my cock hardens, pulsing as the beautiful doll across from me twirls. Once. Twice. Five times while her hips undulate to the beat, the bottom of her strapless dress swirling around her mid-thighs.

She's beautiful. Utterly indecent perfection.

On the last turn, her eyes wander my way and lock on mine. Light grey on my cognac, a bolt of volcanic need rushes down my spine. Licks at my skin. I'm aroused and hungry and near clawing at my flesh, but I stay right where I am.

My eyes traverse her short frame in a minuscule blush-colored party dress. I take in how the fabric shimmers, almost glowing around her with each tempting move. From her dainty, high-heeled feet to her slim waist and thick hips—to those larger-than-a-handful tits pushed up against the thin fabric—I find her to be the physical embodiment of sin. A temptation I won't deny myself.

Not when her lips quirk up into a shy smile.

Not when a touch of pink sweeps across her cheeks.

Not when she subtly squeezes her thighs.

I see it. Her. Every delicious inch makes me throb, and pinning her beneath me is all I can focus on.

"Are you even listening to me?"

"No."

"What's got you so...*oh*. You found her."

"What the fuck are you talking about?" I ask Daniel, but my eyes remain on her, taking in how she bites her lower lip before accepting the shot the girl beside her offers. The little flower throws it back without pause; a small shiver runs through her—nipples pebbling into stiff little peaks as I watch her stand beneath soft lighting. I catalog the rapid rise and fall of her chest. The clenching of her small fingers around the glass. "You know her?"

"I do."

My head snaps in his direction and my eyes narrow. "Explain?" I grit out, the malice behind my tone clear. For the first time in all our years of friendship, I want to shoot him, snap his neck, and all because the grin on his face holds a hint of salaciousness. Of a familiarity. "Talk, man, before conclusions are made that are not in your favor."

"Why so possessive?"

There's a tumultuous storm brewing within, a thick cord that snaps and I pull my gun out, finger on the trigger before rationalizing my actions. "Now isn't the time to test me."

His hands go up and his face loses all trace of humor. "Parce, this is—"

"Who. Is. She?"

"My gift."

"Gift?"

"Yes." He swallows hard, eyes on my finger over the trigger. The same one that's twitching. "That's Solimar Quintero, my friend. The president's daughter."

4

Solimar

I'M AN IDIOT.

Crazy.

A dead woman if my father finds out I let my cousin drag me out to Codicia tonight, and more so without my guards. But then again, that's the least of my worries. I'm terrified of him, of his reaction if he knew that Laura is sleeping—in love—with Signio Cortez when the arrangement for my hand has already been made.

I don't love him. *She does.*

I don't even like him. *She's completely smitten with the jerk.*

My heart breaks for her, but the decision was taken out of my hands a few minutes after the strike of midnight on my twentieth birthday by his father and mine. It's a political move between the two countries. The creation of a stronger alliance by two overbearing and archaic-thinking presidents.

Because of their greed, I've become a pawn in a game I never wanted to play.

Unfortunately for Laura, she'd been chasing him for over a year at that point with nothing more than the title of *friends with benefits* safely within her grasp. No one knew this. No one suspected. And while Laura pines and he sleeps around, I'm caught in the middle of this unwanted love triangle after her confession with tears in her eyes.

I'm damned no matter which way I turn.

I'm left forcing a smile and praying my disgust doesn't show.

I'm left imagining another face every night that is forbidden to me.

"Thank God we're not married yet," I mutter under my breath for the ninth time as our group—a few women I barely know and her one childhood friend I can't stand—are ushered toward a VIP table near the very back of the rooftop terrace. The other section is already occupied, but I know better than to look. To be nosy or worse, get caught by the kind of clientele Sergio caters to.

It's not a secret. The pompous jerk doesn't hide it. My father's given him immunity, and he's using it to his full advantage.

However, the closer we get, the more I'm tempted to.

There's a pulsing energy that grips me.

A near overwhelming presence that makes my skin hyperaware. Sensitive. And I find myself near floating and not understanding the why.

Each step I take feels as though I am being pulled closer by an invisible tether, a connection that's making my pulse race and knees feel weak. *What's wrong with me? What was in that shot I had back at Laura's?*

"Hurry up, Solimar," my cousin calls out and my head snaps up; I've frozen in place a good ten steps from them. "My Signio saved us the best seat in the house, and it's an open-bar night for our group. He's the best!"

My Signio isn't meant to be a personal jab at me, but to others, it comes across that way, and the few snickers that follow are proof of that.

She doesn't think.

She's too impulsive.

She forgets that our engagement has already been announced and the media is counting down the days to my demise. That if her secret gets out, my father's wrath will destroy us both.

"Go on," I say with more bite in my tone than I intend, and at once, the smile drops from her face. Her expression is contrite, and she mouths *perdoname*. And while I know she's sorry, that it's not intentional, the urge to choke her is near maddening. I want to make her understand that this isn't a game, but I don't. Instead, I force another fake smile—one I've become the master of hiding behind— and avoid making a spectacle that could end up in the tabloid section of our newspaper. *The president's daughter can never be anything less than perfect.* "I'll be right behind you."

"You sure?"

"Yeah." Just like I know coming out tonight was a mistake. *Just like I know this—your mess—will burn me in the end.*

With one more apologetic look thrown my way, she turns, and the others follow. The six of them head toward our area and I let out a long, tired sigh. I take those few extra seconds to gather my emotions and breathe. To close my eyes and pray.

Papa Dios, please grant me the patience I don't feel blessed with tonight. Please don't let us get busted or into any kind of trouble...amen.

It's then that I feel eyes on me. More than one set, and I look around.

The people around the dance floor and small tables littered throughout stare. They recognize me, and the whispers begin. It's somewhat subtle at first, but then it's always the same:

What's the president's daughter doing here?

How do I get close?

Not giving anyone the chance to be brave and intercept me, I rush toward our table. Because while I believe Signio isn't stupid enough to leave us unprotected and have anything fall back on him, my security isn't here. We're stupidly out alone while everyone believes we're at Laura's highly-secured apartment, a twenty-floor building where only the affluent enter and whose lobby and entrances have armed guards standing at their post.

It's also where the trackers once inside my phone are now pinging from, thanks to an acquaintance of hers, an ex-intelligence officer who helped us out of the building for some extra platica and a kiss on the cheek from my cousin.

"This place is so berraco, Lau. He's a keeper and deserves a woman like you." I catch the words, the thinly veiled insult my way, but roll my eyes. None of these women matter to me, and the one speaking is her oldest friend, a jealous idiot from a banking family who's as narcissistic as my father, but it goes to show that Laura's words have clout. That rumors will spread because of her idiocy.

My cousin glares at her. "Watch it, Penelope. I won't warn you again."

"What did I do?" *Don't punch her in that overdone smug mouth, Sol.*

"Quit your nastiness." Laura comes to my side and entwines our fingers to show solidarity, while I give the girl a bored look. Because you never let them see your weakness. She wants to get a rise out of me and will fail; I know better than to give in. "You'll never be her."

"Laura, how can you just—"

"Ladies, cut it out. We're here to get drunk, not fight," another chick interjects, handing out shots that I decline. Laura and Penelope don't move at first, but eventually back down and take the offered drink. And while they toss it back and grimace, I move away a bit and let the music playing be my reprieve for a while.

I'm not here to get wasted or sleep with the first guy who pays attention to me. Tonight's about forgetting:

My family. My obligations. My future.

The man I will never be with and who would doom me if our paths ever cross.

This nightmare that I can't find an out from as the clock ticks and the weight on my shoulders becomes heavier—the noose on my neck tighter. Moreover, the sole reason we're not married yet is my schooling, but how much longer will that hold?

It's part of the contract. A clause. This holy grail of a stipulation added at the very last minute by my mother to a literal contract that shouldn't exist. She's on my side, trying to help me find a loophole, and by demanding that I earn my degree in political science first, the inevitable has been delayed.

It was all my father would agree to.

Let it go for tonight, Sol. Just dance and be free.

Closing my eyes, I let the pulsing rhythm coming through the speakers flow through me. My hips sway to the island beat, this dance-hall-like flow that makes me gyrate, smile as the stress begins to dissipate.

The girls around me laugh and I open my eyes, catching sight of Laura doing her version of a running man. It's the one place my cousin has no grace, and a giggle escapes as she looks like a choking chicken while flipping me the bird.

I try to help her. Show her how to move her hips from side to side, but dancing is something that you either can or can't do, and unfortunately, she's horrible. Simply has no rhythm.

"Prima, like this!"

"I'm doing it!"

The others are laughing, imbibing in the free spirits, while I try to show her how to gyrate her hips while turning. And then try again. But on the fifth time, I give up and let her do her thing, my eyes going around the room once and then of their own accord, they stop across from our group.

On a handsome man.

On a dangerous man.

On a man who's starred in every fantasy I've ever had while

simultaneously being my destruction, and I have bigger problems than simply sneaking out to a rooftop bar.

I know who he is. There's no mistaking his face.

Alejandro Lucas is an enemy of my father and a known killer. Someone with no scruples.

He's also looking at me in a way that sets my body ablaze, and I feel weak. Trapped. Engulfed by his heated stare that lingers over areas that no man has touched.

Turn around and leave...

He licks his bottom lip, and my thighs tremble.

He slowly rubs two fingers over his lips, and my mouth becomes dry.

He's a predator and I'm the innocent lamb caught in his trap, afraid to so much as breathe for fear that he'll pounce.

My father and grandfather have always warned me about him. About his family. About the threat they pose to the citizens of this country and abroad—the many lives lost due to their greed and corruption—but he failed to warn me about this man's natural ability to turn women into willing victims without uttering a single word.

Across the VIP section and sitting in a chair fit for a king, Alejandro owns the room. Owns my attention, and looking away isn't an option. I just can't; he takes me in, and I do the same.

I'm memorizing his handsome face with a sharp jaw, the perfect five o'clock shadow, and an inviting mouth—those eyes the color of cognac that seems to glow in the low lighting and ensnare me. Alejandro says something, his head tilting a bit to the side, but not once does he look away.

There's a back and forth, his facial features becoming hard the more he listens to whoever is answering him. At the same time, someone beside me laughs, their arm bumping into mine, but I ignore them. They tap my shoulder to gain my attention, but I simply hold a hand up to where a second or two later, they place a shot glass between my fingers. I grab it tightly. My fingers molding around the small object and I blindly throw back its contents without asking what it is.

Who cares at this point. I welcome the automatic burn that builds and then settles into a warming embrace. It doesn't calm my racing heart or the thoughts in my head that can't ever be—curiosity killed the cat and I refuse to travel down that road, no matter how much my body awakens beneath his perusal.

There's no denying he disarms me. Always has.

He's been my crush for years, a secret that no one, not even Laura, knows about.

My saving grace has always been that my fascination never deviated from something I did behind a screen. Googling him. His appearances. His ties to the mob and roles he plays in the opioid crisis around the globe; the good, bad, and why he's untouchable as of now.

Pharmaceutical companies hold clout in places other than just the US.

Alejandro's lips thin, and he hisses out something I can't make out from where I stand. I'm so busy watching his lips move that it takes me a minute to notice the gun in his hand and the barrel pointing at the chest of another man with him. He's demanding something, the expression on his face now murderous, and finally, he looks away from me.

His hand holding the gun doesn't waver.

His eyes narrow at the man who holds two hands up.

I can't watch this. He's going to kill him.

I'm moving before anyone can ask me where I'm going, my feet rushing toward the elevator as my lungs fight for air. It's on the other side of the floor and I see people waiting for the cart, and just as I plan to join and blend in, someone close says his name.

I dart past the now opening doors, making my way through a sea of bodies dancing, doing things that shouldn't be permitted out in public, and dart inside the women's bathroom in an alcove-sized hallway that's only big enough to fit three people max.

I'm lucky no one's standing there or waiting to use the facilities, and once inside with the door closed behind me, I let out the breath I've been holding. *I knew coming here was a bad idea.*

Opening the faucet, I let the cool water run before grabbing a few paper towels and dipping them beneath the stream. I'm hot and my heart's racing and I can't allow myself anywhere near him. To see if his lips taste like heavenly danger.

He's a criminal, Solimar. He tried to kill your abuelo—Alejandro Lucas is the reason we left Colombia to protect you, your mother, and abuela.

Dad's words ring in my ears as I rub the damp napkin across the back of my neck. They are a mantra I can't ignore. The look on his face as he said them matched the pure venom each syllable was coated in.

Our families don't mix.

Our families are enemies.

"I'm going back to Laura's apartment. I shouldn't be here." With the tips of the paper towel, I swipe across my forehead and then down my cheek before tossing them aside. Looking in the mirror doesn't help my predicament, and the cool water did nothing to help me look less affected.

My light eyes show excitement with just a hint of fear.

My skin is flushed, and goose bumps sweep across my sensitive flesh.

My lips are curling up at the corner and into a tiny smile as I apply a bit of gloss over them.

"This is not good. Really not good." I push away from the sink, my wristlet falling to my side as I close my eyes and breathe. I need a plan out of here, and asking Signio or the ladies I'm here with is out of the question.

They'd ask too many questions. Some hold no qualms in selling me out either.

"Enough time has passed." I'm closing my eyes as I say this and taking in a very deep inhale. "Count to twenty and walk out, get on that elevator, and call Laura from a cab. You can do this." Another inhale and I mumble out numbers one through ten slowly. I'm trembling. Breathing hard. "Christ, I beg you to help a girl out here." There's the creak of a door and I freeze, but the two male voices are coming from outside and I sigh because it's the men's bathroom. "I promise to go to mass this week."

The voices fade as the door closes, and I wait another few seconds before continuing with my counting. I'm on number fourteen when my phone vibrates inside my wristlet. My brows furrow as it stops, only to start up again. *Has to be Laura wondering where I ran to.*

"Aren't you going to answer that?" a voice says from behind me. It's masculine and rich and my eyes snap open, meeting an amused pair of cognac ones in the mirror above the sink. "Well?"

"You." That's all I say. It's all I can get out.

"Me." Alejandro takes the few steps between us, stopping when his chest presses against my back. His arms cage me in. His hands grip the counter's edge beside my own as he sweeps his lips over the shell of my ear, releasing a rough exhale against my skin. "And it's very nice to meet you, too, Miss Quintero."

5
ALEJANDRO

HER LIPS PART, but no words come out.

Instead, she's watching me through the mirror, her expressive eyes saying everything that she can't:

She's afraid.

She's curious.

She's confused.

This little flower is wondering how the fuck she's found herself within the grasp of her father's enemy. Staring at a man she should be running from, and yet, Solimar Quintero won't.

Miss Quintero is drawn to me. She's proven as much while watching me from her area of the VIP section, smiling and licking her lips—unconsciously taking a few steps in my direction.

Nothing made her look away until she saw my gun.

She'll soon learn that running from me is unacceptable. You don't hide. You don't leave my sight.

"How did you..." She swallows hard as I press closer, the feel of her curves against my harsher planes burning me as I anchor her to the modern countertop. "You shouldn't be in here."

"And yet I am."

"Why?" The million-dollar question. *Why am I here?*

The truth is that I'm intrigued by this member of the Quintero family, and where the usual reaction is anger, with her it's the opposite. She's set off a different kind of desire, and those eyes, a unique shade of grey, make my pulse race as they watch me. She's made me hungry for a taste of her soft, tanned skin and cherry lips.

There's something about her that's drawing me in, and I want to figure out the *why*.

I need to decipher why her beauty has been physically hidden from the media. From me.

I want to own her. Ruin her. Take her innocence and corrupt her.

"We need to talk, Miss Quintero." Shivers rush down her spine as my lips leave an open-mouthed kiss on her neck. "You need to explain a few things."

"There's nothing we need to discuss." The last word leaves her on a hiss as I nip her ear. "Our families—"

"Have history than runs deep, and I want my pound of flesh, Preciosa." At my words, goose bumps rise across soft flesh and her thighs clench, a minute movement I feel, and I fight back a smile. Instead, my lips hover over her pulse point. "I will call, and you will come to me."

"I can't."

"You will."

Her eyes narrow, and my cock jerks behind my zipper. "No."

It's the wrong thing to say to a man like me. Her denial only enhances my fascination. The need to bend her to my will is a heady pulse flowing through my limbs.

"You're a dangerous little thing, aren't you?" My lids lower and I watch her through narrow slits, a groan slipping past my lips when her nipples tighten. The stiff little peaks make my mouth water. They're pressing against the thin fabric of her dress, demanding my attention, and the soft blush on her cheeks is the icing on this taboo cake. "The sweetest motherfucking temptation, Preciosa."

"You shouldn't be in here." It's a whine that emits a desperate plea. That causes a few beads of pre-come to slide from the head of my cock and down the underside.

"But I am." One hand releases the marble and I grip her hip, my eyes flashing open just as she bites down on her lip to hold back the moan fighting to break free. It doesn't work. The most delicious little mewl slips through, and I follow the tremble of her mouth. My hunger is unhidden, and I lick my own while tightening my hold. "I'm here, and cornering the daughter of Colombia's president inside of a bar owned by her fiancé—"

"Don't call him that," Solimar whimpers, hands shaking while lowering her eyes. *Diosito, please get me out of here. Don't let my attraction control my actions.* It's a whisper under her breath, almost too low to hear, but I do.

Her confession burns me.

Those words seal her fate.

"Is it a lie?" Brow arched, I dig my fingers into her flesh, leaving behind what I know will be a bruise. My mark. The first of many, because Solimar likes my rough and possessive touch—to be manhandled. The way she gasps and slowly gyrates against my hard-ness shows me as much. "Does he own you?"

The thought of her belonging to anyone doesn't sit well with me. It angers me. Turns the blood within my veins into molten lava. *What is it about you, Solimar?*

"No, it's not…" at her words, my jaw ticks but I don't interrupt "…not all is as it seems."

When it comes to her family, it never is.

"You're right about that, Miss Quintero." Grey eyes focus once again on my lips, following their movements. I shouldn't like the way it makes me feel. The temptation she presents or the adrenaline knowing who she is brings forth. "Many truths hide behind angelic veils."

"What's that supposed to mean?"

"It means you'll be seeing me again, and soon."

"That can't and won't happen."

Before Solimar's next intake of breath, I flip her around and tip her face up with two fingers. It's a firm hold but not painful as my eyes bore into hers, lips a hair's breadth from hers. "I wasn't asking, Preciosa. This isn't a negotiation."

"My father—"

"Will not be an excuse to hide from me."

"Why are you here?" she whispers, eyes shifting toward the door as if expecting it to open at any moment. "What do you want from me?"

"All will be explained, but not here." Releasing her chin, I wrap my hand around Solimar's neck, fingers flexing as she swallows hard —arches against the sink, head tilted back, but doesn't tell me to move or let go. I skim up her ribs and the side of her breast before curling the ends of her dark hair between the digits of my other hand. One forceful tug and she hisses, the slight sting making her shiver. "You will come to me when I call. You will never deny me your presence." Her lips part, the rebuttal sitting on the tip of her tongue, but the words don't come out as I silence her protest with a nip to the corner of her mouth and pull back. Daring her to defy me. "Is that understood?"

"I'm not a pawn."

"And I'm not a patient man."

"Be reasonable."

"You won't deny me."

"Alejandro, I want no part in your war against my family."

A chuckle leaves me and I release her, taking a few steps back. "Follow directions, Preciosa. That's all you need to do to survive."

"I—"

"Will not disappoint me." With that, I turn around and walk to the door. Hand on the handle, I turn and look back at her. From head to toe, I memorize her just like this. Like the deceptive angel she is. "Go back out and have fun with your friends, Solimar. Don't tell anyone. Don't let them know that I'll be watching."

For a few beats, she doesn't move, her eyes frozen on mine, and I feel a pang in my chest. I don't like this emotion bubbling within— her distress hits me in the chest, and all I want to do is comfort her. Pull her against me. *Soon.*

Her lips part; there are things she wants to say but thinks better of it and nods. Solimar walks to me, only stopping once her hand lays over mine on the door handle. Those eyes, a gorgeous grey, stare at me for a minute.

She's studying me, her sweet little pants fanning across my chin and lips.

"Go on, Miss Quintero." Turning the door's fixture, I open it and leave just enough space for her to pass. "Let's not make things any more difficult than what they are."

"Any more and it might break me," she whispers under her breath, but I hear it loud and clear as if she shouted it from the rooftops. Our attraction is mutual, a complication neither of us expected. "Goodnight, Mr. Lucas."

"Noches, Preciosa."

And then she's gone. Out of the room and following my directions.

I follow a minute later.

Close enough to see the sensual sway of her hips and the way every head in the room turns in her direction. Some with envy. Some with lust. Both sets quickly look away once they catch sight of me.

"Did you find what went missing?" Daniel asks when I retake my seat, his speech slightly slurred. He pours us each a drink, spilling a bit on the table and foregoing Geronimo who's watching the room closely. The man is quick to handle unwanted visitors with a single shake of his head—make the group of women trying to dance a few feet away back up. "Did she recognize you?"

"How did you know she'd be here?"

"Signio likes to talk." He passes me a drink before throwing his back. "Was all but shouting it to everyone before you arrived...he's a low-plumage peacock trying to puff out his chest to anyone that would listen. He's marrying the president's daughter, fucking the cousin, and everyone knows this."

"Her father is aware?" Daniel nods at my question and I close my eyes for a second, breathing in deeply to get a hold of the sudden urges dominating my senses. Ire burns me. Disgust churns in my gut. But more importantly, I have this insatiable need to protect her. "That sick fuck."

"Quintero doesn't care about her or the kind of man Signio is. He's more preoccupied with passing the legislation that lets him run for another term after the previous president abolished it."

"I heard." Scrubbing my jaw, I flick my eyes toward the precious flower and find her forcing a smile. Ever dutiful, Solimar's pretending to fit in with those around her but sticks out like the diamond she is. No one sees her discomfort. The need to flee in those expressive eyes while her cousin continues to pull attention her way, relishing in the way the others surround her. *I see you, beautiful.* As if she heard my thought, her head turns my way and our stares lock.

Genuine innocence.

Alluring grace.

Slowly, her lips curl up and it's a complete contrast to the previous smile. This one is soft. Sweet. It's pulling the tail of this predator who's seconds away from doing something he shouldn't...*yet.*

Hi, she mouths and rolls her eyes toward the group. There's also a small yawn that escapes.

Go home, beautiful, I mouth back, and she nods, more than happy to oblige me in this, and I make sure no one stops her. I stand, and this time signal my men to turn with their back to the outside. People look our way, trying to figure out why they're being blocked, and Solimar takes the opportunity to leave without saying goodbye to anyone in her group.

I'm sure she'll send them a text.

"Geronimo?"

"Yes, Patron?"

"Make sure she's not followed and gets home without incident."

"Do I contact—"

"Yes. She's to be met at the curb and her night out covered."

"As you wish."

Goodbye for now, Miss Quintero.

6
Solimar

THIS IS BAD. *Really bad.*

  So bad, that I don't know how to react or decipher our stolen moment now that I'm back inside my cousin's apartment. Now that there's no haze of attraction clouding my mind. No crazy need dominating my actions.

And yet, I can't find it in me to be upset.

Worried? Yes.

Scared? A little.

Sorry that I skipped out on Laura and sent her a text once I was away from Codicia? Not in the least.

"This can't happen. I can't see him again," I whisper low, dropping my keys in a bowl near the entryway before toeing off my heels. It feels good to be barefoot, and the plush carpet beneath my feet is like heaven after running away from the very man I've crushed on since my adolescence.

Christ, having him so close was both heaven and hell—a dream and reminder of what I can never have because of who my family is. Because of a war that I've never been a part of.

My life's path has been chosen for me. Love isn't in the cards.

Taking a couple of steps toward the kitchen, my knees wobble and I fall back, placing both hands flat against the wall behind me for support. I've been a shaky mess since walking out with Alejandro's permission, luckily with no one following, and getting into an already waiting car.

I didn't question why the all-black SUV was waiting.

I didn't question why they didn't accept my payment.

I didn't question why my security guard and friend were there to guide me inside without reproach.

All I wanted at that moment was to get back here and hide from the world. There were traces of my shame mixed with desire and something else that I just didn't know how to explain. He made me feel alive inside that bathroom. He made every fantasy I've had of him since the age of seventeen pale in comparison.

And while I knew I could never have him, that didn't stop my daydreams.

My attraction to him has always been a mixture of forbidden and idiotic, and more so after I stumbled upon an old interview online he'd done for a fashion magazine that crowned him the most eligible bachelor in the world. Those thirty minutes changed me, but it was the glimpse of the accompanying photoshoot—his bare chest glistening with a few strategically placed suds while inside of a clawfoot tub—that ruined my innocence. He left his mark on me without so much as being in the same room.

It was right after he made a lucrative deal with an American pharmaceutical company. The proverbial flipping off to my grandfather.

His fields produced most of the world's opioids. He'd gone from a criminal to untouchable. From someone my father disliked to an obsession.

"He's not the only one who's obsessed." A truth I'll never admit aloud to anyone. Most of all him. *Diosito, please help me out of this.* My rapid heart calms after a minute or two, and so does the shaking of my limbs. Enough so that I'm able to stand upright and walk to the guest bedroom without incident or getting the bottle of water I originally wanted.

I'm on autopilot. Lost inside my head while my clothes fall off in a haste.

One minute I'm trying to remind myself that life isn't made up of wishful thinking or kismet opportunities, and the next, cold water slides down my heated skin.

It awakens my senses. Slams back into reality what I let him do to me.

His touch. His voice. The demands he made that I dutifully followed.

"*Oh God.*" It's a throaty moan, giving in to the feverish sensations that I bit back when his hands gripped me and now I can embrace shamelessly. My hand slips between my thighs, fingers grazing over my clit, and I clench. The sensibility—the pleasure rocks me with one simple touch and I circle the trembling bundle of nerves again. And again.

I can't control the movement of my hips. They gyrate without my consent, forcing my fingers lower where they find their place at my entrance. Two slip inside to the first knuckle and I slam my free hand against the marble tile as the water beats down my back. I'm bucking against my hand, riding my fingers, as his earlier words run through my mind.

Taunting me. Making me crave more. Wishing he was here.

I will call, and you will come to me.

The sweetest motherfucking temptation, Preciosa.

You won't deny me.

"Alejandro," I moan low, gritting my teeth as pulsing waves crash into me and my body slumps against the shower wall. It's a euphoric high that leaves me panting, heart racing, and with the knowledge that I'll never be the same again.

I've never come so hard and fast by my hand, and the man responsible isn't here to take care of me after. *He never is.* I'm a virgin and deviant all in one. I've never let another hand touch me, but I always come with his name on my lips.

It takes me a few minutes to calm down, to wash away the evidence of my shame, but I manage and then take my tired body to bed. Naked, I crawl under the soft sheets and as I'm settling in, I feel a vibration near my thigh.

"The hell?" It stops and then starts again. Then again. Reaching down, I come across my wristlet and phone, not recalling when I tossed them here. It vibrates once more in my hold, screen illuminating, and I notice eight missed calls and one text.

My cousin, and an unknown number. All eight belong to Laura, but it's the text I'm both terrified and excited about.

Sweet dreams, Preciosa.

7

ALEJANDRO

"**P**ATRON, SHE'S LEAVING her home now. She has two classes today at the university, and then a dancing lesson after."

That's a little tidbit I've learned in the last seventy-two hours since Codicia; the little flower is both studious and flexible. A dancer. A bailarina well-versed in both salsa and tango.

She is poised and sensual, and watching her move fluidly as she practices on my computer screen has been the greatest foreplay. A naughty little gift I've given myself.

Because a little money in the right hand grants you favor. A little persuasion—a gun to the temple—will earn you their fear. Both are useful, and more so while forcing the sale of the dance academy she's a student of.

One visit is all it took.

One choice: money or bullets.

And because of their smart decision, I'm now the owner without anyone's knowledge.

I watch her from the cameras I've installed. I've fucked my hand while Solimar moves to the rhythm of her chosen session.

Every gyration is a pump of my fist over my engorged flesh. Every smile when she completes a newly learned step pulls a pearl-like bead to the slit and down my shaft.

I've never wanted to fuck a woman more. To lick the very sweat from her cheek.

And more so after having her file delivered to me the morning after our heated exchange. I won't deny that using her to piss off her father has crossed my mind. That it's one of the reasons I followed her into that bathroom, but one look into those equally hungry eyes up close—the feel of her against my chest—changed that.

Pissing off Matias Quintero is just a bonus now.

She's one of the good ones, and there's something about her I can't ignore. A pull. A draw.

Solimar is beautiful, smart, and never toes a foot out of the line set in place by her father. She's the dutiful first daughter every second of the day, and I want to break those chains holding her down. I want to set her free just so I can catch her. I want to build her up. Own her.

Possess every delicious inch of her forbidden fruit.

"Thank you, Geronimo. Don't lose sight of her." At my words, my right-hand, Chiquito, gives me a perplexed look. He's been away in Barranquilla taking care of a problem with a local dealer—the personal retrieval of a low-level wannabe who's watched one too many movies to understand his reality. You don't approach a man's business associates and undermine his authority without repercussions. "Do you have the package?"

"Yes, sir. Just give the word, and I'll deliver it personally."

"Good. Await my call." Ending our conversation, I place my cell atop my desk and sit back, looking at Chiquito. I'm home for the next three days, a private hacienda sitting atop a mountain at the center of farmland privately owned by me. It's no-mans-land with over two hundred acres of heavily guarded terrain. A location I don't hide from my enemies, associates, and is the amalgamation of my wealth—the pharmaceutical sale of my poppies and the dealings with the cartels. It's where I plan to retire one day, and I have every commodity fit for royalty. "Where is he?"

"Sitting out back by the pool."

"Alone?"

"Having a drink with new friends." Chiquito's paramilitary uniform is crisp, not a speck of dirt, and yet his gun holster has a few spots of dried blood. I see the bruising of his knuckles while he's busy eyeing my phone, his dark brown eyes flicking between my face and the blank screen.

"Speak up." Opening the drawer to my right, I pull out a knife and two bullets. That's all I'll need for this sit-down. "I only have an hour to meet with Mr. Marin."

"Who are you having followed, Alejandro?" he asks, voice hesitant when my jaw ticks. "Is there something I should know?"

"None of your concern at the moment." I'm looking at him through narrowed eyes, hand on the blade's handle. At once, his hands go up in a peaceful motion because he knows better than to question me. It's not something I accept from my own mother. He has his position because my brother and Daniel have responsibilities that come first: to take care of family. Those that I consider *my family*. And while I've known him for years and trust him, I keep him around because he follows orders without questions. However, one wrong step out of line, and I'll slit his throat without remorse. "Your curiosity isn't needed. If and when I decide to explain, it will be at my discretion. Watch yourself, Salazar. Understood?"

"Yes, Patron. No disrespect meant."

"Fresco, it's just a warning. Remember your place." Pushing my chair back, I stand and begin to undo the buttons of my linen shirt, letting it slip down my arms before placing it over the back of my desk chair. And while I gather my weapon of choice and the two accompanying bullets, Chiquito is up and over to my office door, opening and standing just outside the entrance.

No words are spoken as I exit.

None are needed as I stride toward the backyard with him a few steps behind.

I welcome the change in energy flowing through me as I get closer to my guest. My skin—every muscle in my body—vibrates as the blood in my veins thickens. It's a yearning, a certain need that I've developed over the years. Since the day I took my first life.

Because there's something therapeutic about the act.

How meticulous yet artistic the demise of each prey can be. How beautiful the first slice of my knife against pliant flesh feels. How the cries of forgiveness bring forth a calm that nothing else has provided as of yet.

It's my vice. A release.

Laughter meets my ears the closer we get to the covered lanai where Marin is sitting. He doesn't see me, but my men take notice. The amusement falls from their faces as the idiot, a man with a mouth bigger than his body, continues to spew bullshit on a topic I couldn't give two shits about.

Holding a finger to my lips, I shake my head at my soldiers. The action takes less than five seconds, and they return to normal as if nothing's happened.

"You need any help at your post, Señor Marin?" the guy to his right asks, and my guest's head turns. He doesn't see me when I enter and take a seat in the vacant chair at the head of this seating arrangement. His cockiness will be his downfall. Trusting my men will be the last stupid decision he makes.

"Are you asking for personal reasons?"

"Maybe."

"At the moment, I could use a few good men to protect my product. Too many thieves in this business...you should know." He chuckles, completely ignorant of how silent those around him have become.

The man isn't drunk, but it seems that after a few beers, he becomes mouthy, a little too boisterous over his mediocre accomplishments. "I mean, look at Alejandro and his family. A coffee farmer's son one day and the next, the boss of bosses. He's feared and wanted by our government, but untouchable due to global connections. You have to be one shrewd animal to go from a culicagado to this level of berraco."

"Is that so?"

Marin's head snaps in the direction of my voice and his face drains of color, but it's his eyes that amuse me. The expression in them—the fear and awe as he flicks between my face and the large tattoo of a hydra that takes up the majority of my upper body from pecs to the waistband of my pants.

The large creature, a mixture of dragon and snake with seven heads, is intimidating—bold, with each separate body curling around a long staff while baring their teeth. All accept one. Their master. He's wise and untouchable, and this is the perfect representation of my fearlessness and the danger I pose to others.

That while many work for me...

They dirty their hands for me...

I'll always remain on top. Their boss.

"Parce, please continue with your assessment." He swallows hard, beads of sweat now across his brow, and I smile. I'm amused by how quickly he lost the false bravado in my presence. "It's always good to know how the public perceives me."

"Alejandro, it's good to see...*fuck*!"

"Answer only what the patron asks," Chiquito hisses, hand wrapped around Marin's neck from behind. He's squeezing tight. Tight enough that his face becomes red and his lips a noticeably light shade of blue.

I wait for a beat or two before nodding at my right-hand. "Release him."

"As you wish, sir." Salazar steps back but doesn't move from position. A man is covering each of the idiot's sides and all avenues of escape while I sit directly across. A small rattan center table is all that separates us.

"It's a lovely day out, isn't it?" There are varying responses from my men. Some say yes, some say it looks like it might rain, and the one to my guest's right shrugs indifferently with *it's okay*. They all answer, *but* Marin. *Another one with mierda for manners.* "Do I need to repeat my question, Santiago?"

"No."

Nothing else, and I let out a rough exhale. "Put him on his knees."

"Wait! I'll—" The gun at his temple shuts him up.

"You want a second chance?"

"Please."

"Then stand up and come kneel at my feet." Ten seconds pass and Marin remains frozen, looking at me with panic in his eyes. Long gone is the hotshot bullshit. The kingpin mentality.

Now, I see the man—the child he is.

I give Chiquito permission to strike; a single blow to the back of his skull and Santiago falls forward, landing on his hands and knees. His forehead grazes the edge of the rattan table, saving him from slamming head first into the floor while forcing the furniture to move up a few inches. It doesn't cut him but hurts, and a pathetic whimper slips past his lips.

It's unacceptable. The sound pitiful. *Disgusting.*

"Enough," I hiss out, lips curling over my gritted teeth. "Crawl."

His head snaps up at my command, eyes wide and limbs shaking. "Alejandro, there has to be...hijueputa!" A kick to his midsection from the guard on the left stops his moronic train of thought. Once. Twice. Six times my soldier strikes and only pauses when I hold a hand up. "Por favor."

"Please what, Patron," I say, tone mocking now. Taunting. "How can this *poor farmer's son* be of any assistance to your excellency?"

"I've done nothing to deserve this." It's low and full of pain and almost comical. But then again, this is what happens when confronting an imposter.

They have no backbone. No balls.

People seem to forget that the dog with the loudest bark doesn't equate to the most damaging bite. Be afraid of those who move in silence and not the flashy or attention-seeking, because a killer doesn't announce himself before lining the streets with cadavers.

"Are you sure that's the route you'd like to go? Choose wisely."

"I swear, Mr. Lucas..." he swallows hard, eyes widening in horror as I lean forward, picking up the knife I brought with me "...please don't."

I flick it open, sliding my thumb down the sharp end. "Don't what?"

"This is a mistake!" He tries to sit on his haunches but makes the better choice to stay as is when my eyes narrow. *Pussy.* "Whatever it is, I'll pay it off."

A sardonic chuckle escapes me. "How would you know it's a mistake if I haven't accused you of anything?"

"Why am I here?"

"Tell me, what will you be paying without being charged?" I ask instead of answering his redundant question. "Are you confessing sins?"

"I thought the invitation was for—"

"Crawl." I'm holding the tip of my knife's blade between two fingers. "You have exactly five seconds to do so."

8

ALEJANDRO

"**W**HY ARE YOU—"

"One." At the first number, he does as I asked and begins to drag himself toward me. His movements are slow. His dread is palpable. "Two." The most miserable sound leaves him as I say *three* and I smile, patting my leg for the pathetic man not good enough to shine my shoes. "Four."

He pauses for a second and his hands clench on the ground because of the emasculating gesture. Marin is at the most three steps from me and breathing hard. "I'm not a dog," he says lowly, the tone meant to be threatening but in reality, is weak. However, I do admire the fact his spirit isn't completely gone...*yet*.

I'm going to enjoy breaking him down piece by piece, starting with his mental stability.

"You're whatever the fuck I say you are."

"Listen, Lucas—"

"Five."

His head snaps up as the blade leaves my fingers, slicing through the air faster than he can react. One blink and the pointed edge embeds itself into his shoulder about two inches deep.

"Fuck," he howls, arching up, which only stresses the wound and forces the blade to dig deeper.

"Crawl, Marin." I sit forward, snapping my fingers once. It does the job and his focus returns to my face, gritting his teeth from the pain. *He has no idea what agony is.* "Bring me my knife."

"Please, don't kill me."

"That's completely up to you." Tilting my head a bit, I give him a pointed look. "Do as you're told, Marin. Last chance."

"Yes, sir." His head goes down and shoulders drop. It reminds me of an animal when submitting, and slowly, he crawls toward me as his reality sets in.

My invitation wasn't based on a unification of businesses. It's not because I like him or think he's useful or whatever other bullshit he sold himself.

This is a trial.

I am the judge.

It'll be his execution.

Once he stops beside my right foot, I reach a hand out and ruffle his hair. "You made some costly mistakes, Santiago." His response to my words is whimpers. The low mumble of what I recognize as a prayer. "Explain yourself."

"I didn't—"

Marin stops, eyes widening as I grasp the knife's handle and push it in and out a few times. "Don't feed me the mierda you sell your clients. The truth this time."

"I stole from you."

"And how would you categorize that move?" Releasing the blade's handle for the moment, I pat his cheek, the slap loud in the quiet backyard where the only sounds you hear are those coming from the pool's water and my dogs nearby. "Successful or idiotic?"

"Not my brightest idea."

"I'll agree with you there." My eyes snap to Chiquito and I nod toward the exterior dining area not too far from us. At once he walks in that direction, disappearing a bit from view as he picks up a nondescript box and brings it over. "And what, pray tell, did you take from me? What's it worth?"

"Street value is high in the US via Mexican traffickers. I met with—"

"A hired transporter, Santiago. He wasn't a capo, nor was he important." That knowledge is like adding salt to an open wound, the proof of his stupidity slamming into his processors. "The man you met is here to deliver a payment while exchanging merchandise. He's someone I know, and immediately came to see me after you interrupted a meeting."

"I'm sorry," he whispers, his head down now. It's a cop-out. It pisses me off. "Had I known..."

"You wouldn't have?" I finish for him, gripping the knife once again and tapping the carved wooden handle. With each second that ticks on the clock, my drumming becomes rougher. Less patient. "Is that the bullshit you're trying to feed me?"

"Señor Lucas, I did what any man in my position would." And yet as he says this, the man in question still won't look me in the eye. Doesn't have the cojones to.

"Look at me." My grip tightens. "At the very least have some fucking dignity while spewing that weak explanation."

"It's the only truth that I have."

"That's where you're wrong, Marin." One tug and I pull the bloodied blade out, slicing down his flesh with the motion—the gash from shoulder to elbow is quickly bathed in red. His blood is pooling on the floor below as a pain-filled *fuck* leaves him. "You did what stupid men do. What all ignorant culicagados do." Chiquito brings forth the box and places it on the floor beside him. At his proximity, Santiago tries to pull back, but my knife at his temple puts a pause to that. "You underestimated the law."

"No more. I get it."

"You underestimated me."

"I'll never do it again." He's sweating profusely, fighting the instinct to bolt. "I swear."

Oh, I know he won't and just smirk. My head tilts toward the box. "Open it."

"Please don't make me." His hands are trembling, knees shifting on the terra-cotta floor, but he doesn't make a move to follow my instructions. *That won't do.* From temple to just below his chin, I dig in the jagged edge, slicing down his face. It's deep enough that the skin flaps a bit at his chin as I move it across to the other side. "Son of a bitch...*fuck*!"

"What was that? You'll open it now?"

"Yes, sir."

"God boy, Santiago. I'm proud of you for using your words." And to show him that I mean it, I sit back with a now-closed blade in hand. "Go on. It's my gift to you."

He's trembling so hard his teeth chatter, pulling the strip of tape off and then opening it one flap at a time. His entire body goes rigid, eyes horror-stricken as he takes in the contents inside.

Two heads. His idiot accomplices.

"No...NO!"

"This is the result of stealing a shipment of poppy extract meant for the Mexican Cartel near the US border." Standing, I tower over him and fist his hair, pushing his face closer to the proof of my appreciation. The rivulets of red dripping from his facial lesions fall over their shocked expression, mixing with the dried splashes already there. "You fucked up, Marin. You decided to play God and killed the driver—*my* employee—delivering *my* merchandise, and then tried to sell it as your own with the backing of a secret investor." Placing the blade at his cheek, I push it in and come out on the opposite side of his face, twisting the handle. He's skewered. He's also pissed himself. *Nasty.* "You ended a good, hardworking man's life and left a two-year-old without a father and a poor woman without her husband."

"I didn't—"

"Think I'd catch you, asshole." From the corner of my eye, I see Chiquito pull out his gun and empty the magazine before replacing it with the single bullet atop the table. "It's what you told your girl-friend, Maria…no? That I was a dumb fuck too busy playing with my dick to notice the stolen underground connections or goods? That you were protected because of who you've recently allied with."

"How do you…" a sob catches in his chest, head shaking from side to side. "Is she?"

"Very much alive and enjoying the reward for turning you in."

"She sold me out?"

"Yes."

Marin nods, and with shaky limbs brings his hands up and closes his eyes. His lips part and hushed whispers follow as he begins to recite the Padre Nuestro prayer. And it's as Santiago begins to say the third line that Salazar hands me his gun.

I let him finish.

I let him ask God to save his soul and forgive all offenses made while in this world.

"Will you go after my family?" he says after finishing, head bowed and posture defeated.

"They will not be harmed. You have my word." I'm pointing the barrel at his head, finger on the trigger.

"Thank you."

"You're welcome." That one bullet is all I need, and with a few quick pulls of the trigger, it lodges itself into his head, ending his life. Santiago Marin slumps forward as small fragments of skull and brain fly through the air, staining the furniture close to us and my pants. No one moves until I lower my arm and hand the gun back to its owner. "Clean it up and return him to his family along with a severance check. Tell them he died while out on delivery, a horrific robbery gone wrong."

"Consider it done, Lucas." Chiquito stays behind as I turn and head back into my office, already barking out orders as the men outside begin to scrub the outside terrace. He'll take care of the mess and replace what needs exchanging; I have a more important matter to attend to.

My cell phone is right where I left it, and I press number four immediately.

It rings once.

"Patron?"

"Deliver it now."

9

Solimar

"**I** SHOULDN'T BE doing this." I've whispered those same words to myself three times in the past hour. They've become my mantra. My attempt at keeping my sanity while still making idiotic decisions. To prove to myself that I'm in full use of my faculties because as of late, it's been one unwise choice after another.

Going to the club.

Letting him corner me in the bathroom.

Accepting this invitation for dinner at his condo a week after we met.

"What are we doing tonight? You feel up to—"

"No, Laura. Just no." We're walking down the hall after class and heading toward the exit. People around us look, a few try to garner my attention, but I ignore them and let my security further deter any attempts.

It never changes no matter where I am.

No matter where or who I'm with; all my life I've been a circus attraction without my consent. I play a role. I never set a foot out of line.

"But you didn't even let me ask!" *Her expression is one of annoyance until my eyes narrow. Pushing me right now is the worst thing she can do, especially after the fiasco Codicia turned out to be. Between her infatuation and lack of decorum—meeting Alejandro— my night was a jumpy, fearful mess. Laura sighs after a minute, seeing how I'm not backing down.* "Just dinner?"

"Where?" *Exiting the building, I squint while reaching into my bag and pulling out a pair of sunglasses.* "I've got a dance class all afternoon and will be exhausted after."

"Is that a yes? I swear, nothing fancy."

I pause, looking over at the guards just slightly away from us. "Carlos?"

"Yes, Miss Quintero?"

"Can you give us a minute? Girl talk, and all that jazz." *Those are the magical words. At any mention of girly things, he fights back a shudder. Probably remembering the time he drove us around the city for two hours straight as we whined in the back of the car about the unfairness of being a woman. Periods, cravings, and tears because we were both miserable and cranky.*

"Of course, Miss Quintero." *Walking over to the black SUV I use as transportation; he turns and leans back against the vehicle and assesses the perimeter. The other two men with us also give us some privacy while preventing anyone from getting close. Funny enough, they don't see the man holding a medium-sized box crossing the street.*

He's familiar. I know I've seen him before.

"...are you even listening to me?"

"What?" *I don't take my eyes off him as he stops beside Carlos and hands him the box along with an envelope he pulls from inside his jacket. His eyes meet mine after and he tips his head in my direction. "Repeat that?"*

"I said, Signio invited us out for dinner."

"Okay."

"Really?" At my barely perceptible nod, she squeals and begins to recount once again why she loves him. Needs him. In reality, I could care less because a second later it hits me. I know where I remember him from.

He was with Alejandro Lucas the night we met.

But more terrifying is the fact that I don't regret accepting the box later that evening outside my bedroom without asking questions. Not when I opened it and found a beautiful champagne-colored lace dress that fell just below mid-thigh and a pair of strappy heels to complement the delicate garment. Both were expensive—sexy—and I was bubbling with excitement when a simple note beneath both items caught my eye. *His* handwriting demanded I accept this lunch invitation. *His* words told me he wouldn't take a no for an answer.

And even now, as his driver pulls into the private underground parking of the luxury building where he has an apartment, there's no repentance. I feel butterflies taking flight—somersaulting in my stomach when I see his handsome face.

This man is the definition of tall, dark, and delicious. *I'm screwed.*

Alejandro is dressed in a perfectly tailored pair of black pants and a dress shirt with the sleeves rolled up and the top two buttons undone. It gives me an unobstructed view of his throat and top of his chest—the sexy way in which his throat bobs as he swallows. There's also a hint of a tattoo that's peeking from the opening and my mouth waters.

I'm also drawn to the bold ink on his arm. I'm mesmerized by the sight of them.

Watching every flex of his hand and then flicking my eyes to his throat—to that biteable grin. There's curiosity brewing within me. A thirst to see what markings adorn his flesh. *This is a bad idea.*

The car stops, and my door is directly in front of him. Thirty seconds pass, and I count down each excruciating moment before he reaches for my handle.

And I feel it when he does, as if his fingers gripped my flesh. A hard shiver runs through me and I bite down on my bottom lip, fighting back the shocked gasp fighting to break free. This unnerves me. Scares me.

But more than that, these tumultuous feelings he evokes set me ablaze.

It's why I'm here. Why when he demanded my presence, I didn't balk or deny him. Instead, I wore his gift and lied to my family with the help of my security, leaving behind the tracking device Laura's friend found in my phone to corroborate my lie.

To them, I'm at the studio for a special presentation by a famous competitive duo from Brazil. Untrue; a tiny little fib that my security will support after accepting money from Mr. Lucas.

I saw it and kept my mouth shut.

They know it and won't go against him.

"Come." One word; his tone is rich and velvety—the deep baritone gliding across my skin as goose bumps rise. As my nipples tighten. Alejandro extends a hand inside the car, the same one with the tattoos, and I'm taken in by them.

I don't let him take me out of the vehicle. I can't move. Instead, I'm taken in by the mixture of words and vines that wrap around his forearm, gliding my fingertips over each one.

A door opens and closes in the background.

His breathing becomes heavy.

"These are not what I expected." It's the first thing I say, recognizing each line from a famous speech given by an ex-President of the republic. One, my family hates because the man single-handedly revoked my grandfather's past declarations of law. Because he fought to end a constitutional amendment that let the president-elect serve more than one term if he chose to.

He was also responsible for the release of Alejandro's father from prison and dropping all charges.

Fight for tomorrow and never take a step back.

"Not all things are as they seem."

"I've heard that line before," I whisper, letting him pull me from the car a few seconds later. His hand never leaves mine. His grip is tight yet comforting as we walk up two steps that lead into an empty lobby. Not a single person can be found—employee or resident—and the elevator doors are open wide as we slip inside.

"Press the up button, Preciosa."

"Okay." There's a small shiver that rushes through me at his tone; a palpable hunger causes my core to clench as I follow his command. I shouldn't like the way his nickname makes me feel, nor should I allow him to pull me into his lavish penthouse once we reach the top floor of this building, but I do.

My eyes take in every square inch of his place, cataloging the expensive paintings and opulent furniture—the solid gold fixtures and imported rugs. It's magazine beautiful and reminds me a lot of where I live now: cold and impersonal. Lacks the same feeling of warmth that's been lacking in mine for as long as I can remember.

And the further we walk inside, the more I begin to feel uncomfortable. Afraid to move the wrong way and break something valuable. From the foyer to the formal living room, I walk with a stiffness that makes me force a smile and then take my very first relaxed breath once we step out onto the attached balcony. I'm thankful for the reprieve. The chance to stand outside and watch the city below us as people walk by the building and cars zoom past—life carrying on while we simply stand side by side.

"You don't like it." Alejandro's statement a few minutes later catches me off guard, and I turn my eyes to him, finding the caramel-colored orbs studying me intently. The furrow of his brows makes him look menacing yet adorable to me. *I'm certifiable.*

"You have a gorgeous home, Mr. Lucas," is what I say instead, like I've been groomed to do so from an early age, and he chuckles.

Low and throaty. Deep and delicious. "Is there something amusing in what I just said? Did I forget to compliment something specific?"

Alejandro is unfazed by my narrowed eyes and snark, shaking his head with a smirk on his lips. "Not in the least, Solimar. I find you to be many things, but hilarious isn't one of them."

Turning with my back to the veranda, I lean back and let out a heavy breath. "Why am I here?"

"Because I want you to be."

"Can you please elaborate?"

"My words should suffice, Preciosa."

"That explains nothing, Mr. Lucas." They leave me with more questions than answers and I sigh, turning my face from him. There's a woman in his home, a bit older and heavier set, and she's carrying what looks to be iced tea and some pastries on a tray. She sets them down and leaves, her eyes meeting mine once before she scurries away.

I don't know why the simple act makes me wonder how many women he's brought to this penthouse. How many have fallen to their knees or spread their legs? It bothers me. It makes me feel insignificant in a way that brings forth hurtful reproaches.

Maybe I'm just a game to him. A pawn. A way to get back at my father, and like a complete and utter fool I—

"Stop that."

"I think it's best I…" two fingers grip my chin and turn my face "…leave."

"Never take your eyes from me." Alejandro pulls me closer with the firm hold, dipping his face just enough that his mouth hovers over mine. "I don't like it when you do."

My cheeks warm under his intense stare. "And why is that? Tell me why I'm here."

"Will that make you happy?" he asks, licking his lips as mine part. I can almost taste him as I follow the movement. His scent: leather and spice infiltrating my senses, and I swallow back a moan. "Make you less afraid?"

"I'm not—"

"Don't lie to me, little doll. That's a sin I'll never forgive." Gone is the look of lust, and what stands before me is the devil incarnate, the obsessed killer my father warned me about, and yet I'm not afraid. Even as his hand falls from my face and he grips my hip, turning me around to face the fantastic view—pinning me as he moves to stand behind me—I don't want to run.

Not when his lips press against my cheek and his hand skims up my midsection, stopping at my throat.

Not when he wraps those strong fingers around my neck and gives it a small squeeze.

If anything, I like his hold. To feel the rise and fall of his chest against my back.

And while I may be a virgin, I'm not a prude. I've touched myself to thoughts of this very man since the age of seventeen. He's whose face I imagine as my fingers slide across slick flesh. *The reality is more dangerous than the imagination.*

"You don't scare me, Alejandro." It leaves me on a whimper as he leaves a trail of tiny bites across the bare skin of my right shoulder. The feel of him this close has made my thighs slick and core ache. "But I do need to know—why me?"

"You're here because no one has ever left me speechless with one look." Another small bite, this one followed by a kiss. "Because I need to know what you're thinking, feeling…what you taste like." His exhale is rough against my skin, almost pained, and I can't stop the small smile of satisfaction it brings. I'm not the only one suffering. "You're here because life has thrown me a curveball and I plan to catch it and keep it close."

10

Solimar

H E'S WATCHING ME EAT.
      Face serious and eyes hooded, Alejandro takes in the
      way the spoon slips past my lips and the way I groan with
each bite. I'm not trying to be sexual. I'm not trying to seduce him.

This rum cake is just to die for.

"Aren't you going to eat yours?" I ask, giving him a small smile.
My blush gives away how much he affects me. The man has been
indulging—treating me to one of the best lunches I've had in a long
time. Nothing *frou-frou* or foreign or even expensive.

After letting him tug me into his dining room with the promise to
finish our talk, I was served a bowl of sancocho with all the fixings.
The hearty soup with a combination of meats came with a side of
rice, avocado, and the ever-present peppery sauce to give it a special
kick.

My mouth watered as the smells, the comforting gesture, settled in, and I leaned over to kiss his cheek. The action felt natural, his reaction heart-stopping.

His smile was soft with a hint of boyish sweetness that made my heart pitter-patter. At that moment, he didn't look to be in his thirties, nor the feared man most wouldn't dare cross paths with. He was just a guy eating a meal with a woman. No pretenses or fake charm.

And I love it more than I should.

Alejandro licks his bottom lip. "I'd rather just watch you, Preciosa."

"And why is that? You did promise we'd talk over our meal," I say, bringing the spoon of yummy goodness to my mouth a final time. This last bite is overly saturated with the rum-infused syrup, and a little bit dribbles down to my chin as I savor the decadent morsel.

Did I do that on purpose? Maybe.

Is it worth it to see his eyes dilate, fixated on the syrupy flesh? Yes.

"Because you're all I can think about. Because I need to know why all this time you've been hidden from the public view. My view."

"That's not..." My words simply die off, and I swallow hard. Lifting his hand, Alejandro reaches over and swipes the sweetness from my chin and brings it to his mouth. Lips parting, he sucks his finger clean while eyeing mine.

"Delicious." I'm not ready for his groan. For what that sound does to me. Those cognac orbs never leave my face as heat licks at my skin, making me flush from head to toe. More so than before. "The perfect accompaniment to any meal."

"Alejandro, I—"

"Need more of you," he interjects and stands, his chair scraping against the imported floors, the sound loud in the quiet room where all you hear is my rapid breathing. "It's near maddening, to be honest."

"This makes no sense." I'm nodding, accepting the hand he's holding out for me. "Our families hate each other."

A rough exhale leaves him when my fingers intertwine with his. "You're excluded from that."

"Why?" It's driving me crazy. I need some sort of explanation to hold on to—rationality to survive on. "Why me?"

He doesn't talk at first. Instead, Alejandro walks us out of the dining room and toward a room down a long hallway. The door is wide open and the large bed at the center makes my body lock up.

I'm not ready, and my insecurities rise to the surface. I don't know how to—

Two strong arms wrap around me, and I'm pulled against a strong chest. Lips are at my temple. "Calm down, Preciosa. I'm not going to taste the sweet cherry between your thighs."

"You're not?" My tone is breathless relief with a hint of disappointment. There's no denying my attraction to him. I want more of him, but I'm still so unsure of everything else. Of what his motives are.

"No." A tiny kiss above my ear. "You're not ready for me *yet*, Solimar. We're just here to talk."

"Talk in your room?"

"Talk in my bed." Alejandro doesn't give me a chance to protest or deny his request, and on my next intake of breath, I find myself swept off my feet. He's cradling me against his hard body, and I can't help myself, burying my face in his neck so I can drown in his scent.

"I could've walked, Mr. Lucas." It's mumbled, which makes him chuckle, the deep vibration soothing.

"Or ran away." I can hear the smile in his voice, his tone smug.

"Would I have gotten far?" My smile widens at the ridiculousness my life has become, but I still can't regret being here. "Would you have let me?"

"No." No shame. No hesitation. A few steps inside and I'm deposited in the middle of what I'm sure is a cloud. Even the beds at the presidential home aren't this comfortable, and I close my eyes, letting myself sink into the mattress.

Alejandro moves away from me but doesn't go far. He's at the foot of the bed now, hands on the strap of my sandal that he carefully removes, first one and then the other, his thumb running up and down the top of my shins a few times before the mattress dips.

My eyes open and I take in this beautiful man crawling up the bed to where I am, his eyes taking in my expression. He's hovering over me, so close that if I sit up just a bit, I could kiss him, but I don't.

Instead, I wait.

Wait a little more.

And just when I don't think I can stand the heated stare or the feel of him this close, Alejandro shakes his head with a grin and lays a tiny kiss at the corner of my lips. "Breathe, Solimar."

"You're trouble, Mr. Lucas."

"I'm much more than that," he says, moving to lie beside me but leaves a hand on my hip. His strong grip turns me to face him. "But that's something you'll see soon enough."

"You're confusing me."

"Not trying to." At my arched brow he snorts, a sound I would've never thought a man like him would make. "I'm just a man getting to know a beautiful woman."

That's a lie. We'll never be average people.

"You know who I am, Alejandro. Know the men in my family better than I do." My voice is low—a little worried, and yet his expression remains the same. No fear. No concern.

A tsk comes from him before he brings a hand up to cup my cheek. "You're nothing like them."

"How do you know? How do I know you aren't just using me?" It's my biggest fear. That he'll use my attraction against me. That he'll break my heart if I let him in.

"Because had that been the case, I would've fucked you the very next day and sent you home with my come dripping down your thighs." A gasp escapes me, and I both want to smack him for the crudeness and slide a little closer because his dirty mouth is a turn-on. *I'm in so much trouble.* "I'm not a liar, Miss Quintero. With me, you'll always know where you stand."

I nod, but my lips purse. "Were you there at Codicia to meet me?"

"No. I was there on business."

"Okay…" I let out the breath I didn't know I'd been holding in "…I believe you."

"Just like that?"

"Somewhat. This is me giving you the benefit of the doubt."

"Thank you," Alejandro says, rubbing his thumb across my skin before tipping my face slightly up. "And here's my truth in return… that night was the first time I've ever paid attention to anyone in your family that isn't an adult male. Your mother, younger brother, and you didn't exist." My lips part, the questions sitting on the tip of my tongue, but he shakes his head. "Let me finish."

"Okay."

"It was a shock to the system to learn who you were, but nothing changed for me. That beautiful dancing flower with the sassy smile and sinful body caught my eye; I wanted more. More of you. A taste. To feel you writhe beneath my touch." Long fingers grip the back of my neck, holding me in place. "So I chased you knowing who you are because I don't care. Your last name means shit in the grand scheme of things, Solimar. I want you."

"Oh God," I moan, goose bumps breaking out across my fevered flesh at his admission. I believe him; there's no reason for him to lie when he has me at his mercy. I'm here and in his bed of my own volition.

His eyes are sincere as they stare into mine.

His expression is heated, yet there's a hint of softness there that feels privately mine.

"Not God, sweetheart. I'm who you worship."

My father will kill me for this. "This can't possibly work and—"

"I'm not a patient man." No sooner did the last word pass his lips than his mouth slants over mine, taking liberties that no man has before. He's stealing my first kiss; a criminally earth-shattering moment that leaves me at his mercy, and when I moan his name, he slips his tongue inside. It's possessive and hungry and I let him— pulling him closer by the front of his shirt as our tongues caress and I give in. I forget propriety. I forget who he is and who I am while his taste is branded within my DNA. "Motherfuck, Preciosa. So sweet."

"More." It's all I manage to whimper. I need more—everything —and I welcome his tightening grip as he controls my movements, tilting my head back; he nips my bottom lip before licking the abused flesh. "Please, Alejandro."

"You beg so prettily."

"I've never done this before. Felt this uninhibited and desperate." At my admission, an animalistic groan builds in his chest a second before I'm completely pinned beneath his strong body. My hands are in one of his over my head. My thighs are open, my dress nearly exposing my panties as I cradle him where I need his touch.

"Saying that to a man like me is a dangerous thing, little flower." Another rough exhale, the thick length in his pants flexing, and I cry out. I'm sensitive and wet, almost embarrassingly so. "You're not ready for me to take you."

"You asked me to never lie." There's a hint of a whine in my tone and he smiles, his features softening while his grip remains the same. Tight and controlling.

"That I did."

"It's all your fault."

"I apologize, Preciosa. I'll behave."

"But—" I'm silenced by another kiss, softer this time as he explores me gently, yet the fire remains.

It's him.

His scent. His taste. His touch.

Alejandro bites my bottom and then upper lip before pulling back. "You're going to be a lot of trouble, Solimar." He releases my wrist and then brings each hand to his mouth, nipping the slightly pink skin before laying a kiss there. "The kind that could easily be the cause of Colombia's demise."

"How so?" I'm mesmerized by the feel of him against my core. How big and thick he is. By the tender way he rubs my skin with his fingers while keeping those hungry eyes on mine.

"Because I'll never allow you to marry Signio Cortez."

Those words register, and the fog I've been under begins to fade. His threat is valid. My reality is unavoidable.

"It's not up to me." I hate how weak my voice sounds as I say this. How tense my body becomes. "My father—"

"Should be taking care of you, not selling you to the highest bidder and alliance. You're not a pawn."

You're not a pawn.

Christ, those words hit me in the chest, and I turn my face away from him as tears gather at the corners of my eye. It hurts that someone I barely know understands what my father never will.

I'm a person. I have rights.

"Gracias, I—"

"I'm here now, Sol. Trust me."

"I don't know you." I'm still refusing to look at him, but that choice is taken away a minute later when he switches our position. He's below me, my body laying over his and our faces mere centimeters apart. His exhale is my inhale.

"Then I suggest we start exchanging facts about ourselves." Alejandro gives me a soft smile that disarms me. "Every night this week, I'll be calling to play my version of twenty questions."

"Your version?" I quirk a brow up, and my smile broadens at the ridiculousness of it all. I'm here with a criminal, my father is the president, and he's proposing we play a silly game to calm my worries. "Sounds interesting."

"Good..." he pecks my lips once more and then tucks me against his chest, arms hugging me tight "...because I wasn't giving you a choice in the matter."

11

ALEJANDRO

THERE'S A KNOCK at my door two days later, and I'm not surprised. It's why I gave everyone but Geronimo the day off with instructions to head out into the jungle for a training session with Chiquito and my brother.

Out in no man's land. Where those in power here are too scared to venture into.

The Amazon is unforgiving and cruel. It'll take without asking.

"Come in," I say and sit back, dropping the pen in my hand atop a lucrative contract with an overseas pharmaceutical giant. It's a hefty amount on the dotted line that anyone else would sign, but I'm not most. My counter is written out just above the empty signature line, and I won't accept anything less than what I'm asking.

"Hey, Lucas. You have a few minutes to spare?" Signio asks, sitting across from me without being offered a chair. His friend follows, eyes roaming the large office located on the first floor of the building I own in Bogota—where I enjoyed a nice little afternoon lunch with my guest's fiancé two days ago.

I'll put a bullet in his head before he ever says I do.

"No, but I imagine you drove over to share something of importance?" The bite in my tone is lost on both as they admire the picture of Solimar atop my desk. They don't know it's her as I've cut her face from the print, but her body is on full display. Out on the veranda, she stood with her back to the city, arms gripping the bars behind her, and head tipped up to the sun. Her chest—the tempting swell is clear to see, and so is the sinuous curve of her hip, those toned legs seemingly a mile long in the perfect little dress she wore for me.

Before Signio blinks again, I lodge a bullet into the leg of his chair, forcing him to tip forward. "What the fuck!"

When he looks up, the barrel of my 1911 is pointing at his chest. "Keep your eyes off what isn't yours, Cortez. I won't miss next time."

"Understood." He stands from the ruined armchair and places his hands atop my desk. I don't miss the way his eyes shift over the papers in front of me. "We have a similar problem where you poached—"

"I'd be careful in how you finish that sentence, güevon." Lowering my gun, I keep it pointing his way while I sit forward. "There's little patience in me today."

Signio swallows hard and holds a hand up. "I'm not trying to be disrespectful, Alejandro. I just came here to talk man to man." My reply is to wave a hand in the air for him to continue. For a brief second, his eyes shift to his friend, who nods. "Do you know who my fiancé is?"

"You have five seconds to get to the point."

"Solimar Quintero is important to me and—"

He's silenced by the slam of my hand against the wooden top of my desk. "Why the fuck are you here, Cortez? Be a man and spit it out."

"Back away from her."

Laughter bubbles up inside of me. It's loud and non-threatening, the first clue he should be afraid. Shitting his pants. Because while he relaxes and I show an outward amused expression, beneath my skin the ire in me is bubbling to the surface.

The demon in me is clawing its way out, and I smile. "Is that all?"

"Yes." Cortez and his friend chuckle. They're amused and at ease. "We both know you don't need that kind of heat, and between us, she's nothing more than a trophy I need on my arm." They both miss how my hand grips the gun's handle, finger on the trigger. "My father needs this marriage to happen and if I comply, I get a favor in return."

And that right there sums up what Solimar means to him; a means to get what he wants. She's an object. Nothing more.

"How long do you need to stay married and what are the terms?" Every muscle in my body has locked down, the cords trembling with the exertion to stay in my seat and not snap his neck. I want to. I will in the future. However, I've come to learn a few things over the years, and one is that stupid people talk. Give them a sense of comfort and they give themselves away. "For curiosity sake?"

Another laugh. Cocky. "Two years, and she needs to have given me an heir by then."

"Okay." Bringing my other hand to my face, I scratch my jaw. "And why do you believe that I know this girl? What gave you the cojones to come and warn me away?"

Signio tilts his head in his friend's direction. "Samuel saw you follow her at Codicia toward the elevator but lost you among the crowd. He didn't see you talking with her, but you were chasing."

With a brow raised, I stare the friend down. "Is that so, Samuel?"

His throat bobs harshly. "Your eyes were set on her and—"

He doesn't finish as his scream rends the air, the pain-filled sound reverberating throughout every square inch of this office and lobby. A lobby that exists purely for appearance's sake and whose front desk is run by my employees.

The building is mine.

The people within will do anything I ask.

These concrete walls have seen more than one person take their final breath.

And while his friend sits beside him, kneecap blown, Signio doesn't move. He doesn't look. *Pussy.*

"Anything else?" No response other than muffled cries as Samuel bites down on his knuckles. Calmly, I place my gun down. "Are you sure there isn't anything else you want me to know?"

"No." It's low and meek and pathetic. *Fucking* culicagados trying to play men.

"Louder."

"No. Nothing else, Lucas," Signio says, now refusing to meet my stare.

"And you, Samuel?"

His hands grip his fragmented knee, blood pooling below him and onto my carpeted floor. "No, sir."

"Good." Pushing my chair back roughly, I stand to my full height with narrowed eyes. "Now, listen very carefully because I will only say this once. Nod if you understand." They do, looking just like the sniveling bobbleheads they are. "If you ever step foot inside my building in any way that isn't respectful, I will personally cut off your head and mail it to your parents. What I do..." I keep my voice low, but my simmering ire is clear "...is none of your fucking business, and you best remember that. Is that clear?"

"Alejandro, I didn't mean to disrespect you. She's my intended and her father would—"

"Stay away from Solimar, Signio. This is your only warning."

"I can't do that. We're getting married."

Placing both hands palms down atop my desk, I lean forward. "I'll slit your throat before you ever make it to the altar."

At my words, his face pales and hands shake. His curiosity is also piqued. "Why do you care about her?" Signio's voice is low, the words muttered. "Why does she matter?"

"How I deal with each Quintero is none of your concern." His mouth opens; he's dying to ask more or offer some kind of bullshit assistance, but we both know it's fake. I know a lot more than he thinks. Know his true intentions. The things he's done. "This is your cue to leave."

"I—" That's all he gets out, rushing to pull his friend up as my fingers wrap around the gun's handle. "We're leaving. Have a good day."

"You do that." *He's a dead man.*

"Señor Lucas, she's in her room now," her guard speaks lowly into the phone, and the sound of a door closing carries through the line a few seconds later. "It's been a rough day for her."

"What happened?" I hiss out through clenched teeth. My earlier visit with Cortez has left me in a shit mood. He's lucky I didn't end him today, that I'm giving him more time to dig a deeper hole. "Who upset her?"

"Solimar argued with her mother today after lunch." Carlos exhales roughly. "They'd visited an orphanage today, and when a staged reporter outside of the building asked about the pending nuptials, the first lady gave an exclusive."

"What kind?"

"That Solimar has been dress shopping, which is the furthest thing from the truth."

"Why would she do that?" The plastic in my hand groans, the phone's case cracking at the center in my tight grip. "Is there something I don't know, Carlos?"

"No, Patron. That was a lie and Solimar became so upset, letting her emotions out once they were both seated in the back of their SUV."

"What was said?"

"Solimar demanded to know whose team she was on? If she's ever really planned to help her get out of that sham of an engagement."

"And did Veronica Quintero ever have her daughter's best interest at heart?" We both knew the answer, but I needed the verbal conformation on this betrayal. Something is going on with Solimar's mother, and I'm beginning to think she's playing a dangerous game.

"The first lady told her in plain terms to buck up and accept her fate. That there's no getting out."

"Thank you, Carlos." Undoing the first few buttons of my shirt, I release the tie's knot and let the ends hang over my shoulders. "Keep me informed, and I'll have a little something extra for your troubles."

"Thank you, sir."

Disconnecting the call, I walk over to the small bar inside my office and pour myself a drink. I'm giving myself a second or five to compose myself before reaching out to Solimar, swirling the amber-colored liquid around the glass twice before bringing it to my lips.

Her being upset doesn't sit right with me. Eats at me. It makes my chest feel tight.

I throw back my drink and then pour another. And another.

My first instinct is to ram an eighteen-wheeler through the security gate of the president's home and shoot every single fucker inside, except her.

She's different. Innocent.

"My vow of vengeance will never touch a single hair on that little flower's head." Back at my desk with the decanter in hand, I set it down and pick up my iPad, opening the FaceTime app. I'm looking for the contact information her guard gave me a few days back. A quick press to her picture and the phone connects, ringing twice before her beautiful face appears.

At first, she doesn't say anything. There's shock and maybe a bit of awe, but behind the surprise expression, I see amusement. It's in the curl of her lips and the brightness of her eyes. In the way she sighs my name before shaking her head and climbing atop her bed.

Once situated, her back against a headboard with a mountain of white and pink pillows cushioning her body, she arches a brow. "Should I even ask?"

"No, but if you do, I'd tell you." She's appeased by my answer, her eyes dancing between my chest and face. "Does it matter?"

"No. Not really."

"Good." Refilling my glass, I take a sip. "You ready to play?"

"Play what?" The question is coy, the expression on her face inquisitive. *Fuck*, she's beautiful. Solimar is all soft and decadent in her tight, light blue tank top and matching sleeping shorts. She's dangerous curves and a happy smile. However, I do notice the bit of red around her eyes. The bit of wetness that still clings to her lashes. "Is there something I'm missing?"

"Twenty questions, Preciosa. You owe me," I say instead of questioning her. Not today.

"Do I, now?"

"Yes."

"I don't know about that…"

"Are you going to deny me?"

"No." Solimar mumbles *don't think I can* under her breath, but I don't call her out on it.

"First question?"

"Hit me," she replies, nodding enthusiastically, and I chuckle.

"Favorite color?"

She's pensive for a moment, finger tapping her chin. *Motherfucking adorably indecent.* "White. You?"

"Really? White?" Not at all what I thought she'd say. Most women like pink, or red, or even purple.

"Yeah." She giggles. Her fresh face and soft eyes make me want to kiss her. "I like the idea of a blank canvas and embellishing it in diverse ways. Being creative in any way is an outlet I crave."

"Do you like to accessorize, is what you're saying?" Solimar tilts her head to the side, expression bordering on confusion. "What, Preciosa?"

"Never thought you'd understand what accessorizing means, that's all. Men don't go through painstaking hours upon hours to put outfits together." The mirth is back in the small quirk of her lips. "You guys are more grab and go."

"You forget I have a sister slightly younger than you. Shopping is her life."

"Touché, Alejandro."

"I like the way you say my name."

A touch of pink caresses her cheeks and she looks at me from under her lashes, an action I'm not sure she's aware of. "What about you? What's your favorite color?"

"Grey."

Her nose scrunches a bit. "Like a cloudy sky?"

"Like your eyes." Her embarrassment—reactions—are so refreshing. Honest. "Next question…"

"Keep them coming."

"Favorite movie?"

"*The Mummy*." No hesitation from her. "You?"

"*Scarface,* for obvious reasons." I give her a wink, and the flush across her skin becomes more pronounced, the small smile on her face becoming a smirk. "Favorite childhood memory, Sol?"

She shrugs. "That's a toughie."

"Why?"

"Because you don't have a childhood when you're being molded into the obedient child of a presidential family. You don't get to go out and play or be 'normal' like other children." Her voice is flat— no emotion—and I can almost hear her father spewing this bullshit. Drilling it into her head. "You're forced to sit down and learn the rules, expectations, and the reality that what your father says goes, no matter how much it hurts you."

"I'm sorry, sweetheart. No one should live that way."

The smile she gives me is sad. "It is what it is."

"Let's skip that for now. Next—"

"There was this one time my mom put her foot down when I was seven, though."

"Where did you go?"

"We took a trip to Disney World in Florida." Sol is looking at me, but her eyes are miles away. At this moment she truly looks her age, young and impressionable. Sheltered and suffocating. "It was amazing to just be another kid in a crowd. To take goofy pictures and eat junk food and laugh with my parents as we rode every single attraction in the park. There were no crowds crowding or men in polyester suits trying to get my father's attention or approval. For the first and only time in my life, we were just an average family on vacation."

And as the last word slips past her perfect lips, the truth hits me in the chest. There's more than lust and want and revenge singing in my veins. There's an uncontrollable need to protect and take care of her.

To give her back what's been taken.

I'm going to give this precious girl her freedom.

I'm going to make her crave me as I do her.

12

Solimar

ONE, TWO, THREE.

One, two, three.

The instructor claps her hands with each count, signaling the three couples on the floor to start the rehearsed steps to a simple salsa choreography. And while they do so, while I play the part of the audience this afternoon, my mind lingers on my phone call with Alejandro last night.

I don't know how he knew I needed him, but I'm more thankful for that call than he'll ever know. Heartbroken and full of painful anxiety that made it hard to breathe, I'd been cursing my name when the phone rang.

He made me forget.

He made me laugh.

He cared.

"Again, from the top." The instructor's eyes cut to the couple near the back mirror and sighs. "Please try to keep up. This isn't a club downtown or for giggles; dancing is an art and should be respected as such."

Beside me someone snickers, but I pay them no mind and try to refocus on the class.

These are new students. People of affluent wealth. Most are stiff as a board.

However, there's one dancer that stands out—the son of a world-renowned surgeon who's come to Colombia to participate in a medical exchange program before opening his practice in Uruguay.

I know this because it's the first thing he shared with the class, pompous smile on his face. His eyes have also been searching mine out for the past twenty minutes, a tinge of frustration seeping through when I rebuff him.

I'm ignoring him. He's annoyed. It's a game I've learned to excel at with the unwanted attention that comes from my position as the first daughter.

"Very good, Gabriel. That's exactly how you feel the music." She looks pensive for a moment, her feet still moving to the beat. "I'd like to see you dance with a more advanced student. Solimar?"

"Yes, Señora Garcia?" I answer, a feeling of dread settling in. More so when Gabriel's face gives a smug expression. He knows who I am. My family. "How can I be of assistance?"

"Come here and take your place with Mr. Castillo. I want to see what he can do given free reign."

"Of course." My smile is fake, but so perfected over the years that they can't tell the difference. That, or they don't care. Something that over the years I've come to understand.

If it benefits a person, they are willing to overlook another's misery. Because who cares, as long as it doesn't affect their end goal.

His smirk is nothing like the one Alejandro effortlessly wears. "You ready, beautiful?"

"It's Miss Quintero. Please remember that." My voice is low but he hears, and the smarmy smile only broadens as I take his hand and hold the position.

"Of course. My apologies." His arm goes around my waist, pulling me in closer when the alarm in the studio goes off. *Thank God.*

"Everyone out. We'll cancel today and reconvene tomorrow at the same time," I hear her call out, but I'm already using the opening to step back, rushing away and toward my bag on the floor beneath the chair I'd been sitting on. The exit to the building is outside the room's door and down the hall, and I curse my need to please others in this instance. My security's usually across the street waiting for me, something that I've asked them to do so that others don't feel uncomfortable, but as Gabriel calls out my name, I regret it.

"Solimar, wait up." His shout catches the attention of the last stragglers still around. They look but continue on their way; not even the instructor seems to be around. One second I'm walking with the crowd, and the next, I'm alone.

Where the hell did everyone go? "Sorry, I'm in a rush. My guards will...hey!" I'm whirled around by a hand on my arm, the grip a little painful. "Let go."

"What's the hurry? I'd love to spend more time with you." Gabriel doesn't release me. Instead, he walks closer, body almost pressing, but I don't let him corner me. For every step of his, I take one back, all the way until we reach the building's main exit. "Maybe catch a bite?"

"No."

"Don't be like that, Preciosa," he says, and I shudder, hating the use of Alejandro's nickname coming from this idiot's lips. "I'm in town for a few—"

Gabriel doesn't get to finish as Carlos and a man I know works for Alejandro stand over his limp form. They kick him once, twice, before the sudden crack of a bone snapping rings through the air and I lean back against the nearest wall.

Gabriel's arm is bent at an odd angle, his face a bloody mess as blood pours from a gash at the bridge of his nose. Each man is wearing an expression of anger. Each one positioned in front of me so I can't see the full extent of the damage as a pitiful whimper slips past the overeager man's mouth.

I should be afraid, but I'm not. I should be yelling at them to stop, but I don't.

Something warms my body and the calmness that seeps through leaves me breathless for a completely different reason. He's here. I know this. Feel it in the air around us, this dominating force that takes over every square inch of the room and my eyes dart around, looking. Searching. Needing to see his face.

To bask in the knowledge that he's watching out for me. Doing what no one else ever has.

Footsteps come closer from another entrance, a private room that only those who work here are allowed inside. I'm counting down each one in my head. I'm vibrating with nervously excited energy— an overwhelming need to fling the door open and confirm what I know to be true.

Not that I have to wait long. All movement ceases the moment the door is pulled open and Alejandro Lucas steps through, his face and mouth set in an impassive expression as he takes in the man on the floor. There's fury brewing beneath the surface of his calm. I see it, and it grows hotter as he takes me in against the wall, bracing myself.

He doesn't say a single word, just holds a hand out toward me, one that I walk toward without hesitation. At this moment, I don't care who's watching or what they might say; I welcome the safety he brings.

My palm in his, he pulls me closer. "Are you okay?"

"I am now." And I mean it with everything I am. "How did you get here so fast?"

"I'll explain later, little flower." Alejandro leans down, just enough so his lips can skim over my temple. "Expect my call."

"Okay." It comes out breathless and accepting and excited.

"Good girl," he says it so low only I hear, before straightening to his full height. Those soft cognac eyes now burn with fury. And while his hold on my hand remains gentle, the tick of his sharp jaw gives away that the feared man most have nightmares about is very much present. "Carlos, take Miss Quintero home, and no deviations. Report back when it's done."

"Of course, Patron."

There's no protest from me when I'm led out. Nothing.

However, there is a smile of satisfaction that graces my lips when I see Alejandro's fist connect with Gabriel's face before the door closes and the lock is engaged. *What does that say about me?*

THE FAINT SOUND of cutlery scraping against plates as those around the table dig into their meals grates on my nerves. So does the sound of multiple conversations happening at once. Everyone's talking about inane subjects—stock market prices or who has the most expensive car—while I sit here and try to swallow the bite of chicken I've been poking at for the last thirty minutes.

My father's enjoying the attention given by his campaign manager and the head of the political party our family is backed by, while the vice president and his wife listen. While they look at each other every few minutes as the others continue to wax poetry about my father. He's a modern-day revolutionary in their eyes. The suit-wearing guerilla champion of the people.

And yet they don't mention those in need. The poor of this country go without.

The citizens that have been set aside and forgotten because greed and excessive lifestyles are more important.

Every single person at this table outside of the president's children have let Colombia down, and that's only because we have no say. None. We're mere props to make him look better. Give him the illusion of the approachable family man.

"How was class, Solimar?" the woman who's been chatting with my mom asks, and I force myself to swallow before offering a smile. "I heard you're quite the bailarina."

"Thank you, Mrs. Salinas. And to answer your first question, not much happened today." It's the truth, but not enough it seems, and the minute purse of my mom's lips tell me to elaborate. "We had new students today, six in total, and Mrs. Garcia had them run through basic steps. You know, just to gauge their ability and knowledge of counting notes and coordination."

"Were they any good?" She leans toward me as if I have some kind of juicy gossip. As if I'll divulge names and their lack of rhythm. "Or should they be on one of those blooper videos you kids love to watch?"

"They were okay." My face scrunches up, thinking about Gabriel and what occurred after class. My lack of care for his well-being and the acknowledgment that there is a hint of depravity inside of me. "Nothing memorable, but they could improve significantly with some dedication."

"Spoken like a true politician's daughter." The others around us laugh, the joke being me. "What about that fiancé of yours? Does he attend these classes?"

My initial reaction is to snort, but I bite that back when my father's eyes turn our way. Now he's interested. Wants to see if I'll embarrass him. "No…" I add a small girlish giggle as if it's preposterous that he'd be caught in one of my dance lessons "…he's much too busy to join me. His business takes a lot of his time, and its success is all due to his hard work."

The lie tastes like battery acid on my tongue, but the woman buys it and nods. "I know that's right. These men are always busy." She's chuckling while playfully elbowing the man beside her, her husband, who's a known real estate mogul and lobbyist. He's also an adulterer with two children born outside of their marriage and five months apart. "Always starting something new."

That "new" would be the affair made public by a national publication due to the lawsuit by the mistress after he demanded she entertains his associates.

Those around the table laugh at her ribbing. No one calls him out for being a pig, and I shudder internally. It's getting harder and harder to bite my tongue, but I do. I sit dutifully and wait for the next uncomfortable question while my brother rolls his eyes and eats his dinner.

"Claudia, my girl is beautiful, smart, and has Signio wrapped around her little finger." My father seems pleased with my mother's response, entwining their fingers atop the table as she looks right at me. Daring me to not say a word. To follow her lead. *What are you trying to pull?* "So much so that Mr. Cortez is Solimar's date for the gala next week. It's their first public appearance as a couple."

What. The. Hell?

My throat constricts and my chest feels tight as beads of sweat gather at my brow. I know my face is flushed, the heat across my skin making me look embarrassed by the attention when that's the furthest thing from the truth.

I'm angry. Feel betrayed. Hurt.

"Oh, how marvelous! It'll be the talk of every media outlet and society page for weeks." Mrs. Salinas is giddy with the urge to spread the word. Gossip rules these circles. It's how the women entertain themselves. "Have you picked a dress?"

"Yes, my daughter will cause quite the stir with this." It's the first time my father speaks to anyone on this side of the table. He's watching my reaction while rubbing his thumb along the top of my mom's hand. "She's been begging for weeks to make things public, to ease up on some of my restrictions until marriage, and I've obliged. Isn't that right, baby girl?"

"Thank you, Dad. You've been so understanding." To my ears I sound normal, maybe even a little sweet, but on the inside I'm dead. Choking on the pain. "It'll be wonderful to make our relationship public and spend time together."

This appeases him, makes him beam with pride, while Carlos

enters the room with a large box. It's grand and all white with ribbons and a bow atop. *A blank canvas I can embellish.*

Could it be? Would he?

"Sorry to interrupt, Mr. President, but this arrived for Solimar by courier." Could he have waited? Yes. Will my father reprimand him? It depends on the sender. "It's from Mr. Cortez."

"How wonderful," Mom gushes, waving Carlos deeper into the room. They exchange a look, but it's gone before anyone notices their exchange. "Go ahead and place it in her room. Just leave the card."

"Of course, Madam." He bows to the room and walks over, placing the envelope in my hand. His eyes meet mine briefly, just a quick flick, and I see the amusement in them. This is not from Signio. He doesn't like the overgrown kid. "Enjoy your meal, and buenas noches."

And while everyone watches him leave, I tear open the envelope and smile when I read *his* note. This devil with the smile of an angel is letting me know he can reach me at any time. That he's watching.

"Well, Solimar? What does it say?" Mom asks, all smiles yet I see the confusion in her eyes.

With my head held high, I square my shoulders and turn the card around for the table to see.

You will always be my beautiful little flower.
My Preciosa.

13

ALEJANDRO

THE WORLD REVOLVES around perspectives—decisions —interpretations of everyday problems where our capabilities are tested. Some good. Some bad. Some idiotic. These instances all pose a diverse set of problems, but they can't be ignored.

Because for every action, there is an equal or harsher consequence, something that my American hackers have yet to understand. They still think and act like children. Are irresponsible and full of excuses.

"You see, Mr. Lucas..." Shawn fidgets under my stare, looking anywhere but at me "...what happened was that—"

"Silence." I hold a hand up and Geronimo cocks his gun. "Do you, or do you not, have an update for me? Nod if you do." They're still, almost frozen, but I notice the subtle scowl Jason gives Shawn as the louder of the two shakes from his place on the couch.

They weren't expecting me today.

They chose to head out last night instead of working under Shawn's recommendations, drinking until four a.m. with a hooker each perched on their laps. They bought drinks, talked shit with the other customers—Shawn sharing confidential information about our negotiation—while Jason enjoyed the lap dance given to entice him out back for a quick fuck.

They forgot who I am.

Forget what country they're in. Who these people are loyal to.

The apartment they're using is mine.

The money paying for the pussy they used last night is mine.

Every motherfucking thing is mine.

"Mr. Thorn?"

"Yes, sir?" Jason's voice is low and expression contrite.

"What's more important? The hand or the foot?"

His leg's bouncing, hands fidgety. "Depends on the person's lifestyle, to be honest."

"Fair enough." Turning, I walk over to the dining room area and drag a chair back with me, flipping it around so the back faces them. I'm ignoring the duo for the moment as I undo the button of my suit jacket and take it off, handing it over to the guard. He takes it with the hand not pointing a Glock at the idiots, while I roll up the sleeves of my shirt and then take a seat, straddling the chair.

"Patron, if you give us—"

Shawn's lips snap shut at my murderous glare. "My conversation is with Jason at the moment. Not another word." Shifting my gaze away from his shaking form, I level his partner with the same expression. "Now, humor me. The average man who works in an office all day and has a somewhat normal social life. Hands or feet?"

"Hands." Sweat beads at his brow and he wipes the droplets with his arm. "He'll need his hands to work and to take care of himself."

I nod. "Good answer."

"Thank you."

"I appreciate the input." For some reason they both let out a sigh at this, becoming less rigid. It's the wrong move, and on their next intake of breath, my 1911 is in my hand and I'm pulling the trigger. Two bullets, and screams rend the air. Two holes that ooze blood and pool on the floor below.

It's a clean entry and exit that leaves one man with a horrified expression and the other crying, a whimpering mess down on the floor where he's slipped to. A bit overdramatic, but then again, I expect that from men like him.

A cocky, overbearing, and idiotic frat boy with the common sense of a roach.

"Quiet, or the next one will be to your head," I hiss out and Shawn bites down on his bottom lip, hard enough to break the skin. A few drops of blood roll down from the torn skin, but he does remain quiet. "Much better."

Looking over at Geronimo, I signal for him to play for them a recording from last night. It details the night, the people at their table —the talking and laughing. You can hear clearly when Bosdell tells Thorn to be quiet and live a little.

"We work for El Patron, fucker. We're untouchable." There's a small gasp or two, the sound of chairs scraping against the terrazzo floors of the establishment. People are moving, Shawn's voice becoming louder as less noise surrounds them. *"I could literally piss on the owner's cash register and still be protected, Jason. It's a dream come true."*

"Jesus, Shawn! Shut up!"

"It's not like people don't know Alejandro Lucas is a corrupt son of a bitch." There's a bit of a slur in his response, followed by a harsh smack to a solid surface. *"He has no morals, so why should we?"*

"You're stepping out of line—"

"Sweetheart, suck his dick and remove the stick from his ass while you're at it."

"That's enough, Geronimo." A click follows, and I arch a brow. Waiting. "Anything you'd like to say?"

"I apologize, Mr. Lucas. We messed up and should've been more responsible."

"Jason, I appreciate your acknowledgment and apology." My eyes turn to his associate, a man whose eyes are closed and writhing in pain. "Mr. Bosdell?"

"I'm sorry." That's it. No remorse. What he's sorry about is getting caught and chastised like the toddler he is.

Standing from my chair, I walk the few steps that separate us and look down. "Not good enough." His eyes snap open at my response, and now we get an emotional response. Fear flashed across his eyes as my finger twitches over the trigger and it engages, a bullet exiting the chamber. One second. One blink. The projectile enters his skull and his head bounces, the lifeless eyes stuck on horror as they gaze at me.

His blood bathes—splashes across the men standing present, each wearing a fragment or two on their pants as it pools beneath Mr. Bosdell. The puddle becomes larger with each passing moment.

"You were right about choosing the hand, Mr. Thorn. You're useful while your partner was a liability." Placing the gun back in its holster, I smile. "Don't make me regret this."

"No, s-sir. I won't." His entire body is shaking, face ashen.

"Let's hope so." I look over at Geronimo. "Get him the cleanup kit and walk him through the disposal process. It's time Mr. Jason Thorn learns something other than hacking if he's to be of use to me."

THERE'S something eerily calming about taking a boat into the Amazon jungle early in the morning. It's quiet and peaceful and meant to give a false sense of calm. It's untrustworthy yet lulls you into the serene landscape as predators watch from behind the cover of trees.

Or beneath the surface of the calm water. They watch while you lose yourself in the silence.

And if you're not careful, they take your life before a call for help can be screamed.

It's a danger I recognize in myself. A yearning for blood that I welcome.

"We're almost to the embankment, Patron. Will you be calling Mr. Emiliano?" Geronimo says, bringing me a bottle of water and a moist towel to wipe my face. We've been on this river for a few hours now, navigating through the densest section of the Amazon that's within the Colombian border. It's an uncharted area, unexplored because of the dangers it possesses when the nearest hospital is hours away and the chances of something going wrong are high.

Taking the cold bottle of water, I twist the cap and take a few sips. "Bring me the SAT phone. I want him to be there when we disembark."

"Right away." He's gone maybe a minute at the most, coming back with the satellite device and placing it on the bench seat. Geronimo doesn't linger, heading downstairs so I'll have some privacy while the boat's driver is far enough not to hear me.

Opening the case with the phone, I pull out the device and turn it on, leaving the antenna pointing toward the sky. It comes to life within a few seconds and I press the number three, bringing it to my ear as it starts to ring right away.

"Are you close by, hermanito?" My brother's voice is gruff, always sounds annoyed, and I chuckle at the fact he still calls me his little brother. The asshole works for me but uses the term to show some bullshit hierarchy when it comes to siblings.

"Forty minutes or so." I stand from my seat and walk over to the back where the water ripples, the motor slicing through as it propels us deeper into the jungle. Off to the left, there's a caiman on the embankment sunbathing, while another swims up close and then stops. They watch each other, not moving an inch as they wait for an opportunistic moment to present itself.

"Are we meeting by a large tree with the machete embedded?" There's shouting behind him, the sound of a group creating a formation and rifles being shifted in unison. Hands grabbing the metal, it slaps against their palms as they continue to perform a drill and can be heard clearly through the line. "That works?"

"Yes." A fish jumps out of the water and both predators rush forward, disappearing beneath the water. They don't come back up as we get farther away. "And come alone."

"Is there a reason why?"

"Because you sound as if you have something to say."

HE'S THERE when I arrive, arms crossed over his chest and a foot bent at the knee against the tree with the machete. I put it there over five years ago, the only sign of which riverbank I use.

No dock. Nothing but the splash of boot-covered feet as we jump down and walk the few feet to shore.

Geronimo walks ahead of me, gun drawn and after a quick head nod to my brother, continues his trek, and then stops out of hearing range. His back is to us and attention on making sure no one comes close, not even my right-hand, who I'm beginning to doubt.

"You sounded off earlier. What's going on?"

At my question, he nods, gazing out onto the still water. "Things are heating up, Alejandro. Have you seen the new advertisement he's running at the top of every hour?"

"I've seen it." Matias Quintero is pushing for a change in national law. To be given the chance to run for a second term, using the same tactics that helped *his* father win fifteen years ago. Smearing my family. Using fear to antagonize those that are in power and move chess pieces at their disposal. "You moved them?"

"Yeah. All three are at the safe house in San Andres." Emiliano rubs his jaw, eyes shifting to me. He's concerned. "We need to talk."

"Something wrong with…?"

"No. Mom is fine, and so is my wife."

"That leaves Lourdes."

"I think she's seeing someone."

"Does Mom know who?"

"That's the problem…" Emiliano looks at me with worry in his eyes "…our sister refuses to talk to me. She's starry-eyed and found daydreaming around the house but gets nervous when you ask her what's going on."

"I'll talk to her. She's always been honest with me."

"That's not the only problem right now, Alejandro." The worry in his expression turns into anger, hands clenching. "You need to speak with Chiquito, brother. He's out of line."

"What did he do?"

"He almost smacked a female soldier across the face."

14

ALEJANDRO

ALL NOISES CEASE as I step through the trees.

The camp becomes mute—not even the sounds of the jungle's natural inhabitants can be heard. This area is unexplored territory deep in the Colombian stretch of the Amazon and about an hour's hike from the riverbank where my boat is docked. It's off a deviation from the river that runs through these lands, a small marsh that once you pass, opens into an even larger body of water and where a smaller vessel awaits my return.

The clearing where my unit trains is large, an unobstructed terrain that's surrounded by dense bush. I don't say a word as my eyes scan the field, taking in those standing at the head. Chiquito's there along with another soldier, a rifle in the latter's hand, the butt being held up by his right palm as it lies over his shoulder.

Past them, I take account of the provisions being provided. There are huts with food and some for bathroom usage, and then three large structures with a metal roof that house hammocks. Twenty to a unit and each hammock is spaced to give each individual a bit of privacy.

It's their preferred choice; my paramilitary is resourceful and always on high alert. They're trained to move fast, live off the grid, and kill on command. My command.

The group—both men and women—stand at attention with their eyes trained ahead. Out in the field or while on assignment, they're equals. They're ready to die for their country if it comes to that.

The soldiers are divided between two groups with a pathway that lies in the middle. It's long and leads to the small stage, a height advantage needed so every person out on the field can both see and hear their instructors. Their eyes look ahead, trained on Chiquito although they know I'm here.

Breaking command to look over is unacceptable. Something I won't allow.

I walk with Emiliano close behind me, his footsteps heavier than mine, and I turn my face slightly toward him. "Get everything ready for our meeting in the white hut. I'll be there in ten."

"Listo." Emiliano walks away without looking back, but I do catch the way Chiquito eyes him, curiosity brimming in his expression.

"Patron," he says as I climb the steps and then step onto the platform. His hand is outstretched in greeting and I take it, squeezing harder than I would any other day. I'm not happy with him. He's toeing the line into dangerous territory. "They've been running drills all day. Are ready for any standoff with the national—"

"Silencio." My glare makes him take a few steps back. I ignore him for the moment; his atonement will come later today, and I turn to face the group. All eyes are on me. All waiting on my orders. "Come closer."

Feet move on command; they stomp on the ground in unison and the sound is loud across the field. Every single person crowds around the stage, almost surrounding me as they await orders.

"Tonight, we leave for Bogota." Boots stomp, their rifles all turning counterclockwise before they settle the weapon at their feet, barrel pointing toward the sky. "The president of Colombia has left us with no other choice in the matter. Not when he wishes to pursue another term by lying—changing our constitution to best serve his needs. Not when he's negotiating the extradition of our fellow man to other countries to win political favors." Every expression around me is one of anger. Of having had enough. "No more fattening the rich off the bones of the poor."

These soldiers come from all walks of life. Criminals, anarchists, and those that simply dislike how the richer get richer while their families starve. And while I'll never be an innocent and my hands are just as dirty, I do remember where I come from.

It's a promise I made to my mother, and I comply with each year. For every dollar I make, fifty percent goes back to those in need. It's why so many—the poor and hungry—are loyal to me.

"Viva Colombia!" they shout in unison.

"No more suffering in silence. No more fear."

"Viva Colombia."

"No more empty promises or stolen riches. It's time to fight and take back our country." The ground vibrates beneath the feet of my soldiers, their ire radiates throughout every single inch of this campsite. Boots stomping. Men pounding their chest as the women shout out their loyalty to me. Our country. And while I appreciate them, the dedication, I hold a hand up so they're quiet. At once, noises cease and all eyes are on me. Anxious and excited. Ready. "Tonight we show Quintero who we are. Why he and his father will never make Colombia a communist country."

"Viva Colombia!"

"God bless our country."

"You wanted to see me?" Chiquito asks, stepping inside the large hut my brother and I are sitting in. It's the largest, with a round table and a few chairs at the center—a battery-powered radio playing the national news lowly in the background as I sip some rum.

In front of me, there are a few maps of the capital. Everything from the city's major avenues to the back alleyways that lead to an empty building with the façade of an expensive apartment dwelling that the military tombos use as a hideout.

It's where they monitor those coming and going. It's where certain business meetings are held.

Where I know Quintero will be tonight as he meets with a foreign leader and the man he believes will be his daughter's future father-in-law. *They'd have to kill me first before I let any of those pieces of shit anywhere near Solimar.*

I have eyes and ears everywhere.

In every department of state.

At every fucking corner.

"Have a seat, Salazar." He does as I ask, sitting between my brother and me, his gaze shifting between us. For a few minutes, silence lingers, slowly making him nervous. His leg beneath the table begins to bounce, hitting the wooden pole beside his knee. Then there are the beads of sweat that dot his upper lip, the perspiration spreading the longer I look at him.

He's the first to break the quiet, squaring his shoulders and sitting up a little taller. "Why do I feel as though you're upset with me?"

"Should I be?"

"Nothing happened, Alejandro. Heated words—"

"Is lying the road you wish to travel down? Emiliano—"

"Doesn't understand what a firm hand...fuck!" In a flash, my chair tips back and I'm leaning over the table, his neck in my hand. My fingers tighten around the sweaty flesh as he begins to fight for oxygen. "Why?" It's a hoarse whisper, his eyes wide and becoming frantic as my hold doesn't waver.

"You don't ever interrupt me," I hiss out, glaring at the idiot as I drag him over the papers I have spread out, most of them falling to the floor. "Have you forgotten your place?" From the corner of my eye, I see Emiliano leave the hut. "Have you forgotten who I am?"

"No."

"Then why am I here having this conversation with you?" I deepen my grip, his face turning red a few seconds before I let him go. Chiquito slumps back in his seat, coughing and avoiding my narrowed eyes. "Explain yourself. You have a minute."

"I'm sorry, Patron."

"For?"

"Disrespecting you and Mr. Emiliano." My expression is emotionless at those less than convincing words. If anything, the sight of him is irritating me at the moment. "I was out of line."

"Is there something troubling you today? A problem I'm not aware of?" A flash of fear crosses his features, but it's gone soon after. I saw it, though. Just like I took notice of the blood on his holster when inside my home office after delivering Marin to me. "Now is your only chance to get this off your chest, Chiquito. Lie to me, and it's your funeral your wife will be attending next."

"Just problems with the missus. Nothing big."

"You need time off?" I'm not buying his excuse or the clear lie; something's up with him, and I'll find out. "Maybe take her away for a few days?"

"That would be amazing."

"Then you're dismissed." At my words he sputters, almost looks indignant, but is smart enough to snap his lips shut when my brother re-enters the hut a few seconds later with the woman he almost assaulted.

"He told you." Not a question, and the way my brother glares at him makes Salazar shrink back.

"He did." Looking over at the young woman, I crook my finger at her. "Come here."

"Am I in trouble, Patron?" She looks young. Almost too young to be here, but I leave it alone, knowing that the age we accept any involvement within my units is twenty. "I'm sorry if—"

"What's your name?"

"Karla Jimenez, Patron."

"How long have you been with the group, Ms. Jimenez?"

Her hands shake at her sides, but she holds my gaze. "Six months."

I nod. "Karla, if I asked you to do something for me, would you? Without questioning me?"

"Yes."

"Hagale." My eyes shift to my brother, and I nod at him. He's quick to move into position, grabbing Chiquito's arms and pulling back, forcing the man to his knees with his face unobstructed. "Strike him."

"Alejandro, you can't—" Karla surprises him with a backhand across his cheek that leaves my general in shock and enraged. His body tenses and eyes cut fire at her, but before he can even attempt to fight my brother off, I crouch down to his line of sight. Anger still dominates his body language, but the hijueputa is smart enough to stand down.

"I have never hit a woman." His bottom lip is bleeding, and I wipe it with my thumb, then clean it off using his uniform shirt. "I have never hit a woman."

"Patron, I—"

"Karla, please leave and join the others. Thank you for your help, and I ask that this stay between the four of us."

"My lips are sealed, sir."

"Gracias." The second she exits, Emiliano releases Chiquito, who looks at me with fear as he takes his place in front of the door to guard it. My right-hand—my highest-ranking soldier—is shaking. "I HAVE NEVER HIT A WOMAN," I growl out from between clenched teeth as the hand with drops of his blood lands straight across the bridge of his nose. One blow and the bone crunches, breaks, and the blood begins to flow from each nostril. "I have never motherfucking hit a woman, and those who work for me need to follow that rule. If I ever so much as hear that you ignored my order,

I'll hunt you down and expose your organs to the vultures roaming the city streets. Understood?"

"Yes, Patron."

"Good." Standing up, I extend a hand, which he takes, and I pull him up. He's smart enough to keep some distance, but I'm a peaceful man and slap him on the back before returning to my seat. "Now, get out here. You're dismissed for the next two weeks."

"But what about Quintero and…" The look I give him shuts him up. Knowing there's no changing my mind, he picks up all the papers I dropped, putting them in a neat pile before me. "Thank you, and I apologize once more."

I don't say anything, and he leaves after mumbling another apology to my brother.

His actions bring forth a few problems that I'll be rectifying soon. Very soon.

It's time for a change.

———

THE CITY STREETS are deserted at this time of night, and the police aren't paying attention to this building. Not when they need to protect the president and his guests as they discuss foreign diplomacy, fuck a whore or two, and plot ways to fuck the working class.

And while I'm not a saint nor will I ever be one, I do believe in progress. In giving back to those that have nothing as I do business with both sides of the coin. You give and take, keep balance.

Something Quintero hates. Loathes how easily I've made myself into what he'll never be.

Rich.

Powerful.

Feared.

I'm the devil they run from—a criminal in the eyes of *their* law —but loved by those whose stomachs would go hungry without me.

"We're in position, brother. Waiting on your signal."

My eyes shift to the Piguet watch on my wrist and wait. The building where the president currently sits is about seven blocks from here and has the perfect view to witness my retaliation. The SUV's TV is playing the end of a soccer game on a local channel. The referee blows his whistle while holding up a yellow card, and the transmission goes into a commercial break. A family restaurant, a national event, and then my father's name flashes across the screen as piano music plays in the background.

Pressing the two buttons on the right of my communication device, I wait for the beep that signals Emiliano is on the line.

"Listo?"

"Hagale."

Not ten seconds pass when the first of five bombs go off, each one louder than the last. The justice building goes up in flames, the sky a plumage of smoke and fire as the evidence the state has on my father withers to ash. No more using his memory to further campaigns. No more using our name to bullshit these citizens.

The device in my hand beeps three times a minute later, and that's the signal everyone's gone from the scene. Emiliano will take a different route, meeting me back at my place here in the city, while the others have different safe points to spend time at. Where they'll be seen to create alibis.

My eyes shift back to the screen, and I watch as old footage of my father in handcuffs plays out. Lines are fed to the nation—lies that make him and his father looks like saviors and my family to be terrorists.

Newspaper headlines.

False facts.

Empty promises made off the back of a now-dead man.

I've been your president, my family a part of yours, and now I ask that you trust me once more. Please vote yes on amendment one for a change to an outdated constitution. Together we can make history. We can clean up the streets of these modern-day narcos and make them safe again for future generations to come. Our country deserves to be safe. You deserve peace and prosperity.

"Take me back to my apartment, Geronimo, and take the scenic route." Sirens drive past us, heading toward the engulfed building without so much as looking toward my bulletproof vehicle. They're in a rush. Hoping to contain something that won't be easily stopped. "There's much to enjoy."

"Yes, Patron."

15

Solimar

I HAVEN'T HEARD from him in a few days.

Not so much as a note, and it makes me unhappy. A bit moody.

I'm missing him, and it's messing with my head. It makes my chest feel tight.

"You look beautiful, Sol," my mother says, entering my room, and I give a small jump in my seat in front of my vanity. *How did I miss the sound of heels clacking on the marble floor outside?* "Are you ready to head down?"

"Almost."

"Baby, please look at me." The sadness in her tone causes my heart to clench and I sigh, looking back over my shoulder and meeting her eyes for the first time in days. "I don't have much time."

"For?" Her smile slips at my one-word response and practiced grin, shoulders dropping, but I don't have more in me to give. Not when I still feel the sting of her betrayal. When she's lied to me.

"Please don't."

"Don't what?" Turning my attention back to the mirror, I apply my lipstick, a red shade that brings out the hints of blue in my eyes. The combination works for me, and the small moment of satisfaction fades when I remember that Alejandro won't be here tonight to see it for himself. To tell me how beautiful I am or how he can't deny himself a taste.

"Give me that practiced first daughter smile. I hate it." She fully steps inside, and I hear the click of the door closing and lock engaging. There's a beat of silence that lingers, and she comes closer. Mom stops an inch or two from me and I watch her through the mirror as she fights to speak. To find the right words to express whatever is on her mind.

I take the moment to look at her.

Yes, she's beautiful and without a single deep wrinkle on her face at the age of forty-eight. However, behind the makeup and expensive jewelry, there's a sadness I've never seen before. The mark of a woman near her breaking point.

"Mom, what's going on?"

"Can we talk for a few minutes? I can't take your disappointment in me."

"Don't we need to leave soon? Can this wait?"

"Your father and Signio are waiting downstairs." At the mention of their names, I force myself to swallow back the harsh words sitting on the tip of my tongue. Instead, I go back to adding the finishing touches to my makeup, dread sitting heavy in my stomach as the clock ticks away.

My distress comes from having to endure that idiot's attention all night with a fake in-love expression on my face.

My nightmare is having to pretend to love a man I loathe for fear of retribution from my father.

He's on the warpath. Angry. Almost frothing at the mouth after

Alejandro attacked the judicial building four days ago, and more so after the man himself sent him a card with his condolences.

No one has been spared as the country looks at him with distrust. As if he were an imbecile

His ego is wounded. His hopes for a constitutional change is hanging on a precarious thread if he doesn't convince those in attendance tonight. Those with enough money to make it happen even without public support.

Another reason why tonight feels as though it's the final nail in my coffin.

My fingers wrap around the closest perfume bottle. "Mom, now isn't the—"

"I'm leaving your father."

The glass slips from my hold and crashes back down atop the mirrored vanity top. They shatter, shards of glass spreading all around me and the floor, a few pieces cutting my hand. It stings and I gasp, but nothing else registers. *She's leaving him? How? Does he—*

"Baby! Oh shit!" Her cursing pulls my attention back into focus and I clutch her hand, having no idea when I stood up to face her. Nor when she took my injured palm—where the cloth she's using to wipe the few beads of blood came from. The cuts aren't deep and there's only mild pain, but her words stung. There is hurt and confusion, but above all lies and betrayal.

She's ready to leave him but has no problem handing me off to someone just like my father.

"How could you?"

"Sol, he's not the same man I married all those years ago." Her eyes beg mine to understand, to not condemn her. "He's a monster. The things he's planning…" Mom trails off when we hear footsteps approaching, her face becoming ashen. "I promise to explain everything, baby. It'll all make sense."

Her whispered words anger me, and I snatch my hand back. "Am I a diversion while you get away?" It's a low hiss, my grey eyes the exact shade as hers, narrowing. "I get married and—"

"You're not marrying that hijueputa."

"What?" I don't question her cursing. I'm too shocked.

"I'm not leaving you here to marry that man or any other your father has in line."

"But what about what you told the reporters? That lady at dinner?"

Mom's smile is sad as she comes closer, hands cupping my face. "I have a plan, mamita. Trust me."

"Trust you with what?" Dad's voice cuts through and we both turn to face him, our faces a matching calm that evades his perception. Not that he'll notice either way. My father cares more for his appearance than that of his wife or the happiness of his family. His eyes are reading something on the screen of his phone. "Well?"

Still, he doesn't look up, and Mom and I share a quick look. "She says you couldn't notice the drop of blood on my dress. I cut my hand by mistake when a bottle of perfume—"

"Really, Solimar? Can you try and be more careful." It's a command. A decree that needs to be followed. "Is her dress okay, Veronica?"

"Yes, amor."

"Good. Good." Dad walks out and stops outside my door, his face turning toward mine. Our eyes lock. In them, I see anger and hate and a warning. His hostility isn't because of the damage done to the federal building, but because he lost every last bit of evidence the country had against Alejandro's deceased father. There are no copies, nor does he know the intricate details from the case, and the public demands proof to support his constitutional amendment, forcing him to gain support in other ways. "Signio is downstairs waiting, my daughter. Do not make me look bad tonight."

"Dad, I'd never—"

"And you also don't want to find out what happens if you do."

I'VE BEEN HERE a little over an hour and have done nothing more than shake hands and smile. Rinse. Wash. Repeat. It's always a different name. Some dignitary or influential family or a member of the conservative press that sings *President Quintero's* praises.

Over and over.

Same pleasantries.

The same amount of brown-nosing.

I hate this. Every last bit.

"Thirsty, beautiful?" Signio offers me a flute of champagne, sidling up close while all eyes continue to drift toward us. We're entertainment. Young and in love, according to national headlines.

The couple to be married in what they consider to be the wedding of the century, a paparazzi's wet dream, while I want to shrink away and hide.

This sham isn't my dream. He's not someone I want to spend more than ten minutes with.

And yet I'm stuck. This is my reality.

He'll never be Alejandro. I'll never get to choose for myself.

"Thank you," I say, my tone even while meeting his gaze. His eyes hold a predatory edge that's never been so blatant. Yes, he's hit on me in the past, but not like this. Signio tries, but at my rebuff seeks comfort in my cousin. "How kind of you."

"Are we upset tonight? Not having fun?" The mocking edge to his tone pisses me off. The sleazy smirk disguised behind a flirtatious smile makes me want to punch him in the mouth.

I'm not a violent person by nature, but I've thought about it. Breaking his nose or jaw. Maybe even asking Alejandro for help. *I know he'd do it, too, without asking me why.*

Widening my eyes, I giggle and bring the glass to my lips. "I'm going to reserve my answer," I say before taking a few sips. "Women and secrets. They come hand in hand."

"Careful, little girl." His hand grips my arm, pulling me in closer — fingernails dig in and break the skin, but I'm not allowed to show pain. Instead, I grit my teeth and don't give him the satisfaction. My smile widens, and his annoyance mounts. "Don't be smug or taunt-ing. I know too much. Things your father doesn't and would heavily compensate me for."

"I'm not afraid."

With his other hand, he taps my nose. "You should be."

To the outside, we look playful and laughing and compatible; it's a lie. Signio makes my skin crawl, and the only reason I'm still having this conversation is my father's eyes across the room. It's better to keep them on me and not Laura, who's sulking in her seat not too far from him. While he's talking to the vice president, his wife, and Signio's father—she watches him with sadness and betrayal in her eyes. While the men look tense and the women offer a laugh or two as they pretend to like each other, she wipes away the stray tear that falls.

I'm protecting her by not making a scene.

I'm letting the room in on this movie-star quality performance, so questions don't arise.

She doesn't understand the position she puts me in.

She doesn't appreciate how I've covered for her in the past. Excused myself from the last dinner he invited us to so she could be alone with him.

"You promised we could go, Sol. Come on."

"I have other things to do, Laura."

"Like what?" her tone is grating on my nerves. Demanding and pushy, as if I owe her.

"Like not sitting there while you paw at him and he laps up the attention."

She giggles at that. "Are you jealous?"

"Hell, no." It's hard, but I manage not to gag and shake my head. "He's not my type. At. All."

"But I need you there, prima. Please." My cousin puckers her lips, and I want to flick them. I feel bad for her, I do, but other people's happiness can't always come at my expense. If he loves her

*as she claims, then he needs to stop being a dog and man up. Be with
her. "Just one more time. I'll never ask again."*

"That's a lie, and you know it." *At my words, she has the decency
to grimace.* "But I'll cover for you instead. I'll stay at your apartment while you two go out. That's the most I'll do, and only because I
know this is hard on you."

"Oh my GOD!" *Laura throws her arms around me.* "You are the
best and I owe you."

"Then please stop putting me in this predicament. If you get
caught—"

"I won't. I'm talking to him tonight."

At this point, I have to come to grips with the fact Laura's so
blinded by her emotions that she simply doesn't care.

"Don't threaten me."

"Or what, Solimar?"

I don't answer him. Can't.

My lips part, and a stuttered breath escapes because I feel him.
That inexplicable fluttering in my stomach and the throb between my
thighs. Every single inch of me becomes hyperaware, discreetly
scanning the room, but I can't find him.

Alejandro is here, but where?

So close. So consuming.

He's the kind of man who owns the room, and I'm not the only
one noticing that something is different. Signio pulls his hand from
my arm as if I've burned him, pretending to wipe a sweaty palm
while around us a few people laugh, but they too sense the change.

Eyes are shifting. My father's brow is creased.

I need to get out of here.

My chest rises and falls rapidly, and I close my eyes for a second.
"I'm going outside for some air."

"Not by yourself, you're not."

"You sure about that?"

"Your father—"

"Would either of you care for an hors d'oeuvres?" a male voice asks, and I open my eyes, coming face to face with the same man again. He's smiling, while Signio's face is pale and his head shakes minutely. "I have mini arepas stuffed with ham and cheese. Simple and delicious."

"One of my favorites."

"He knows." The man doesn't need to emphasize just who he's talking about. All three standing here know. "He's also not happy with you, Signio."

"Geronimo, he can't be—"

"Walk her outside and disappear, Cortez. That's an order."

My smile widens as genuine relief consumes me. "Would you like to join me outside for some fresh air, Signio?"

His eyes harden, but his grin matches my own. He knows I spoke louder than usual on purpose. "Of course. Let me just tell your father—"

"No need." Dad's voice breaks our stare off, not that he notices just who the waiter is. He's not one to talk with those he deems beneath him, too busy being surrounded by important men: his security team, some members of the senate, and the vice president. They all look tense. He seems pissed. "Why don't you two get out of here and have some fun. Maybe have a late dinner?"

He wants us out of here. What's going on?

"Are you sure, Matias?" Signio's avoiding the look the waiter— that dad ignores—gives him. It's menacing and it makes me shrink back a bit, something Alejandro's employee sees and shakes his head at. The action is so minute that no one notices.

"I'm sure. Get her out of here."

The way he says that causes me to look over at my father with curiosity. I want to ask why. I want to tell him to stop sending me away with this creep.

My mouth opens, the questions sitting right at the tip of my tongue when Signio grabs my hand and tugs me closer. "Right away."

"Good. I'll call you later." Dad turns and walks away without another word, the group with him following close behind. No good-night. No "be safe." Not a damn thing. They exit the room while those in attendance continue to drink, eat, and dance.

"You heard him."

"Get your hand off me." I need to find Alejandro. Ask my mother what's going on.

I'm scanning the room but find no trace of either. This night is making no sense.

"Solimar...baby, why don't you let me take you back to—"

"Outside to the terrace. You have two minutes."

"Look, just tell him you missed us. I'll triple your pay and..." He trails off at the sight of Geronimo's gun tucked at his hip. Just the butt of it makes him shake beside me.

"A minute and a half left."

"Okay." He doesn't want to be reminded again of the dwindling clock. Without stopping, he walks me outside by the hand and then closes the door behind us when we enter the terrace. It's dark, the only source of lighting coming from the moon, and yet, I still see him the second my eyes adjust.

Standing in the middle of the terracotta-paved patio is Alejandro Lucas in a tuxedo, and my knees feel weak.

His eyes are hard and his body tense, but he's more beautiful than anyone has the right to be.

His mouth set in a thin line, and the way his jaw ticks makes my heart thump harshly inside my chest.

He's angry. Looks like the devil incarnate.

I've become a hussy for this man.

"I warned you."

16

ALEJANDRO

AT THE SIGHT of me, he releases my little flower's hand and takes three steps back. It's still not far enough. Nothing short of buried six feet under will ever appease me.

"Alejandro, I can—"

"Quiet," I hiss out, fighting to control my temper because Solimar doesn't need to see that. She'll never witness my wrath. The devil that resides within me. "I warned you, Cortez. Warned you, and yet you decided to not listen. This is on you."

"He made me do it. They're planning to—"

"I know every fucking step he takes." My eyes shift to Solimar, and I shake my head at her. Her eyebrows pucker at the center. I know she's confused, but now is not the time for this conversation. The sound of guns being cocked surround us and while Signio looks around nervously—I mouth *later,* and she nods. "Here or traveling, it doesn't matter. Even now, as he sits inside his office surrounded by men that want my head on a platter, I stand without fear. Remember that, güevon, I have eyes and ears everywhere."

Signio's mouth opens, but before he can utter a single word, I snap my fingers twice.

My guards step out from under the shadows, all ten that accompany me tonight, while Geronimo walks behind the idiot. One strike with the butt of my guard's Glock to the back his skull and the idiot goes limp, his unresponsive body a heap on the ground. As Geronimo steps back, another soldier steps forward and grabs Signio, tossing him over his shoulder before all traces of the would-be fiancé disappear.

Then, it's just me and her.

"You ready, Preciosa?"

"Ready for what?"

"I'm whisking you away for the weekend, Solimar." Her lips quirk up into a salacious smile while those warm grey eyes admire my attire. Something that I find myself doing to her. Her satin, floor-length black dress is modest in the front yet provocative with a backless design that exposes a large expanse of tempting skin. Then, there are the sexy and strappy heels in the same color as her garment that make her perfect ass perkier. The long, soft curls draped over her right shoulder tempt me to wrap them around my wrist and take possession of her body.

However, it's those ruby red lips that make me throb the hardest. They make the blood in my veins scorch with a near demonic desire that I'm left fighting to control.

The shade against her sun-kissed skin and striking eyes is delicious.

"Do you trust me?"

"I shouldn't..."

"But you do."

"What about my parents? They'll know something is wrong if I don't come back tonight."

ELENA M. REYES

"I doubt your father is expecting your return until Sunday." It's the truth, and we both know it. That piece of mierda doesn't care about her safety; he wants her in Cortez's arms. And if that union fails to happen, both fathers have a back-up plan.

Two more contenders are waiting.

Cortez is interested in an open marriage arrangement between them and the first ladies.

"But my mother will." She comes closer, just a couple of steps, and then stops with a hand on her sinuous hip. "She'll want to know I'm okay."

"Then call her when we reach our destination."

"That easily?"

"You'll always be taken care of with me. Anything you need, no matter how trivial."

"I believe you." Her scent is luscious. Intoxicating. This delicate hint of freesias and a unique sweetness that is naturally hers. "And it's why I'll come with you."

"Who said you have a choice?"

"I did."

"Is that right?" Chuckling, I take the remaining steps between us and wrap an arm around her waist. One tug, and she's flush against me. Chest to chest. "Because that not how it's supposed to work."

"How is it supposed to work, then?"

"Like this." Before her next intake of breath, I pick her up bridal style and walk us around to the private exit used by her father where just beyond the gate, my is car waiting. Solimar is giggling in my arms, wide smile across her lips when she sees Carlos holding the passenger side door open. "Thank you."

He nods and steps back as we approach. "I'll await your call to pick up Miss Quintero, Patron."

"Enjoy your night off."

"Have a good night."

Sol cups my jaw and turns my face to hers, lips lightly brushing. "You thought of everything, didn't you?"

122

"Yes."

"Good." A quick peck and then a nip. Playful and bold. "Then take me away. I'm all yours."

"Your wish is my command."

"Are you going to tell me where we're going?" Solimar asks after a while, tone teasing from beside me. It's just the two of us inside of my all-white Aston Martin One-77 as I drive out of the city, heading a few hours out of Bogota and toward my home in the country.

It's somewhere very few are welcomed, but her, *her* I want in my space. Her scent infiltrating every square inch, her tiny fingers touching my things and leaving tiny fingerprints behind in a trail for me to remember.

"No." I shake my head, a chuckle slipping out. "There's no fun in that."

"Fun for who?" Her huff is cute, and the way she crosses her arms over her chest is tempting me to pull over and devour that sassy, inquisitive mouth. Something we both need.

And while I won't take her innocence tonight, I'll satiate this hunger we're both drowning in.

"Fun for me." Another huff from Sol, and from the corner of my eyes I see those supple thighs clench as the car slows at a light. "But by all means, don't stop begging, Preciosa. I enjoy it."

"Is that so?" She shifts in her seat toward me and I turn my head, matching her raised brow. "Why?"

"In due time."

"Please," my little flower begs so prettily, her pouty lower lip jutting out, and I smirk. She's nothing like I thought she'd be, or how she seemed that night back at the rooftop bar. Back there, Solimar was shy and a bit nervous—afraid, but the more we're together, the more I see the woman behind the title of first daughter come forward. This woman wants to live. To fully experience life without barriers or rules, to be herself. And while I find myself drawn to her natural sweetness—this goodness that radiates from her every pore— she's just as equally hungry for my darkness. To find her balance. "Pretty please, Mr. Lucas."

So dangerous, I muse while scratching my jaw. "One clue. That's all you get." Solimar opens her mouth to protest, but I hold a finger up as the light turns green. "Patience, and you'll get your reward."

She giggles. "Maybe you should take me back."

"Maybe you need to be taught a lesson in patience." The SUV with my security stops at a four-way crossroad a few minutes later, and I take the opportunity to teach my flower two things: I say when, and two, I own her.

"But, Alejandro...of *fuck*," she moans as my hand grips the back of her neck, my hold tight, and I bring her closer. Right to where those beautiful lips belong, against mine. Her exhale is my inhale. Her body is mine to take.

"Even the way you curse is innocent." Miss Quintero's eyes close, and her sweet breath fans across my lips; I lick them, and by proximity, hers. It's a small taste. A decadent violation of my senses and I take her mouth, slanting my lips over hers as she mewls from the back of her throat. This kiss is hungry and rough, tongues twining and hands caressing; her body's angled across the center console as she grips the lapels of my tuxedo jacket. Her tongue is small and soft, lapping at mine—she's fighting for a dominance I'll never hand over, and I love it. I love the challenge she presents at every turn.

And to prove my point, I slow the kiss to a few soft pecks. She whines. "Want more."

"That word coming from your lips should be illegal."

"What word?" Her lips are swollen and eyes heavy-lidded. "Maybe I'll say it again if you tell me."

"Behave, little flower."

"But—" I place a finger over her lips and shake my head. My men have pulled slightly off to the side and step out in what is normal protocol. Solimar notices this and pouts, not liking when I release her and much less when I nod for her to sit back. However, she does what I ask and looks toward my men carrying out orders they know by memory.

And while they pause traffic, rifles pointing at cars in every direction but mine at the four-way stop, I take that moment to enjoy her. She fidgets under my scrutiny but doesn't ask questions, something that I know her mierda father instilled in her from an early age.

You don't ask. You don't see. You don't repeat.

The road is cleared for my caravan to move through a minute later, but I don't change gears. I'm too busy taking in her reaction. Admiring the swell of her breasts as her breathing hitches once more.

Not in fear. No.

The two little perfect tips poking through the soft satin fabric are enough of a tell. Even if she doesn't acknowledge it yet, my life excites her. The fact I'm the complete opposite of her forced fiancé makes her fidget in her seat.

I've noticed how her thighs clench.

How her lips part, tongue peeking out while I throb behind the zipper of my slacks.

I'm not hiding who I am. I'm not pretending to be anything but the man people fear.

Car doors close and those with me wait for my signal to drive.

"Do you trust me to take care of you, Preciosa? To not let anyone hurt you?"

"I do."

"And will you let me handle everything from here on out?"

"I do, but I have some questions that need answers."

"Good girl. Always ask questions," I say and take her hand in mine, laying them atop my lap. "Now, let's head home. We'll finish this conversation in bed."

"In bed?" Head cocked to the side, she raises a brow. "Won't that be a distraction?"

"That's why it'll be after. Much fucking after."

FOR THE REST of the ride, she remains quiet, dozing off after we hit the open road. She never woke up when I stopped at a gas station midway to our destination to refuel and remove my jacket, cummerbund, and bowtie, leaving just the white long-sleeve beneath.

Not when I took a few sharp curves up a mountain's winding road. Not when I put my window down and lit a cigarette, pondering my next few moves.

Her father will be coming for me after the explosion that demolished the federal building. He's furious. Embarrassed. Looking for anyone in my employ to hold responsible.

It's also why I need to get Solimar out from under his clutches. Desperate men make careless decisions.

The roads are empty this time of night and in the distance, I hear the mooing of a few cows as I cross a stretch of land known to have roaming cattle. Farmers around here let their animals graze openly and keep them marked with distinct patterns shaved into their coats just to differentiate.

My life has always been out in the countryside. Near the mountains and fields where coffee grows and life is simpler. Quieter.

It's how my father lived.

His father before him.

And had Jose Quintero not accused him of using the Finca for a non-existent drug operation, it's where we'd all be. On that same land. Running the same business started as all those generations before.

"...*divorcing Dad?*" Solimar murmurs beside me and I look over, not liking the way her eyebrows pucker in her sleep nor the frown on her face. "*Don't leave.*"

"Who's leaving, Preciosa?" I mutter, but somehow, she hears and turns her head in my direction. Her eyes are closed and breathing still even, but the sad look remains. Her words also don't make sense. She can't be talking about—

"Mom is. Told me today."

She talks in her sleep. Adorable. "Does your father know?"

"No." Frown deepens. "He's going to be pissed."

"I'll protect you." We're nearing my home, and I make a left onto a secret road that runs right to my front door. Nothing but green surrounds us, trees and lush fields, with the occasional guard at his post. No one comes in or leaves without my permission after entering.

"But what about them?"

"Them who?" I have an idea of who she's speaking about, but before I make a move, I need confirmation. We reach the main gate and find it open, a soldier on each side, and I drive through with the other cars behind me. They'll be parking around back and emptying the accompanying cargo. Signio will be joining us for the next two days.

He'll be persuaded into offering his assistance in creating an alibi for her.

Her hand shakes a bit, fingers squeezing mine as I park the car a few feet from the stairs that lead to my front door. I turn and meet wide-open eyes, a hint of fear in them. "Them who? Umm, what are you talking about, Alejandro?"

"We both know, and I need the truth."

"I don't—"

"Never lie to me, Preciosa."

She lets out a heavy sigh, but nods. "My mom told me tonight that she plans to leave Dad."

"When was this?"

"While I was getting dressed."

There's worry in her eyes, and I don't like it. "What do you need me to do. Say it, and it's done."

"He won't let her, and I'm afraid of what his reaction will be."

"And when I said earlier I'd protect you, that includes those you love."

17

Solimar

I DON'T KNOW why I told him that, but I'm relieved. The news has been nagging at me since earlier, like a tiny splinter that progressively gets worse as the hours pass.

My mother is leaving my father, something that isn't allowed inside of our social circle. First families don't split up. You don't air your dirty laundry for the world to see.

Instead, you shut up and suffer in silence.

The husband is the head of your familial unit, and his decisions are the law.

You have no word or say. Nothing comes before having the perfect unifying appearance for your constituents to envy.

But why now? Why is she doing this after confirming a wedding I want no part of?

"I don't like it when you look sad." His voice pulls me away from my thoughts. "All you need to do is ask, and I'll fix it. Tell me what you need."

"You are nothing like I thought you'd be." My voice is low inside the car, my attention solely on him and not the world around us as his employees retake their posts and the ones who're in charge of Signio's well-being have disappeared to another section of his property.

Something that should worry me but doesn't. I don't care about him in the least.

And while Laura's blinded by pretty words and empty promises, I've always known he was just another opportunistic abuser. Another man like the ones whose blood runs through my veins.

Alejandro exits the car, a chuckle escaping right before closing his door. I watch him as he comes around to my side, his natural swagger holding just the right amount of cockiness, and the smirk on his lips is maddening. In an amazing way. In a panty-destroying way. He's enjoying my perusal while making me wait—not that I'm made to sit here for long—at the most thirty seconds pass when my door is opened and his hand appears in my line of sight.

There's not a single second of hesitation from me as I let him pull me out. No regret as he wraps an arm around my waist and keeps me flush against his chest, lips hovering over my temple. A tiny kiss, and I shiver. A firmer grip and I bring my arms up, wrapping them around his neck, something that without these high heels I'd never be able to do.

Tipping my head back, I meet his warm eyes. They crinkle a bit at the corner with his smile. "Hello, Mr. Lucas."

"Hello, Miss Quintero." The long fingers of his unoccupied hand embed in my hair, pulling out the few bobby pins on the right side where a section was pulled back before wrapping them around his fists. "What did you think I'd be like? What did you know about me?"

"A woman has a right to her secrets."

"Not when it comes to us."

"Is that so?"

"Yes." His lips kiss a path down the side of my face until reaching the corner of my mouth. "Now answer the question, Solimar. What did you know about me?" The way he's looking at me as if he already knows about my childhood crush makes me flush. It starts at my hairline and sweeps down in a telltale sign of my obsession. "Why are you blushing?"

"Can we skip this part of the evening?"

"I might be persuaded to push it back until later for a kiss."

"How many and where?"

"That's a dangerous offer to make."

"How many and where?" I've never been so bold in my life, and what's more dangerous is how naturally it comes with him. Even earlier today when Dad was sending me away with Signio, the urge to tell him how I felt was strong and had the man my father chose for me not pulled me away, the words would've slipped without a second thought. That courage comes from Alejandro. From being allowed to be me without fear of repercussion. "Time's ticking, Mr. Lucas."

"Five in total, and one on the mouth for now."

"Deal—"

"But I choose the time to pick up this conversation again."

I roll my eyes. "Yes, *Patron*."

"Sassy little thing, aren't you."

"Sometimes...Alejandro!" It comes out a mixture between a giggle and a scream as he lifts me and throws me over his shoulder, marching up the steps of what I assume is his home. "Put me down!"

"No." We're not in the city, maybe a little over two hours out, but I'm not sure in which direction. I should've been paying better attention, but didn't. Instead of looking at signs or taking notes of mile markers, I watched him drive. Took in the way his arms flexed as he changed gears. The tick of his jaw as my thighs clenched.

"Are you insane?"

"Yes." His warm hand slides up the back of my thigh, bunching up my dress in the process. He stops just beneath my rear, fingers massaging my flesh. "Now behave, Miss Quintero. I'm trying to be a gentleman."

"You are?"

"I am." Alejandro never puts me down but does adjust me before ascending the stairs. Now he carries me bridal style, his hold on my thigh possessive and his cognac-colored eyes show his hunger. His eyes are heavy-lidded and his mouth so close to mine as we make it to the top and turn right where a long hallway ends with a set of double doors.

And it's when we make it through those doors that I follow through on my promise.

There's something about being in his room, his private domain, that sets off my own need and I fist his hair in my hands, pulling on the soft strands as I kiss him. I'm not afraid or timid or careful. Instead, I take, slipping my tongue past his lips and swallowing the almost feral hiss that builds in his chest when I nip his bottom lip.

"Dangerous fucking flower," Alejandro growls, his hands wandering as he walks us over to the large bed at the center of the room. It's dark and the sole lighting comes from the moon above, filtering through the sheer window curtains—bathing us in a soft glow as my back meets the plush comforter. His body covers mine, a predator pinning a willing prey. "You're not ready, Sol. Not yet."

"I want you, Alejandro. Always have." It's the truth. I've always known there was more to this man than what the media or my family portrayed. There's always been something about him that calls to me, and I don't want to deny it anymore.

What I'm doing—seeing him—is crazy and probably idiotic, but denying myself will hurt more. We need to talk and discuss what this is between us, but not now. I need to feel him close. To experience his ardor.

"You're the sweetest temptation." With one hand, he holds himself slightly off me. Alejandro licks his lips, and I moan low. "You'd let me do just about anything to you."

"Yes." No shame. Am I nervous? Yes, but I want this. With shaky hands, I pull the skirt of my dress up slowly, not stopping until the soft material is bunched at my hips and my lace black thong is visible.

"Motherfuck." Then, I'm cradling his hips. They fit perfectly against mine, grinding while my eyes roll back. "So beautiful."

"Oh God," I whimper, feeling every solid inch of his cock as it throbs against where I need him most. Where I'm wet and swollen. Where I've fantasized him taking me. Another gyration and I shake, fingers clawing at his shirt while his lips skim up my throat and chin, stopping their exploration when he finds my lips. This kiss is softer. Slower. A complete contradiction to all the others while the intensity remains, heat licks at my skin.

"Please." It's all I can manage as he presses me further into the mattress, length flexing against my core. Two thin layers of clothing separate us, and I despise each. "I need—"

"I know," he says, voice pained as he pulls back, and I immediately miss his warmth. My lips part, the whine sitting on the tip of my tongue, but they die when I feel his nose skimming my upper thighs. From the left to the right, each leg is given the same treatment. A lick. A nip. A kiss.

I'm shaking and gasping. I'm sensitive and unable to make a single coherent sound as his mouth travels higher, just to the juncture of my thighs, and he exhales. My core clenches and I lift my hips in offering, and it feels natural to do so. An instinct I don't question.

No shyness.

No doubt.

I let him see my yearning, and his harsh breathing against me is all the reward I need.

I've never been so turned on in my life.

It's painful. Driving me crazy.

"Alejandro, I can't—"

"Mine." One word, and the accompanying action steals the very air from my lungs. One lick, the flat of his tongue running over the lace covering my pussy, and I seize. For a second or ten, I can't breathe as pleasure rocks me from the very tip of my toes to the last strand of hair on my head.

I'm coming for him, and the man has barely touched me. Wave after wave is crashing over me as he curses, but I'm too gone to understand the words.

Languid and satiated, I find myself sleepy. So gone that I don't open my eyes when he lowers my zipper and manages to pull off my dress. Not a single peep when my shoes and panties follow, and without my wearing a bra tonight, I find myself naked and snuggled against a bare chest.

When he undressed, I have no clue, and I'm too comfortable to care.

The last thing I remember is his warm chuckle against my neck as I drift off.

THE ROOM IS pitch black when my eyes open again. The curtains are closed and for a minute, I'm disoriented. This isn't my room or bed, and the body next to mine is unfamiliar until the last twenty-four hours come rushing back to the forefront.

The party.

My mother's confession.

Signio.

Being swept away…

The body moves and his warm arm wraps around my stomach, tucking me against his side and making me aware that I'm now wearing some kind of shirt. His scent is undeniable and body warm; I never want to leave this moment. The feel of him against me is heaven, and God knows how many nights I've dreamt of this.

Pretending that we were together while ignoring a reality that hurts.

This is real. You're here.

I'm in Alejandro's bed.

Heat blooms across my cheeks, and I smile. Inside the darkness of these four walls, no one will witness my girlish moment. And had I been alone, there's no doubt I might've squealed and hugged my pillow. It's everything I've ever wanted—to choose for myself—and while I know it's not a promise of forever, I want to grab the moment and not think.

It's why I move slowly and disentangle myself from him, slipping further down the bed until my face is over his stomach and I count each indentation with a finger, caressing each slowly as I descend toward his happy trail. There's six in total, and the large tattoo of a hydra is something I didn't notice last night.

You fell asleep before the man could remove his clothes.

It's his fault, though. The orgasm Alejandro pulled from my body with a single lick over my lace-covered slickness left me weak. Satiated and happy. One minute I'm falling over the edge headfirst into nirvana, and then, I don't remember much after.

There were murmured words I couldn't make out.

There were gentle touches that pulled me further into sleep.

It was perfect, but...

"I want more. So much more."

18

ALEJANDRO

"I WANT MORE. So much more."

Little does my girl know that I've been awake the last two hours watching her rest. Counting each breath and sigh, taking note of the way she wiggles her right leg to rock herself into a deeper slumber. It's an adorable habit. But then again, I'm completely fucked over for this slip of a girl.

There's no denying the attraction, but I'm not dumb nor do I ignore that things between us run much deeper than lust. There's something about her that gets under my skin and burrows deep. She calls to me. Her mere presence moves the ground I stand on.

Slipping from my loose hold, Solimar moves lower until her breath fans across my abdomen.

She's mumbling to herself as her slim finger trails over each ab. There's the mention of numbers and a whimper as she slips just a little lower, pushing the strewn-about bed sheet down toward my feet.

I'm hard for her—throbbing—as beads of pre-come pool at the slit of my engorged head and disappear into the pajama bottoms I slipped into late last night. It's been this way each time she moves or squirms or simply breathes.

I've been biding my time while the faint taste of her wetness still lingers on my lips. I've counted each crescent moon shape left behind by Signio's hold on her earlier this evening, and for each one of the seven, he'll bear his own marks before the weekend is through. I vowed this to her while she burrowed deeper and her hand reached out for mine subconsciously while she slept.

It's also why I'm not flipping her around and sinking balls deep yet.

I love her. It's an emotion that with her, I welcome.

Three words that up until now I've only said to my family on rare occasions, but with her…

Christ, she's in deep. They come naturally and bring no doubt or fear, and I want her here in my home—sharing my life. Something I'll make a permanent situation after my trip to Guatemala in a few days.

It's a visit years in the making and the start of the end.

Their death is our beginning.

I love her.

This is her decision, and I'll give her what she needs. My time. My attention. My love. Solimar wants me to fuck her and I will, but only after she cries out for me. I want her to give herself completely and admit that I own her.

Freely. Openly.

Because once I claim her innocence, there is no going back.

"I'm in trouble," she breathes out, her hot little gasp seeping through the thin cotton stretched across my thick girth. "It's going to hurt."

Christ, she's perfect.

An untouched treasure.

I want to assuage her fears and deliver the pleasure she seeks, but instead, I lie still and pretend to sleep. Not that she's paying attention to the man biting his lips as she explores without interruption. She can't see me looking down nor has she taken notice of the pillow below my head, propping me up just enough to have the perfect view.

The moon's soft glow illuminates the room, but only catches the bottom of my bed. It's enough for me to see her, and at the same time not be seen.

Those same fingers glide over the waistband and lower, pressing against my hardness. My cock flexes and she lets out the smallest little moan, lips getting closer.

They part and her tongue peeks out, sliding across her bottom lip as I give another jerk for her benefit. She's so lost to the sight that my movements haven't brought her eyes up to mine. No. Instead, Solimar pulls the waistband back, farther and farther, and then down until my cock is exposed and straining toward her mouth.

Closer, and I feel the featherlight touch of her fingers as she traces the underside and then fists my hard flesh. Her touch is firm but not tight enough, and I fight back the need to ask for more. I'm enjoying her like this more than I ever thought possible. The inexperience—how overtaken Sol is by the proof of my hunger for her is sexy.

Delicious.

Two pumps and I grit my teeth, holding still when all I want to do is demand she open wide and hold her tongue out for me. A twist of her wrist, and I notice the change in her breathing and the small gyration of her hips.

"Just a little taste," she whispers before licking the slit and humming low in the back of her throat. The sight of her pouty lips just over my cock is a thing of beauty, but the feeling of her warm, little pink tongue on my flesh is nirvana. Pleasure rocks me and my abs contract, heart beating fast as I replay the vision again.

Her hot mouth. Her body trembling. *Just a little taste.*

Fuck, I want her. Today and tomorrow.

There's no getting away from me now.

Before my little flower realizes I'm awake, I lift her and flip our positions. I'm hovering, lips on hers in a bruising kiss while she writhes, clawing at my back to pull me closer. Her legs part, cradling my hips. Her back arches, pushing her chest against mine as my hands begin to explore.

She's sinuous curves and a beautiful smile.

She's heavy-lidded eyes and trembling thighs.

"Such a naughty little thing to do." I nip her top lip and then the bottom, leaving a trail of tiny bites until I reach her neck and suck the skin between my teeth. "Teasing a man like me is a dangerous thing to do, Solimar, but you knew that…didn't you?"

"Yes." It's a hiss followed by a low keening sound when my teeth dig in deeper. "I was hoping you'd wake up."

"Is that so?" Releasing her, I sit back and grip the bottom of my shirt she's wearing. My brow arched. "Why?"

"Because I want you, Alejandro."

Those five words make me shiver. "Say it again."

Solimar sits up, her hands reach up and cradle my face. "I want you, Mr. Lucas. Let me choose you."

"*Christ*, I…you're perfect." Turning my face, I kiss her right palm "But we do this my way. Understood?"

"Yes."

"When I say."

"I want to be yours." *Silly girl.*

Pushing Sol to lie back, I lower my body and rub her nose with mine. "You already are." One tug, and the cotton T-shirt covering her body tears down the middle exposing her abdomen—her heaving chest, and the way the muscles contract beneath my heated stare.

"Please, Alejandro. I need—"

"Me." My mouth descends on Solimar's for a quick, hard kiss before lowering to her throat. She's sweet there, and I can't get enough. The soft scent of her perfume lingers in the background while her decadent essence teases me. It's unique and mouthwatering and I flex my hips against her heated core, rubbing my exposed cock against her bare lips.

"Alejandro," she moans, clinging to my forearms—nails breaking the skin—as her back arches and I take the opportunity to pull the tattered remnants of my shirt off and toss it. It falls somewhere near the bottom of my bed as I roll my hips again and her eyes close.

"Look at me," I grit out, pausing with my hardness over her wet slit as my pants join the ruined shirt somewhere behind me. At once they open, heavy-lidded, and full of passion. The way she watches me beneath those long lashes pulls a few beads of pre-come from my tip and down over her engorged clit. "Never take those beautiful eyes off me."

"I can't."

Grabbing the base of my dick, I slap the tip where she's the most sensitive. "You can."

Solimar sucks in a breath, teeth biting down hard on her lower lip as a light sheen of sweat spreads across her chest. Goose bumps rise and her limbs shake as her tender flesh throbs beneath my touch.

I've barely touched her, and she's panting.

I've barely touched her, and she's soaking my sheets.

"My body…it's…oh, God!" She's slick, taking her pleasure from me as I slide through her labia and over the trembling bundle of nerves. Seeing her lost in pleasure is the most erotic thing I've ever seen. Watching her follow her natural instinct is almost enough to make me come.

Almost.

"Motherfuck," I hiss out through clenched teeth as I grab her upper thighs and pull them further apart. This brings her tighter against me; my cock is just a quick flex from slipping inside that tight little pussy.

I don't, though. Not yet.

Not until she learns my land and accepts my offer. Until then, I want her crazed and wanton.

Near desperate.

Bringing my hands to the swell of her hips, I thrust harder—sliding through her wet folds and across her trembling clit. My fingers dig in. My hips pump faster as she bathes me in her juices and I leak across her slit, rubbing it in as she trembles in my hold.

Solimar's lips parts and sweet little pants escape; I can almost taste her pleasure. "I'm so close, Alejandro."

"You want to come, Preciosa?" I flex against her heat, a harsh shiver rushing down my spine as another rush of wetness coats my length. "How badly do you need it?"

"Please." It's a whine of frustration when I pin her down with one hand, keeping her immobile.

"Please what?" My eyes sweep her delicate frame, from the splayed strands decorating my pillow to the curling of her toes. From the heaving of her chest to the obscene sight of her little pussy—all pink and soft—beneath my cock. Her juices and mine mix. Her low moans mixing with my grunts. "Tell me what you need."

"You." One word. Three letters. And they motherfucking flip my world on its axis as I grip my dick and run the head over her opening. I pause there, just feeling how her tiny hole flexes in search of me as the truth behind her confession makes me shiver.

My chest expands and I close my eyes, breathing in deeply as pleasure rocks me. There's a tightness in my abdomen and my balls feel heavy; I grip myself tighter. My hips punch forward just a little bit.

"Say it again." I need to hear it again. One more time.

"I need you, Alejandro." Soft grey eyes watch me from beneath long lashes, her lips still swollen from our earlier kiss. She's never looked more exquisite.

My thrust is shallow, a soft punch forward, and the head slips inside. Fuck, she's tight. Almost painfully so.

It's heaven and hell and I pull out, only to enter again. And again.

Solimar's mouth drops open and her back arches, thighs trembling on either side of my waist.

She's close. So close.

With every shallow thrust, I softly touch her hymen but don't break it. Not yet. Her innocence is something I want to explore and soon, but I want her free and wild and with no barriers that impose the bullshit notions that have tied her down for far too long.

Tomorrow.

"Come for me, Preciosa. Give it to me." Pulling out, I tap her clit twice with my head and slip inside just deep enough to kiss her innocence with the few beads of pre-come beading. "I need to see you come."

Pouty lips open and her eyes roll back as the first wave of pleasure slams into her. There are no screams or curses, but I feel every shake beneath me and the pulsing wetness that covers me down to my thighs. Her pleasure is beautiful. *Her body is mine.*

And it's that thought that brings me to my peak as I pull out and with a tight grip, fuck my hand. Two pumps and I groan, watching as a thick rope of come lands across her clit. Another stroke and the next covers her pink lips on the left and I make sure the rest of my seed covers the neglected right.

It's a gorgeous sight.

She's wearing me. Smells of me.

Came for me.

"You look very proud of yourself." Solimar's voice pulls me from her perfect core, and I raise a brow as our eyes meet. Her words are a bit sassy and playful, but the blush spreading across her cheeks and down her chest is bashful. "You broke me and I'm still a virgin."

Christ, this girl.

"Soon, Miss Quintero." Not giving a single fuck about the mess on her body, I lower mine across hers. Cover her from head to toe and nip her bottom lip. "I'm just getting started with you."

LEAVING her to take a shower in my room after a few chaste kisses, I take one myself in the guest bath downstairs and head for the kitchen to start breakfast. There's no one working in the house this morning, per my request, and I have plans to show Solimar the grounds before Carlos picks her up late tomorrow afternoon.

I'm not hiding anything from her. I want her to know exactly what kind of man she chose.

Because there is no going back for us.

Fate is a cruel mistress. She placed me in the path of this innocent woman, knowing I'd become obsessed with her. That I'd kill to consume her. To own her heart.

And if I were a better man, I'd feel bad about it. But I'm not, and I don't.

Knowing from the staff inside of the presidential home that my little flower loves coffee, I start there. The beans have been roasted but not ground, as I prefer to have that done freshly each morning. I still have the special machine my mother used at home from our days on the coffee plantation and I walk over, grabbing the container with the specialty blend.

It's cultivated on a farm I own that's run by a friend of mine. I don't sell the product to anyone. It's for private consumption, and I have it delivered once a week to four of my six properties around the country.

The machine turns on, churning as I add enough for a few cups throughout the day if need be. With that going, I turn my attention to something simple for breakfast. Cooking is something my mother loved to do and instilled in all her children, making sure that no matter where we'd go in life, we wouldn't starve.

Moreover, while I have staff in all my properties, I still cook a good amount of my meals.

Walking to the fridge, I take out what I need and set it on the counter. I'm keeping it simple today, something Solimar likes: scrambled eggs with tomato and onions accompanied by an arepa with fresh cheese. That sweet girl can appreciate a fancy meal but yearns for comfort and ease.

I saw it in the way she enjoyed our lunch date.

I saw it last night when Geronimo offered her a quick bite only available to her during the gala.

Something so simple brought a smile to her face that lit up the entire room. Doing that for her made me feel ten feet tall.

The soft padding of feet meets my ears as she descends the stairs. "Alejandro?"

"In the kitchen. Turn left and follow the corridor," I call back, grabbing a cutting board and knife to begin prep. Sol finds me quickly, coming to a stop beside me as I dice the tomato first. My face turns toward hers and I bend over a bit, laying a kiss on her cheek. "Morning, Preciosa."

"Buenos Dias."

19

Solímar

I'M STANDING BENEATH the waterfall shower head in his bathroom, eyes closed and fighting to get my breathing under control after he left. I'm alone with my thoughts now, missing his touch while accepting how weak I am when it comes to Alejandro Lucas.

His scent is addictive.

His touch is a soul-destroying catastrophe.

He owns me, and the truth is I don't think I'll ever get enough.

"I'm screwed." It's my reality and fear. Our relationship—this crazy affair—is forbidden and while I see no happy ending in sight, I don't care.

My family won't approve. I've been promised to another—an obnoxious jerk—without my permission, and all I want is to choose him.

Alejandro is who I want. *I deserve to be happy.*

And wearing him between my thighs does that. Feeling his lips on mine while my hips cradle his, gives me the sense of home and comfort I've been missing.

I cried out for more.

I never want to leave.

For once, I'm doing what my heart tells me and not following an order and I've never felt freer. Unbidden. Calm.

"Why him?" I ask myself, even though I know the answer. It's been there all these years as I followed him through the media's eyes. Through my father's hatred. There's always been something that draws me in and holds me captive.

That keeps me coming back.

I'm a stalker.

I'm weak.

I'm his.

My eyes close as the sight of him above me replays through my mind. How his lip curled and grip tightened. The way his cognac eyes never left mine as he marked my skin with his release and then kissed my lips.

Lost in my desire, my right hand travels down my stomach and lower, not stopping until the proof of his lust covers my fingertips. It's a heady feeling and I shiver, his release and mine coating my labia, and I'm tempted to slip my slick finger inside.

To coat my walls with his essence, but I don't.

Not like this.

Instead, I focus on the memory I want to relive again. And again.

I'm sensitive to the touch, and my clit trembles beneath my soft touch. My thighs tremble and core clenches.

So close.

Just one more—

"No. Not without him," I hiss out, pulling my hand from between my thigh and slapping the white marble tile inside his shower. I'm sensitive and turned on but don't want to come without him.

I need him.

"Then go find him."

MY HEART THUMPS harshly inside my chest the moment I step into his kitchen. It beats at a fast cadence while goose bumps rise across my flesh, and the sight before me makes me want to pat my own back.

I rushed through my shower. I almost ran down the stairs.

This is my reward.

There's something so sexy about a man that can cook.

Maybe it's the fact he can take care of himself. Maybe it's the sight of his arms, the thick cords of muscles rippling as he wields a knife against the chopping block while preparing a meal. Or maybe it's the heat in Alejandro's eyes when he says *good morning* after kissing my cheek.

He's trouble and fire, and I'll proudly dance inside those flames for him.

"Buenos dias." It leaves me on a breathless whisper and his lips quirk up. Alejandro doesn't hide his smirk, nor is he apologetic in his perusal of my body. From head to toe, he takes in my lack of clothing choice with a spark of mischief in his eyes.

I'm wearing an old shirt I found in his dresser with nothing beneath; my dress would be uncomfortable, and my panties are drying in his bathroom after I hand-washed them. So with little choice in the matter, I opened his drawers and snooped a bit before grabbing an old, threadbare *El Pibe* jersey and slipping it on. It's smaller in size than his other clothing and definitely from his youth but fits me loose with the hem falling just above my knee.

It's soft and smells like him, and I won't deny loving the woodsy scent surrounding as I stand here.

"I'm hungry, Solimar." Alejandro places the knife down, pushing the cutting board with chopped tomatoes and a whole onion aside, and turns to face me. The grin on his face should be illegal, and I lean my hip on the counter for support. "Are you?"

"Famished." I take in a deep breath and his heated stare follows the rise and fall of my chest. *Christ, if he touches me now, I'll beg.* "What are you making? Do you need any help?"

"Something you'll like, and no." Alejandro takes a step closer and we're chest to chest, his hands finding purchase on my hips. Grip firm, his fingers hold me in place while his face lowers to mine. Mouth hovering. "All I want is for you to take a seat and watch. Nothing more."

Without conscious thought, I lick my lips and he groans. "Where do you want me?"

"Innocently coquettish." A peck is all I get before I'm being lifted and placed to sit atop the countertop. A cold countertop that makes me hiss on contact and for his brow to raise. "Is there something you want to show me?" At his question, I blush. The heat sweeps across my skin, and I shake my head. "Don't be shy, Preciosa. Are you wearing anything beneath?"

"No," I whisper, and his salacious grin tells me he heard. His hands leave my hips and travel lower to the top of my thighs where he steps between them and squeezes—higher and higher, pushing the soft cotton up until the top of my bare mound is exposed. "Alejandro—"

"*Fuck,* beautiful." Those large hands clench, and I shiver. I'm near panting as I silently beg him to touch me. To take what I so willingly give. "What you do to me." His fingers skim a little higher and pause right over the top of my clit. *So close.* "You're a temptation I crave. My destruction and salvation."

"Please."

"Please what?" A featherlight touch over the hood and then lower to my entrance. Not entering, but caressing. "Tell me."

"Touch me," I whimper and then blush for a completely different reason as my stomach suddenly growls from hunger. It's loud, and I'm embarrassed; the fevered spell we've been under is broken.

Alejandro pulls back, chuckling as his eyes come up to meet mine after my plea. "So, I guess it'll be food first."

"No." It's a whine, and my lips pout when my hunger makes its presence known again.

"Behave." The rebuttal sits on my tongue. I don't want to stop, but he shakes his head before I can. Instead, I'm given a pointed look and a soft caress across my thighs as he fixes my shirt and covers my neediness. "Let me feed you, and I promise to eat that pretty little pussy afterward."

My core clenches at his words. "I'm not that hungry."

"Is that the truth or a lie?"

"Maybe."

His shoulders shake with silent laughter. "You're adorable." He's not laughing at me, nor does he seem upset that I *killed the mood,* so to speak, by needing sustenance. If anything, the boyish amusement on his face shows he's okay and his hardness now pressed against my thigh tells me I'll be enjoying him later. "All right, Miss Quintero. I cook, and you watch."

"Can I help with anything? Speed things along."

"You can sit and look pretty..." at my mock glare, he leans forward and gives my bottom lip a quick bite "...or pick something to listen to."

"Where's your radio?"

"One sec." Alejandro turns from me and walks over to the counter on the opposite end of his kitchen. There's a large portable device there that I recognize from our kitchen at the presidential home; a portal that controls most smart functions, and his cell phone. Picking up the latter, he brings it over and places it beside my right hip. "Here you go. Play whatever you want."

"You sure?" That's a dangerous offer for two reasons: his phone could contain things he doesn't want me to see, and two, I know just the song to pay him back for leaving me hanging.

"Go for it." No hesitation or concern. He pecks my lips a final time and steps back into cooking mode. Still hard and throbbing, his cock flexes beneath the confines of his pants, and I have to look away or I'll pounce.

A truth that smacks me in the face once again.

With him, I lose all control. My inhibitions are without regret.

"Get it together," I mutter low, but he hears something and clears his throat.

"You said something, Sol?"

"No."

"You sure?"

"Yup." Keeping my eyes on his phone's screen, I pull up the music app and type in the name of what I have in mind. It's an old song that blew up and is popular amongst the wedding/any-kind-of-celebration crowd. The opening notes begin to play, and I bite back the giggle fighting to break free.

His shoulders bunch and head shakes. "No. Please don't."

"Why? It's so catchy." Jumping down from the counter, I begin to shake my hips as the male singers begin to clap. I ignore the cool air caressing the wetness between my thighs, focusing on his reaction and not how sexy the man looks standing a few feet from me and now running a hand through his thick, dark hair. The clapping coming through the speakers is fast-paced and I join in, moving just like the women do in the original video. Then, I'm humming, and he grimaces. I'm smiling so big, and he's shuddering. "Want to join me?"

"No."

"You said I could ask for anything and—"

"But this." Cognac-colored eyes are begging me to not push. It's hilarious to see this strong man try and back out from doing a simple dance. There has to be a story behind this reaction. "Ask me to do anything but the Macarena."

"Why?"

"How about some of my specialty-blend coffee," he offers instead, and it's my turn to shake my head. "Una arepita with ham and cheese?" In response, I hold a hand out as the male singers belt out the first line. "Or we skip breakfast and I make you come on my tongue."

At once my hands drop to my sides and lips part. "That's not fair."

"Bend over the counter and I'll show you just how *fair* I can be." Alejandro's expression is smug. He knows I want him to touch me and decides to fight dirty. However, two can play at this game, and I take on a different approach.

Pursing my lips, I lower the volume and hop back onto the countertop while he watches me with an amused expression that is dripping with cockiness. *Papi is about to learn a lesson.* Once situated, I cross my legs and give him a sweet smile. "How much longer before breakfast is ready?"

"Run that by me again? I don't think I heard you correctly." If anything, his velvety tone deepens, and it's smooth like whiskey. "Now you want to eat and deny me."

"Pretty much." I'm nodding, fighting back a laugh at his narrowed eyes and thinned lips. "You offered, and now I want it."

"I also offered to make you come."

"Something you could very well do in an hour."

"You're going to pay for teasing, Miss Quintero." Once again invading my personal space, Alejandro takes my face in his hands and skims his lips across mine in a kiss that's innocent yet decadent. That simple touch makes my heart thump harshly and a smile to curve against his mouth. "Now, behave while I cook and feed you."

"Yes, Patron," I breathe out, and he groans, giving me a final nibble before leaving me to continue his prepping.

In mere seconds we went from sexy to playful to back to scorching, and I like it. It also leaves me with two noticeable problems.

The first being my lack of worry for Signio and if he's alive.

The second being how much I crave this kind of attention from Alejandro. It makes me needy and happy and I... *I love him.*

20

ALEJANDRO

"**M**ORNING, GENTLEMEN," I say, stepping inside the garage-like structure behind my home while Solimar gets ready for our afternoon tour of my property. The building is past the pool house and the line of gardenias my groundskeeper planted last spring. It's large enough to house five cars, three holding cells, and a fully functioning apartment on the second floor with the staircase at the rear of the building that my men use to crash for a few hours when needed.

Sweeping my eyes across the room, I notice the lack of vehicles and how all the lights are on. I take in the empty food plates and the few bottles of water atop a small table at the center. How the last cell on the left wall's inhabitant is shrinking back from the metal doors, keeping him within, and all eyes are on me.

"Buenos dias, Patron," three male voices reply in unison while my guest remains quiet, shivering, although he's fully dressed and untouched. No facial bruising. No bloody limbs.

I nod at the men, yet my attention remains on my guest. Signio is avoiding my eyes, trying to stay within the shadows of his temporary room.

"Mr. Cortez, I suggest you put into practice all those years of expensive education and use your manners. When someone greets the room, you respond accordingly. Understood?" Still, I'm met with silence. Another *culicagado* brought up with money and has mierda social etiquette. "So be it." Meeting the eyes of the guard to my right, I nod in the direction of Signio. "Bring him out."

"Wait!" His face appears between two bars on the door, hands gripping the metal tightly. "Alejandro, there's no need for this. I wasn't going to hurt her or defy you."

"So you do know how to speak?" My jaw ticks as I recount each little scar left behind by his nails digging into Solimar's arm. How red and swollen the delicate flesh was. "You fucked up, kid. I warned you."

"Let's talk this out," he says, eyes on the guard walking over with a key in hand. "I can help you."

"Help me?" I ask as Geronimo steps inside with a burner phone in hand. "Explain yourself."

"It's just that…" He swallows hard and tries to keep the door closed, pulling it toward his body after my guard unlocked it. "I know things, Alejandro. Things you don't have a clue about are happening as we speak."

"Sir?" my employee calls out, knowing I didn't want excessive force used last night. Past tense. Today is a new day, and Mr. Cortez is going to learn a very cruel lesson in life. A golden rule his miserable father and too-afraid-to-speak mother failed to explain.

You don't touch a woman with anger.

"Let's give him a second to collect himself." Eyeing his shaking limbs, I tilt my head to the side. "Go on. Tell me how Quintero is venturing into the sale of illegally harvested organs with your father and a silent partner from Russia. Tell me how he sold Solimar to your father in exchange for military alliance once he implements a dictatorship society in this country. Tell me that he's plotting my death in a public execution next month."

Signio's face pales and head shakes side to side. His eyes are wide. "How?"

"Be specific." For a few beats, there's silence in the room and I give the signal for extraction. One hard yank of the door and he tumbles out, landing on his hands and knees on the concrete floor. There's a sharp gasp of pain as his hands give in and palms scrape against the rough, unpolished surface. It's that way for a reason on that side of the room, and the torn skin and bloody fingertips are the end result. He whimpers, and I crack my neck. "Get up."

"Alejandro, this isn't necessary. Come on, man..." Signio attempts to push himself up but fails, now adding small lacerations to his cheek. He looks up at me from his place on the floor, a few beads of blood rolling down to his stubbly chin. "Dad will pay you whatever you want. I'll even leave the country."

"I can't hear you from down there."

"I can't...it hurts." You'd think I'd broken his leg or used my knife to run a line down the center of his chest with the way Cortez is crying. *Pussy.*

"Would you like some help?"

"Please."

"Help him." At my order, Geronimo points at the man next to him, his nephew Lino, to get Signio up off the floor. The younger man is still a bit rough around the edges and yanks him up by the hair, all but dragging and then tossing him at my feet. Then he moves back into position as if nothing happened and waits for his next order. "Gracias, Lino."

"I'm at your disposal, Patron. Always."

"Hagale." A bloody hand grips my pant leg and I look down, noticing the tears already forming in Signio's eyes. "Are you ready to be honest with me? To explain the idiocy from last night." He's nodding before I finish asking my questions, bottom lip trembling. "Good boy."

"They made me do this." His eyes land on a special addition to the property on my right that arrived a few days ago with a certain person or three in mind. The Judas chair: medieval and dark with large spikes over every surface and four leather straps to bind the unfortunate under castigate. It's a black-market purchase made after my lunch with Solimar in Bogota, after uncovering the president's plans for my little flower.

"Of course." My tone drips in sarcasm, in the barely contained ire flowing through my veins, but he fails to pick up on anything past the horror my purchase creates. "Are you afraid? Intrigued by my furniture?"

Those shitty orbs snap toward me, and his chest rises and falls fast. "Are you? Am I?" Signio swallows hard; he's fighting the fear crawling beneath his skin and the shivers that are proof of his pathetic worth. "Please don't."

"Get up."

"Alejandro, I'll disappear. Just gone."

"Let go of my jeans and stand up, Cortez. Can you do that?"

"I need help," he says lowly as a few beads of sweat roll down his face and the cuts there.

"Big boys can do it all by themselves. No hand-holding."

"I didn't mean harm, Alejandro. Por favor, tell me you believe that."

"This is the last time I'll ask you to stand," I hiss out, yanking his head back by the hair until he's almost on his haunches and the strands rip from his skull. There's a small bunch in my hand while his scalp is a lovely shade of irritation red. "Quit whining and take a seat. We need to talk."

"Oh, God…I-I don't want to die. I'll do anything—"

"Quit crying before I strap you on the Judas myself." Signio manages to get up without using his hands to propel him, he's starting to look a mess and lethargic—his legs are shaky—but it's not enough. Nothing short of his death will be, *but* not today.

There's something I need him to do for me first.

His mouth will be his demise, and I am counting on the slip.

Geronimo moved two chairs over from the wall and placed them on opposite ends of the table. I point to the seats, knowing he saw, and walk over to the set of monitors I keep in the building. It's there to supervise those in my house, and today, I use it to see what Solimar does while I'm not there.

After entering my private code, I walk back and take a seat—lean back and follow the moving red dot on the screen. She's out of the room and taking the stairs down to the first floor.

A few more steps and she'll have a decision to make. Right or left. My office or the living room.

The dot stalls at the bottom of the stairs and after a few beats, it turns toward the living room.

Good girl.

Her trust in me is appreciated and will be rewarded.

Signio sits down and groans, pulling my attention from the screen. "Something wrong?"

"What do I need to do to walk out of here alive?" he says, voice betraying the bit of bravado he's trying to exude.

I arch a brow. "Who says you aren't?"

"Then why—"

"Because you'll be of use to me."

"How?" His hands clench and he grimaces. "What do I need to do?"

"You can start by taking off your shirt and tie," I ask and wait. His eyes widen and body shakes again, the entire scene becoming too repetitive for my liking, and I slam a hand atop the table. "Take it off and fold it neatly atop the table. Then you are to tell me your side of the story. Every last fucking detail. Understood?"

"Yes." Shaking hands follow my order and once it's off, Geronimo hands over the phone in his hand. "What's this for?"

"Call Quintero and tell him you and Solimar are heading out to Santa Marta for the weekend. You'll have her back bright and early on Monday."

"You're sending her back?"

"What I do is none of your concern."

"Yes, sir." Grabbing the cell, he dials a number I know by memory and waits. Two rings and someone picks up. "Matias?"

"Where the fuck are you? You were supposed to call me last night," Quintero spits out, the sound of a door opening and closing coming through the line as the noise around him dissipates. "Well?"

"We're on our way to Santa Marta for the weekend." Cortez swallows hard, eyes nervously on mine. "I thought it was the perfect opportunity to get to know my bride."

"You fucked her? Cause you know that'll cost your father a pretty penny before the wedding, kid. If she isn't pure..." So cold. No anger. Instead, his chuckle shows amusement with a slight tinge of curiosity. *Sick fuck will pay for how he's treated her all these years.* "Answer me, güevon."

"No. I haven't."

"You don't sound sure."

"I haven't touched her that way."

"Yet you continue to fuck Laura every chance you get." Another laugh: it sounds like he's drinking from a glass as ice clinks. "That one has no shame or morals."

"Easy pussy."

"My wife's family is pathetic, and her father has no control of the women in his life," Quintero spits out, then the line goes quiet for a few seconds. "I'd shoot my daughter before I let her run around as my niece does."

"Then why do you let her spend time with Solimar?"

"Because it gives you easier access without raising suspicion. No one knows you bend her over, and my daughter's public image is intact."

I'd heard enough and slice a hand across my neck so he ends the call. Signio nods. "Hey, I hear her coming in from the patio. I'll call you later tonight…just wanted to give you our whereabouts."

"Never take this long again." There's a knock on the president's door and he muffles a curse. "Call me when Carlos picks her up. I'm close to closing in on my target and need the family out of sight. It's bad enough that hijueputa blew up a government building, but if he hurts any of them, I'll be publicly crucified."

"Should we be concerned?"

"No. I have a finger on the button." The call disconnects and Signio sits back. His mouth opens and closes a few times, but nothing comes out.

"He's watching my mother's house on the outskirts of Medellin."

"You know?"

"I do."

"And what is your plan?"

"At the moment?" He nods, and I pull out a simple blade from my pocket and place it on the table. His brown eyes are on the all-black matte handle, shifting in his seat as perspiration dots his upper lip. It's almost comical how someone can go from calm to complete and utter fear within the span of a few seconds. "I'm going to make you count to seven as I repay you for marring Solimar's skin."

"What?" Signio's voice trembles, eyes shifting around the room. They stay just a few beats longer on my torture chair. "I didn't…I would never—"

"So you don't remember breaking her skin by digging your nails in while at the gala last night? How you manhandled her?"

"Don't kill me."

"I'm not…" he breathes out a sigh of relief "…*yet*." No sooner has the last word passed through my lips when two of my guards grab his arms and force him face down, bent over the wooden top. Signio struggles. Cries. I'm not moved by his pleading. "You didn't listen."

"Please. I'm sorry."

"So you do remember?"

"No." At his lie, I stand and walk around behind him and place my blade at the base of his spine beneath his neck. "Okay...maybe. It was an accident." Another lie. *Motherfucking idiot.*

Pushing the tip deeper, a small drop of blood appears as I slide lower and pause mid-back. "Is that the version you want to stick with?"

"Por favor."

"The truth," I spit out through clenched teeth, forcing the blade in a little deeper. "Be a man and confess your sins."

"I hate her for not wanting me." It's spoken low, almost indiscernible.

"What was that?" A soft pull and the blade cuts lower, the opening another inch longer.

"Please stop."

"Say it. Why were your hands on her?"

"Because I hate her for not wanting me!" he yells out, tears slipping from his eyes and onto the tabletop.

"Thank you."

"Will you let me go now?" Signio is shaking, failing at moving away from my blade.

"No." Pulling the knife from his back, I lean down close to his ear and smile. "That's number one." The second and third cuts are to the left of the original on his spine and aren't are small. They're easily five inches long and bleeding profusely, but not deep enough to cause any serious problems. "You ready for number four?"

"I'll never go near her again."

"That wasn't my question..." Dragging the tip across to his right side, I slice another jagged line down to the top of his ribs "...*parce.*"

"No more."

"Count the next one. What number are we on." Signio doesn't respond, and I hum. "If you lost count, I could always start again. One?"

"No! No." His eyes snap shut and his bottom lip trembles. "Y-you're on number five of s-seven."

"Good boy." Number five and six are small and very shallow, just deep enough for a drop or four to pool at the center with the other lacerations. "You ready for the last one?"

"I'm sorry."

"You are getting off easy, Cortez. Now, thank me for my leniency."

"Gracias...*fuck*!"

I embed the blade fully to the handle, right between two ribs, and leave it there. "You're welcome." Looking over at Geronimo, I nod toward the back exit where the stairs are. "Get him checked and comfortable. He'll be leaving the premises Monday morning and we don't want him to be in pain during the ride."

"As you wish, Patron."

"Hagale." There's a small sink near the electronic lift to change the oil of my cars and I walk over without sparing the bleeding man another look. There's blood on my hands that needs to disappear and a beautiful girl I plan to worship after turning my monitoring system off.

I miss my beautiful little flower.

21

Solimar

I LOVE HIM.
    I love him.
    I love him.
  I'm screwed.

Those words continued to run through my mind as we ate the breakfast he prepared and then when I went upstairs to change and encountered another surprise: a closet stocked with everything I'd need and a few things that make me blush.

"What did you do?" I ask, mouth gaping like a fish as I take in everything this crazy, gorgeous man bought for me. There's so many pieces of silk, lace, and delicate fabrics; Alejandro chose well and plenty with me in mind. My sizes are right and the fabric soft; I would've chosen these items for myself.

There's activewear, loungewear, and a few dresses for various occa-

sions. Jeans and simple tops and more shoes than I've ever owned in
my life. There are also a few things that I've been tempted to try on in
the past and didn't have the courage to. I had no one to wear them for.

Risqué and indecent, the lace bodysuit with cutouts in private
places is beautiful. But more than that, I want to wear it for
Alejandro and have him rip the delicate fabric with his teeth.

"With me, you'll never want for anything. I'll always take care of
you."

"Always?"

"In this life and every single one that follows, I own you and
you me."

I shiver at those words—the declaration behind his possessiveness—and he kisses the area just below my ear. "You cold?"

"No," I say and try to focus on the here and now as I'm given a
private tour of his home. He was gone a while this morning, taking
care of something I never cared to ask about while I relaxed on his
couch. Could I have snooped? Yes. No doubt. However, I don't want
to learn a single private anecdote or personality trait from his
belongings.

I want him to tell me every last secret.

I want him to show me what makes him happy.

"You sure?" The landscape in front of me is beautiful—every
inch of his land is, and more so when I take it in with his rich timbre
whispering in my ear. He's explained every little thing I've seen, his
chest vibrating against my back with each word.

"I am." My nipples are hard, and I try to contain the whimper
fighting to break free. Moreover, a part of me is sad we're dressed in
T-shirts and jeans because I want to feel his skin on mine. Bask in his
warmth.

"Hmm?" It's a low hum in the back of his throat, and the sound is
dangerous. Sexy. "We can always head back and pick up a light
jacket."

"I'm okay." More than, but I don't voice how much his thoughtfulness means to me. The man continues to surprise me at every turn, and I find myself loving every layer I uncover.

The sweet. The devious. The danger.

I love him.

I should be scared and surprised and begging him to take me back home, but I don't. My attraction to him isn't new; I've hidden this from everyone, buried my desires for so long, but the more time we spend together...

I've fallen.

I see this side of him that's sweet and caring. Every interaction—every stolen moment has made me his.

He's my person, and I truly don't care about his business or the fighting with my father; I choose him. I know that deep down, it will always be him.

"Good girl." He kisses the back of my head, tapping the horse's side with his boot. We're on the north side of his terrain and riding his prized *criollo* horse, my back nestled tightly to his front. "We'll be there soon."

"Okay." I'm willing to follow him, no questions asked. However, while he continues to talk, I focus on the feel of his thigh muscles flexing while he directs *Azul* further into the pasture.

At first, I didn't understand why he called this ebony criollo *blue*, but after taking him out of the paddock and giving him a few nose scratches, I saw it. The stallion's eyes are like two azure gems: pure and clear. Azul holds a commanding presence that's drowned in protectiveness for its riders, and I can see why Alejandro favors him.

He's gorgeous, just like the owner.

"We're almost there, little flower. Are you tired?" His arm around me tightens, pulling me impossibly closer as we reach a large wooden gate. So far, I've seen his stables, livestock, and met a few of the ranch hands—noticed the tight security at each stop and the guns in holsters—but there's still so much more. At least that's what he said after we left a small creek halfway from the barn and where we are now.

Throughout the tour, it's been lush greens and vibrant wild-flowers.

It's been birds chirping and the sound of hooves meeting the terrain.

"Not at all. This place is amazing," I say, leaning my head back against his shoulder. I'm warm and feel safe. Completely enveloped by his earthy scent. "If I lived here, I'd never leave."

He nuzzles my hair. "That can be arranged."

"Don't tempt me."

"One day you just might find yourself kidnapped." There's an edge of danger to his tone, and I shrug with complete nonchalance. "Not afraid?"

"Not in the least." Turning my head, I kiss his jaw and then look forward again. "I'd be more than okay with that."

"Careful, Solimar. You're tempting the wrong man."

"I know." Azul stops at the gate and pulls on a thick piece of rope attached and tugs, leading us through the opening without Alejandro giving him instruction. He just trots slowly through the known pathway in the grass that's wide enough for a truck and stops a few feet in. "Wow."

"Welcome to *El Jardin de Sara*."

"You are becoming too perfect in my eyes, Mr. Lucas, and that's a hazardous thing for my sanity."

Alejandro chuckles, thumb rubbing circles on my arm. "Why is that?"

"Because I love the fact you dedicated a garden to your mother, and more so, that you're sharing it with me. You're different with me, Alejandro. You're not hiding who you are, and I find myself defenseless in your arms."

I'm blushing. Can feel the heat as it spreads across my cheeks and then down my throat and across the top of my chest. My confession slams into the forefront once again. How easily I've fallen for him. I'm embarrassed, heart almost beating out of my chest, and yet I don't regret my honest answer.

Not when his lips quirk up and the sight of Alejandro's boyish grin makes me feel light and free. Foolish and strong. Unafraid and more than willing.

Jesus. I look away for a second, needing a moment to collect myself while his heated stare remains on me. It's there, burning my flesh while his masculine scent infiltrates and dominates my senses.

This thing between us scares me.

Makes me feel alive.

It'll break me in the end.

22

ALEJANDRO

SOONER THAN SHE'S ready, I'll overwhelm her world more than I already have.

There's no avoiding our future and the sacrifices she'll have to make. Because while my Preciosa claimed to choose me last night, I'm not sure she understands what life as my queen will entail.

Who she'd become at my side. What she'd give up.

With me, there is no in-between. No middle ground.

Solimar needs to intimately know both sides of my coin: the monster and then man.

I'm not a saint, but I'll worship her and always be there. I will kill to protect.

Because while I'm no good for her, I am selfish enough to never let go. Because one thing is hearing stories on the evening news, and the other is living my reality.

Pressing my lips to the side of her head, I dismount and offer my hand. "You still trust me, Miss Quintero?"

"Yes." Not a single second of hesitation and then her small fingers entwine with mine as I help her off and then step into her personal space. That tight little body slides down over my hardness and her feet touch the ground, a soft sigh escaping those bee-stung lips. "I do trust you."

"Good girl."

"I love it when you call me that." She clutches my shirt trying to reach my lips, but I kiss her forehead and step back. *Soon, Preciosa.*

"And you call me the dangerous one?" I wink and turn her toward my mother's garden, not paying attention to the exaggerated pout or the huff she releases. Instead, I walk us to the center of the passion fruit grove. "Come with me. There's one more thing..."

"More than this beautiful garden? This place is perfect."

"Thank you." Standing behind her, I kiss the crown of her head and pull her back to my chest. She shivers as one arm wraps around her midsection. My girl lets out a lovely hum when I bring my cheek down next to hers—nuzzling her. "I planted this grove the year my father died so Mom wouldn't go without. You see, it's her favorite fruit drink, and he holds the blame for this obsession." I press my lips to the area just below her ear and smile when she mewls. "It's the first thing he bought her when they began to date, and their chaperone stopped to buy fresh fruit at a stand. My great grandmother wasn't an easy woman, but that little detour from their walk in the park changed their lives. She loved it so much and promised to stick by his side as long as he provided a few of these each week."

"That's a very sweet story." Her expression is happy; seeing her take in something as simple as this cluster of fruit trees after dismounting my horse—hearing my story—is adorable. The sweetest treat after her pussy. "But what about when the fruit isn't in season?"

"I have a few distributors for those occasions."

"It's sexy how you've covered all your bases, Alejandro. Always going above and beyond."

"The Lucas men are known to be possessive and equally giving."

"How giving?" she says while turning her face in my direction, the pink on her cheeks coming from more than just the sun exposure today. It's innocent curiosity. It's need and hunger.

"Bend over and you'll find out."

"*Christ*." Now her voice is low and breathy—sinful as I bite the soft skin of her chin. Not hard enough to leave a mark, but enough to feel me. "You…I…oh, God!"

"Let me show you." It comes out gritty and hungry, the length of my cock pressed against the small of her back. "Come with me."

"Anywhere."

"Right answer." Taking her small hand in my larger one, I walk past her and pull us deeper into the pasture. My eyes shift to look at her as I follow a familiar path, wondering what she's thinking. If she'll forgive me one day for what I'll do to the men she calls family.

My feelings for her will not deter me from slitting her grandfather's throat when the day comes, but I will consider her feelings. I'll console her. I'll earn her forgiveness.

But two things are certain:

They will die. She is mine.

"Shit!" Solimar suddenly trips on fallen fruit and stumbles into me, clutching my shirt to keep upright. My grip on her hand tightens as I turn, yanking her to me as I help her stay upright. She gasps as our eyes meet, lip caught between her teeth.

"You okay?"

"Yeah."

"You sure?" Gripping her hips, I lower my face to hers. "Because you seem out of breath and shaking." And she was. The second my fingers take hold and pull her against my chest, those striking grey eyes become heavy-lidded. "Be honest. Tell me what you're thinking."

"You're going to destroy me."

"And then I'll put you back together again." My mouth slants over hers in a quick yet harsh kiss before she can question or rationalize my statement. I taste her desire for me in each moan, in the way she immediately tries to wrap herself around me, but I have more to show her and slow us down to a few soft pecks. *Almost.* I lay my forehead against hers. "I'll do everything in my power to always fix us."

"Why?"

"Because I can't see myself without you in my life." Solimar's lips part to respond, but before she can, I put a tiny bit of distance between us. Her hand is in mine, all soft and delicate, and I kiss the palm before moving us toward the final destination and past the wall of trees that separates one plantation from the next. A few steps from where we stand side by side, the pasture opens into two separate crop areas and with a different product in each. To the left are poppies, rows upon rows of my strand of flower—the line I produced after twining three different seedlings from contrasting countries and climates.

It's why it's so popular. Stronger than what others grow in my market.

"Thank you for showing me this part of you." Solimar's awed voice pulls my attention down to her as she takes in my experimentation crops. She's facing me now and her arms come around my neck, fingertips playing with the hair at the nape. My little flower is completely unaware of my final surprise just a few feet from us. "I appreciate your honesty and willingness to not play a fictitious role."

"I'm not hiding who I am from you, Preciosa. Everything they say about me is true." Lowering my face to hers, I run my nose down her cheek and pause at the corner of her mouth. "I'm a killer. A criminal."

"You're so much more than that." The late afternoon sky is beginning to give way into the evening, and it's a little cooler now. The blue over the horizon is a bit more pronounced and the wind around us is picking up, dancing over every leaf and flower, and yet, nothing stands out more than the beautiful grey of her eyes. They shine with emotion and lust; two gems beckoning me closer. "I see you, Mr. Lucas. All of you."

"I'm not a good man, Solimar." Gripping her hips, I walk us back a few steps. Right to the edge of each plantation where my two worlds—family and business—come within a few feet of each other. The good and bad. The illicit and legal.

On one side is my mother's fruit trees and on the other drugs, and yet, the middle is neutral. It's where I plan to make her mine.

Out in the open. Where I'm at home.

Because I'm a man of the land and have always been.

"Nobody is perfect."

"No. Nobody is," I agree and bring both hands up to cup her cheeks. *So soft and warm. So mine.* "But this life isn't for everyone, Sol."

Her brows furrow and lips purse. "Are you trying to dissuade me from wanting you?"

"I'm not letting you go."

"I'd never give you a chance to—" I don't let her finish. My lips cover hers and I taste her desire for me, revel in the way she moans into my mouth and the goose bumps that rise across her flesh. There's no hesitation or asking questions as I walk us toward a large tree that shades the earth between the two pastures.

On one side is a symbol of my family, and on the other the kingpin she craves.

"Fuck, you're beautiful," I groan, taking her bottom lip between my teeth and pressing down. She hisses but doesn't complain, the fire in her eyes a challenge for more.

Another detail I never got the chance to show her, but I remedy it now as I stop us just as her foot meets the soft blanket on the ground. Then I'm placing soft pecks down to her chin before turning her around. There's a soft gasp that escapes at the sight laid before her; a picnic for us and our names carved into the wooden trunk of the large oak where the basket with our snack and a few pillows sit against it.

"This is beautiful."

"Nothing is enough for you…" skimming my hands down her arms, I entwine my fingers with hers while my lips hover at her temple "…but I'm going to spend the rest of my life laying the world at your feet."

"Alejandro, I—"

"Turn around, Preciosa." Sol does as I ask, only letting go of my hands long enough to face me. Grey orbs meet mine and in them, there's anxiousness and desire—hunger. There's also need and an emotion that both grips my heart in a painful squeeze and causes a shiver to rush down my spine. I untwine our fingers and cup her face with both hands, tilting her face up to mine. A little closer. Lips brushing. "I love you, Miss Quintero. I'm owned by you."

It's my truth. She's come into my life and rocked the very throne I sit upon. This between us is fast and all-consuming, but also comes with a set of complications we can't ignore.

I will kill her father, and she will wear my ring.

Solimar's knees weaken and tears gather at the corner of her eyes. "I love you too, Mr. Lucas. Since before I ever had the right to."

"At the club."

She shakes her head, a delicate blush spreading across her cheeks. "Since the day I stumbled upon a picture of you in a bathtub and watched the adjoining interview. You stole my heart with that first cocky smirk."

Christ.

That was...

"You naughty little thing." That interview in question was a little after I took over Don Andres's business dealings. She had to have been no more than fifteen or sixteen and rebelling—

"I've never been able to help myself where you're concerned. You're worth it to me."

"And I'm going to marry you one day." It's all I manage to growl out before slanting my mouth over hers. This kiss is heated and near desperate as I undo the top three buttons of her top. My fingers skim over every inch that becomes exposed, following the swell of her chest and then lower where I grip the material in my impatience and rip the rest off; the tiny white fasteners scatter on either side of us. "Right here on this land, Solimar. Just like I'm making you mine today, I plan on binding us in front of God and the citizens of this country soon."

"I'll proudly walk to you wearing white," she moans, fumbling with the buckle of my pants, hand trembling as it opens. I stop my exploration and watch her, take in the nervousness and then how her pupils dilate when she realizes I'm not wearing underwear beneath my jeans. There's a low whisper of *so hot* and *oh God* as the head greets the cooling air and her fingertips.

I don't think she's aware of the soft caress or the raw hunger in her expression.

"Your place is beside me, Solimar."

Her gaze snaps up to mine and her expression softens. "It's all I want. To be with you."

"And you will be." Taking her hand from my pants, I bring it up to my mouth and kiss the palms. "Always."

"Promise?"

"In this life and the next." Gripping her hip, I lower us to the blanket below and skim my lips down her throat. "I'll always be near, Preciosa. Nothing could keep me away from you."

"Alejandro." It's a keening sound: happy and needy.

"Just feel me." Nipping her collarbone, I follow the path down the center of her chest. I'm leaving behind tiny bites—the perfect indentation of my teeth that I'll use as a guide after to love her flesh with kisses. Her chest rises and falls rapidly. Her nipples pebble against the lace fabric of her bra.

One hard pull and the clasp breaks, tits spilling out.

"I need you," she hisses from between clenched teeth, eyes rolling back and writhing beneath me. Her hips lift and thighs spread to welcome my hips. "All of you."

She's fire and love.

She's mine to protect and fuck.

The open shirt and tattered bra come off in a few swift tugs, flying behind me and onto the grass. Her upper body is flawless; perky breasts and smooth skin with a few tiny freckles leading me toward the waist of her jeans.

I undo them and then lower the zipper with my teeth. "I'm yours." Delicious shivers rush through her as my fingertips roam her exposed skin and then dip lower, caressing the thin material of her panties as I sit back to admire. "Only yours."

"Mine." Solimar counters my confession. The possessiveness in her tone creates a heady feeling—a throbbing animal which before only hungered for blood. At this moment, looking up at me with only her jeans covering her innocence, I'm her prey. Her only desire.

"Motherfuck," I grit out, shaking as Solimar bites that luscious bottom lip, and my fingers dig into her denim-covered hips. My grip is tight and I'm breathing hard. I'm throbbing for her and dripping pearl-like beads on to her pants. "Say it again."

Heat flashes across her gaze as it drops to my cock and back to me. "I love you, Alejandro."

"My Preciosa." There's nothing gentle in the way I yank her bottoms off. Nor am I civilized when I lower my head and rub my nose down her covered slit. She's wet. Her arousal soaks through the thin fabric, coating her inner thighs that glisten for me.

I turn my head and lick a path from thigh to juncture, slipping my tongue just beneath her panties.

"Oh God...*please*...don't stop."

"Motherfuck." Eyes snapping closed, I inhale deeply and count to ten. Then twenty. This is her first time and while the pain is inevitable, I'll do what I can to prepare her for my size and girth. "You're going to be the death of me."

"And I need you to lose your clothes."

I nip her mound. "In a rush?"

"I'm desperate to feel you."

"Patience, beautiful." But I do lose my plain white T-shirt and toe-off my boots and socks, tossing both aside. My pants stay loose around my hips as I resettle with my lips over her pussy; taking her sweet scent deep into my lungs. "I'm in no rush."

Her body trembles.

Her hips lift in invitation.

"Don't be mean, Papi." Another gyration, and I'm quick to nuzzle her. I love her calling me that. "You've been teasing me all day and I've been patient."

"You have been a good girl, haven't you?"

"The best."

"Then pull your panties aside and show me that pretty little pussy." Solimar brings her hand over her mound and pauses. She's nervous, but the look in her eye is anticipation mixed with lust. Excitement. "Give me what's mine, Preciosa."

She pulls the thin material aside. "I've always been yours."

23

ALEJANDRO

THOSE FOUR WORDS fill me with peace, but it's the sight of her bare pussy that causes me to snap. My mouth waters. My cock gives a hard jerk.

"Christ, Preciosa." I lick her from slit to clit; one long pass with the flat of my tongue and a groan rumbles in my chest. She's sweet and decadent—the literal incarnation of pleasure—and I bury my face between her thighs.

I'm obsessed. My hunger is uncontrollable.

"Fuck," I growl, dipping my tongue in her entrance as another rush of wetness seeps out. Her taste robs me of my senses as I catch each drop before parting her labia and reaching the throbbing bundle of nerves.

Her hips lift and back arches as I flick it with the tip of my tongue. Her hands fist the blanket when I scrape my teeth over it.

"So good. Need—"

"Me. Only ever me." My cock throbs—hurts, but I keep my focus on her. Every swipe of my tongue over her swollen pussy is sweeter than the last.

"Don't stop." It's a plea. A cry of total surrender. "I'm so close."

"You need to come?" I slip a finger inside to the first knuckle, in and out, and her opening clenches. Tries to pull me in deeper. "Tell me."

"Please," she whispers, body flushed and chest heaving as Solimar holds my stare. "Please make me come."

Fuck she's beautiful.

Laying like this, wanton and free with my land surrounding us, she takes my breath away.

This is her at her most natural. No titles or propriety. No one directing her actions.

Just her. Just a woman enjoying a simple pleasure.

Solimar, my beautiful little flower.

I pull my finger out and give her clit two quick slaps. "So pretty and swollen. Wet for me."

"Alejandro, I..." Her words die as I lower my jeans past my ass and kick them off. My hand lazily works my cock, fist tight and wet with her juices.

We're out in the open with nature surrounding us and my dirt just a few layers beneath our bodies. Seeing—having her like this on my land is what I've been missing all these years while I lived in chosen solitude. She's what I've needed without knowing. She's my home and sanctuary.

"I want to hear you scream my name." With my other hand, I rub her, running my fingers up and down her slit. "Can you do that for me?"

I'm keeping her close.

Want her tears and cries of frustration.

"Yes," she hisses when I slide the blunt of my cock up her slit to nuzzle her clit.

"God, little flower." *Motherfuck,* she's slick. Her wetness coats me, marks me. "My Sol."

"Yours." Flexing my hips, I slip just the head inside her tight opening and pull out. And then again. Solimar throws her head back and lifts her hips to pull me in deeper. *Bad girl.* My response is a smack to her bundle of nerves with my cock.

Her body seizes, breath caught in her throat. She's on the precipice, eyes squeezed shut and that won't do.

Another two slaps and her lips part, a stuttered breath escaping.

"Look at me." They snap open and lock on mine, drunk on pleasure and full of want. "I love you."

That's all she needed as her orgasm slams into her—shaking us both as she writhes beneath me. "Alejandro, make me yours. I—"

"You are mine and I am yours." At my words a keening whimper escapes her, fingers digging into my biceps as I slam in to the hilt. "Fuck, baby," I grit out, fighting every cell in my body that demands I move. She's tight; a motherfucking vice grip, and as much as I want to fuck her like a wild beast, I hold back.

Solimar's my priority, and I focus on soothing her pain as she adjusts to my size. Grey eyes look at me with both wonder and pain, with happiness and love.

"I'm sorry, Preciosa." Gently, I skim my hands down her body while kissing her lips. It's unhurried and languid; we're sharing the same breath as the rigidness gives way to a needy state.

The more I stroke my tongue with hers she calms, keeping me in place as she wraps her long legs around my waist. I slip deeper inside and she sucks in a breath, experimenting with the small gyration of her hips beneath me.

I close my eyes and exhale roughly at her unhurried movements, pulling me a quarter of the way out and then back in. She's using me for her first taste of pleasure, taking control, and I wait patiently for her to adjust.

Sweat beads at my brow, the drops rolling down the side of my face as my stomach muscles clench and cock flexes within her heat. My entire body burns from holding back.

"I'm not." A warm hand suddenly cups my chin, and I open my eyes to meet her stare. Her expression is sweet and happy as a few tears fall. I'm quick to wipe them away. "I'll never deny that it hurts, but you're worth the pain, Alejandro. You've always been it for me."

"And you've become my world. What tethers me to this life." My truth makes her clench, shift her pelvis, and the tiny hiss that escapes isn't of pain. No. This sound holds a hint of pleasure, the same tantalizing cry of rapture from last night and today when I licked her little clit.

"I'm yours." She gyrates again, her face contorting as my pelvis rubs against her sensitive clit. "Please."

"Stay with—"

"Oh, God...I need you to..." Sol pulls me in deeper with the heels of her feet on my lower back, forcing me closer. To bottom out once again. "I need you to move."

Leaning down, I take a nipple between my lips and flick it twice. "Are you sure?"

"Yes!"

Her hooded eyes are on mine as I pull out and hold just the tip inside. "Your choice, Preciosa. Soft and sweet or rough and demanding."

"I just want you. Nothing but you."

"I love you." The last syllable hasn't passed through my lips when I slam back inside, causing her body to seize. "Even when I fuck you, we're still making love. Everything we do comes from that emotion, and I'll spend the rest of my life making sure you never doubt how I feel for you. You're my world."

"And I'll always choose you."

The wind around us picks up. It moves a stray piece of hair across her sweat-slick forehead, and I push it aside with my lips while my hips never pause in their search for completion. I ride her hard and without mercy, pounding her pretty little pussy with wild abandon while the trees and flowers around us sway gently with the breeze.

It's the perfect backdrop: beauty and her savage.

My eyes squeeze shut, and I pull back as another rush of heat envelopes my cock. Her wetness runs down my shaft and onto my balls that are heavy with come. My body is strung tight as she clenches—her walls fluttering in the most agonizingly beautiful cadence around my girth.

Grey eyes watch me from beneath long lashes before following the path down to where we're connected. I follow her line of sight, and a growl builds in my chest. "Son of a bitch."

She's so delicate compared to me. A sinful little doll.

Mine to love. Mine to fuck.

Gripping her hips, I raise her up and settle her ass on my thighs. The change in angle causes a shiver to run down her spine and limbs, for her walls to try and pull me in deeper. The tiny hole flexes, her walls massaging, and I groan, more so when I catch the smile on her face.

It's an innocent exploration.

Following her natural inclination to torture me.

"Behave," I grit out and give her one quick stroke, the head of my cock hitting that special little spot that makes her cry out. Solimar doesn't listen, though. Instead, she tightens and releases again and again. My response is to snap my hips forward and pull her at the same time down on my cock by the hold on her hips. I ride her hard for a few strokes—punishing the coquettish move.

"Please don't stop. That...I...*fuck*," my Preciosa screams, fingernails digging into my arms pinning her in place. A light sheen of sweat decorates her skin as her brows furrow and lips part; she's stunning in her pleasure. Takes my breath away in her pure trust.

She's offering her soul.

She's offering her life to me.

"Say it again," I grit out, picking up speed as I piston in and out of her. "I need to hear you say them."

"I choose you. Always." It's low and a little slurred, but I hear her. Those words are a balm to my soul and my balls grow heavy, my orgasm teasing at the corner of my senses.

"Alejandro, I'm so close."

"I know, little flower..." Her grip on me is near painful and when she squeezes again, I grit my teeth. "Give it to me."

"I'm—"

"Mine," I groan, and she lets go. Wave after painful wave assaults her and when she whimpers my name on a prayer, I follow. "Christ, girl. You feel like heaven and taste of sin—perfection." Hips stroking deep into her, I draw out every last drop of pleasure from our bodies. Slower now.

No words are exchanged as our combined juices slip from inside her and the mess we created stains the blanket below. It's still early enough that I take my time and enjoy her like this.

No rush and wearing that post-orgasm glow that makes me want to start again. That causes me to twitch and her eyes to widen before a tiny smirk appears.

Solimar has no idea how innocently teasing she is.

"You're dangerous." The rebuttal is sitting on her tongue, but I silence her with a look, by cupping the back of her neck and laying over her from head to toe, and taking her lips in a kiss.

We have a lot to discuss. To plan.

I want her here with me always and will make that happen even if it means unleashing my wrath on her family sooner. I'll kill them and marry her on the same day if that's what it takes.

She's my home. My peace. My reward.

I'll kill anyone that tries to take her away.

24

ALEJANDRO

"**R**EMEMBER, ALEJANDRO. WHILE *everyone gravitates toward the easy path, you follow the winding road. The more difficult a product is to cultivate, the more your buyers will pay; the exotic always equates to a higher-end crop. Stick to that motto, and you'll go far.*"

Looking over at Don Andres, the largest poppy distributor in South America, I scratch my jaw. "Is that why you travel to Turkey and Costa Rica to bring back seeds? I've seen the shipments."

"I'm a man who likes to create, kid. My product can't be duplicated because the extraction process with my machines creates a unique product that's exclusive to me." He claps me on the shoulder, his expression smug, and I turn my attention back toward his large field. Rows upon rows of poppies are growing and will be ready to harvest by the end of next month. Their reddish and purple hues make for a pretty picture—they seem harmless to the naked eye, but

the reality is that their death toll continues to rise, and the price goes up. "Most in this business grow whatever they get their hands on and repeat the process through the use of their last cultivation; I don't. I mix the two strains to create one that's stronger...more attractive to the cartels in Mexico."

"What about selling to a bigger market?"

"What do you have in mind, parce?" Don Andres is intrigued, body language at ease.

"Pharmaceutical companies."

"Is there something you'd like to tell me?"

"There's more profit in the legal route, Andres. More security with each transaction."

"And how do you know this? Can we trust—"

"I know because I've done my homework." His eyes narrow at my interruption, hands clenching, but he is smart enough to let me finish. Curiosity outweighs reprimand at the moment. "Because I met with an interested American company, and the contract on the table is very lucrative."

"Why would you do this without my knowledge?" Don Andres spits out, his hand moving toward the waistband of his jeans, but I'm quicker. The first bullet from my Glock embeds in his hand, blowing two fingers clean off, and his eyes widen in horror-filled pain.

The second is to his chest.

The third is to his knee, blowing the bone and forcing his body to the ground.

Then, I stand over him, my eyes on his. "Your first mistake was hiring me. Your second was making a drunken pass at my mother."

"Alejandro, son...please don't do this."

"Your last mistake was thinking I'd stay an errand boy, Patron." The last bullet snaps his head back, bouncing off the ground as blood quickly pools beneath his body. He's dead, and the tiny hole between his eyes makes me smile as those out in the field begin to clap.

"Someone's a little distracted this morning. You okay?" Sol says, bringing me back to the present as she wraps her arms around me and presses those sweet lips against the center of my back. She peppers kisses...

Up and down. Left to right.

And then finishes with a nip over my spine, which she licks. *Naughty little thing.*

"I am." A smile curls at my lips and my hand covers hers, just holding the warm flesh against mine. "How about you? Any soreness?"

"No."

Turning my head, I look at her with a raised brow. "Are you telling me the truth?"

"Why would I lie?"

"Fair enough." Bringing one of her hands up to my lips, I kiss each knuckle. "Are you hungry?"

"Not yet, but I am content and at peace." There's a pause that follows her statement, a lingering quiet that's not uncomfortable or worrisome because I know what she's experiencing. Those two states of mind are her gifts to me each time my girl is near. With her, I find my calm. I'm happy. "To be honest with you, Alejandro, I feel at home here. As if this were my everyday life and not some passing moment before reality sinks—"

"Do you trust me, Miss Quintero?" I interrupted, keeping my voice low and even while reaching with my free hand for her hip and keeping her against me.

"I do." Her lips against my skin curve up into a smile. "Even though I shouldn't."

"Why is that?"

"Because you never give yourself completely to what can destroy you."

"Wise words, Preciosa..." with my grip on her side, I pull her around to stand in front of me "...but useless on me. I'm not going anywhere, and I'm in this for the long haul."

"Until we're old and grey?" Fuck, she's beautiful. No makeup and sleep rumpled, Solimar's breathtaking while wearing nothing but a white sheet wrapped around her small frame. She's the perfect backdrop to my morning, and nothing in the vast land behind her compares to the exquisiteness against me.

We're just a few yards away from the marijuana and poppy plantation on the back end of my Finca where a small cabin sits. It's where I come to escape and be alone. Where I plan.

The small, 3,000 square-foot property has everything you could need without the added distractions of the internet and apps. This place is quiet and relaxing, and it's also where I devoured my queen's pussy late into the morning hours before exhaustion took hold and Solimar passed out on me.

And even then, I still kissed and licked her tender flesh until finding my release with her taste on my tongue and a few pumps of my hand. My hunger for her is insatiable, uncontrollable, and I chose to walk outside and let my mind wander while she slept.

I'm a man of few words.

I'm a planner.

The man who I killed to dethrone had taught me to look past the conventional and seek what others fail to account for, and I know what's coming. Can almost see each move being made while I sit back and wait.

"Until my lungs expand for the last time and I begin my search for you in our next life."

"For someone who's known as a criminal, you're very romantic."

"Only with you. No one else sees this side of me."

"Thank you." Her expression is soft, but the heat in her eyes shows appreciation for my bare chest and the tattoos that adorn my flesh. They lower—from my stare to my ink—and a blush stains her cheeks. "I'm very hot...happy...I—"

"I'm up here."

"Shut up!" The little flower goes to smack my arm, but I wrap her in both of mine and pull us close before lifting so we're chest to chest. Lips hovering. "This isn't fair."

"Not for you." I kiss her pout, biting the jutted-out lower lip, and pull back. "This is how I always want you."

"Manhandled?" There's a bit of breathiness in her tone and once more she looks down toward the edge of my tattoo, licking her lips while following the bold black ink down to where her chest and mine touch. "Roughly taken?"

"Close."

At that Sol looks up, caging my face between her two small hands. Her thumbs sweep across my jaw. "I can live with that."

"You have no choice."

"You sound very sure of yourself."

"Always." Pecking her lips twice, I set her down and help tuck the corner of the bedsheet a little tighter. "Now, are you still not hungry?"

"Not yet, but I definitely could use some coffee and..." She trails off then, her head turning around while her mouth drops open. "Wow." She's switching between the marijuana plants and my face, another venture I've taken on for personal reasons. "That's a lot of weed, Alejandro."

A bark of laughter bubbles out and I throw my arm across her shoulders, tucking her into my side while we turn to fully face the field. She's a breath of fresh air, and I love how her mind works. "That's your first observation?"

"It is a lot."

"Have you smoked before, beautiful?"

Her grin is cheeky. "Maybe."

"Bad girl." I try to make my expression stern while looking down at her, but the thought of Sol high, happy, and hungry is amusing. It also makes me wonder who popped that cherry under her father's tight grip. "With whom?"

"Laura bought it from some guy she knows out in—"

"Enough said." This shouldn't surprise me either.

The smile drops and her head tilts to the side. "Why did your tone just change? You don't like her?"

"I'm not a fan of anyone who hurts my girl."

"She doesn't mean to. Not really."

"And yet, Laura continues to put you in dangerous predicaments. I know all about her and Signio, as does most of the country." Shame flits across her expression before she schools her features into that monotone look that she's perfected over the years. It pisses me off to watch her shoulders square and the way she takes in a deep inhale and then lets it out slowly; she's going to excuse their behavior. "Don't," I grit out while stepping back and holding a hand up. "If you care about my sanity and their safety, just don't."

"Alejandro, they've known each other a long time and—"

"She owes you more loyalty than this, Solimar. Laura is selfish and manipulative."

"Don't hurt her." Her, not both and certainly not *him*.

The sudden sound of a motor catches my attention, and I peck her lips once in answer. It's not a promise or denial; I refuse to lie when I'd kill anyone who makes her so much as shed a tear. Whoever is driving, though, is getting closer, and no one sees her like this but me so I step back. That, and my men know better than to interrupt unless it's dire—life or death.

"Please head inside and wait for me there."

"Is something wrong?" In the blink of an eye, she's gone from blissful to worried to near frantic, her face growing pale while she begins to wring her hands. "Do you think Dad knows I'm here?"

"No one will harm you, Preciosa. Just give me a few minutes."

"Okay." I can see on her face the need for answers but I appreciate the trust to handle it, and before she turns to head back inside, I pull her back against me with a hand on her nape. My grip is tight, and I angle her head back to take those sweet lips in a harsh and quick kiss that leaves her dazed when I pull back.

"Thank you, pretty girl. I'll be inside soon." No sooner did she close the door than a familiar jeep pulls up and out jumps my brother and Daniel. A sinking feeling overtakes me, and I march across, grabbing Daniel by the neck before either utter a single syllable. "Why are you two here? The fuck is going on?"

Emiliano places a hand on my shoulder, but that only causes my grip to tighten and for my friend's face to redden. "Let him go, Alejandro. We need to talk."

"Then spit it out. Why are you here?"

"Because she's gone. Lourdes disappeared last night."

25

Solimar

HIS SCENT IS *deliciously male, and it surrounds me—consumes me—while his muscular frame overpowers mine. He's strong. Attentive to my every sound while forcing me to face the night's sky; I can feel the way the muscles of his abdomen flex against my back. Feel the vibrations of a low rumble as it builds in his chest and then vibrates against my neck.*

He's kissing the area just below the lobe, just a soft caress across my skin, but I feel it from the tip of my toes to the very last strand of hair on my head.

I shouldn't let him control me so easily, but my body isn't complying with rationality. It's boycotting my every instinct to protect myself and instead, leans back. Moves us closer so I can let his touch burn me.

Consequences be damned.

His hands skim down my thighs, bunching up my dress until he reaches the waistband of my panties. One tug and they rip, the thin lace of my thong slipping down to my mid-thigh. I'm exposed to the city below, but they can't see me from his penthouse balcony.

Calloused fingers skim across my hip and lower as he traces my mound and then clit, not stopping until my wetness coats the tip.

"Motherfuck, Preciosa. I'm going to devour that sweet little—"

Beep. Beep. Beep.

I wake up with a gasp and a hand between my thighs, fingertips soaked with the effects of my dream and the yearning to feel him once more. My thighs tremble and heart races. My lips tingle and nipples harden.

It's been like this for a few days now—since I came back home after assuring him I'd be fine while he found his little sister.

I can almost feel his touch—that dominating power he exudes by walking into a room—it's surrounding me as the last dregs of my dream leave me near tears because I'm alone. Alone, and being watched by my father who keeps asking me questions that make me nervous.

Where did Signio take me?

Was it secluded?

Was anyone else with us?

Stretching my hands up, I turn my face and stare at the clock, seeing it's almost ten. It's the start of another day without him. Another round in this waiting game I'm left with no choice but to participate in.

I can't fault him, though. Not under the circumstances, because had someone I love gone missing, I'd move heaven and earth to find them.

To save. To hug.

Moreover, even in his absence, his reminders are everywhere...

In my room.

In this bed.

In the nightly gifts Carlos delivers that set me ablaze with yearning.

Last night's box sent me back to four days ago when I slept in his arms. Nothing fancy or pretentious; a shirt—*his* shirt—that he wore to pick me up before stealing me away.

It smelled of him.

Of man and need and want. Of leather and earth and home.

"Please come back," I whisper low, throwing my covers off while reaching for my phone. The screen is full of notifications and I scroll through, stopping when I see four missed text messages.

Three are from Laura, and I ignore those for now—her never-ending questions about Signio—and focus on the last one instead.

Unknown number at 8:45 a.m.

My heart feels as though it's galloping inside my chest, and I swipe across to enter my pin. At once, the words on my screen cause a smile to stretch across my lips and a giggle to slip through.

Two days, Preciosa. You owe me a kiss.

"Something you want to share, Solimar?" Mom's voice cuts through the Alejandro-induced fog I've been under.

Tossing my phone aside after closing the screen, I look over at her by the now-closed door. "Morning." Mom eyes my cell and frowns. It's fingerprint protected, so she can't read the messages without my cooperation. "Any reason why you didn't knock? Something going on?"

"Your father just left and won't be back until tomorrow."

"Okay." I drag the word out, raising a brow. We haven't been on the best of terms since my return from the Lucas hacienda, and her secretiveness puts me on edge, especially after dropping the news that she's leaving Dad with no plan or further explanation.

"He has a meeting in Cali today with large donors looking to push an amendment supporting the deforestation in Tama and the installation of an 'eco-friendly' lodge."

"And how do you know this?" Because sharing isn't my father's forte.

"I listened in on a conversation he had with Signio's father last night. They were here to see you."

My hackles rise and I sit up, brows scrunched in confusion. "Why do they want to see me?"

"That's what I'd like to know." Mom walks further into the room, grabs the dainty chair in front of my vanity, and places it at the foot of my bed. "Something you want to tell me, Solimar?" The look on her face is inquisitive-meets-fear as if she already knows the mess I'm in and doesn't have a clue what to do. "Is it the reason my baby girl was grinning from ear to ear and your fiancé looks like someone took a bat to him?"

"W-what?"

"Have you not seen Signio?"

"No."

"Interesting." Her eyes, so much like mine, flick toward the device on my bed and then back at me. "Mind telling me what's going on?"

"Mind explaining your 'coming soon' disappearing act?"

"Touché."

Deciding to be the bigger adult in this situation, I take in a deep breath and let it out slowly. "I met someone."

It's low and nearly mumbled, but you'd think I screamed it from the top of my lungs by the way she jumps up and points at me. There's also a bit of squealing and some *thank you, Jesus,* thrown in the mix.

After she has her moment, Mom sits and primly crosses her legs while watching me with schooled features. "Do I know this young man? What family does he—"

I cut her off with a hand up. "Stop."

"Mamita, this could help you dissolve this engagement. Your dad will have no choice but to let you out of—"

Flopping back on the bed, I sigh. "No. He won't."

The sudden sadness in my tone catches her attention, and Mom abandons the chair for a place on my bed. For the first time in years, she lies beside me in silence, contemplating life, or her decisions, while I try to explain myself without giving anything away.

Silence looms between us for a while, and just when I think I'll blurt it all out, she clears her throat. "I met someone, too," she says so low that I imagine hearing wrong, but when I turn my face and see the guilt, a sick feeling begins to churn in my gut. There is shock and confusion, but I hold no anger toward her. None at all, because the man she married way before I was born is no longer here. He abandoned her for my grandfather's idiotic ideology. "Before you judge, let me explain."

"I'm not."

"He's just a friend and wants to help." I don't miss the softness with a bit of wistfulness in her expression. "We've known each other since our school days and he is offering me a way out of this mess." Mom grips my hand and squeezes it. "Your father's empire will collapse, and I can't allow him to drag us down with him. He doesn't care, but I do. My babies will not end up dead because of his greed."

"Alejandro would never allow that." *Christ.* The words slip past my lips before I can catch myself, but they don't make them any less true. I know he's watching out for me. That Carlos and others are near in case I need them.

She sits up abruptly and narrows her eyes. "What Alejandro are you talking about?"

"A friend."

"Solimar, what Alejandro? What's his full name."

"Why does it matter?" Slipping from the bed, I walk over to the small seating area where a pair of yoga pants lay atop an oversized chaise and grab them. I shimmy into them, doing the universal jump in place routine all women do, before giving her the most honest answer I can without spilling it all. "He's very protective of me, and that should be all that matters."

"Baby, please tell me he's not using—"

"Why don't you tell me your friend's name." Her lips snap shut, and I raise a brow. "Hagale. Tell me yours and I'll tell you mine."

"It's not that easy."

"So make it easy."

A sudden bout of giggles takes over her and she waves off my confused expression. *What the?* "I already know, Sol. Mr. Lucas came to see me the same night you came back from—"

"He did what?" It leaves me on a screech, and I'd be embarrassed if it weren't for the shock of her admission. Why wouldn't he tell me? Text me?

"Quit cutting me off, missy. It's rude."

"Sorry..." my countenance is contrite as I walk back over and sit on the edge where she's perched now "...but when exactly did it happen? Where?"

"Don't worry about that, Sol. I'm more concerned—hurt by the fact you kept falling in love from me. Do you not trust me?"

"Of course I do, but coming to share the news with their history isn't feasible."

"I could care less about some bullshit your grandfather started."

"You really don't care?"

"No."

"Thank God." My exhale is heavy, and the relief is instant. "Keeping to myself and avoiding this topic is exhausting." There's a vibrating behind us and I reach back, picking up my cell and hitting ignore when I see it's Laura calling me. Mom gives me a funny look. "She won't leave me alone."

"Something is up with that one." She clicks her tongue in distaste.

A snort escapes. "You mean, other than chasing Signio?"

"Yes, smarty. Something about her involvement with him gives me a bad vibe."

"Me too." For a beat, we're both quiet, but when there's a knock on my door and Carlos asks if he can come in, I take note of the smile on her face. The way her eyes light up even though his tapping is a bit hurried. "Oh my God!"

"Kid, stop."

"Carlos, Mom? He's who you were talking about?"

"There's nothing to confirm."

"We'll see." With my eyes on hers, I smirk. "Come in, Carlos."

"Sol!"

"Veronica?" we say in unison, and Mom's reaction mimics mine the second he steps into the room. Something isn't right. His expression is one of worry, and more so with her here. "We need to leave, Solimar. Now."

"What? Why?" Mom pleads, but he's shaking his head and walking toward my vanity to pick up a pair of sandals I left there. "Talk to me, Carlitos. Q'hubo?"

My guard stops and turns to face us; he's angry. "Your father knows, kiddo. He knows about your relationship with Alejandro."

26

ALEJANDRO

"**W**HERE ARE YOU?" I hiss out, holding my phone in a tight grip while those in the room watch me. I'm standing with my back to them, not giving a single fuck about what they think while calling my little flower's guard. "Is she safe?"

"We're on our way out of Bogota and toward your home, Patron." I can make out Solimar's voice in the background, but there's a secondary female tone that catches my attention. "No one saw us leave."

"Who else?" There's no need for me to elaborate; I know more than Carlos would like. I'm well aware of where his loyalties lay and why.

There's a small pause and those around him grow quiet. "Mother and son."

"Those were not the instructions I gave you."

"And I take full responsibility."

"I respect that." Accepting the glass my brother offers with a few fingers' worth of rum, I take a few small sips. "It was a smart move and I'm glad you did for Solimar's sake, but next time ask before you react. In the future, I'd hate to have to put a bullet between your eyes."

"Si, Patron."

I disconnect the call and turn once again to face the room. My brother and his wife, Daniel, and my mother along with Chiquito's family are here. His two military buddies are tied up, and his younger brother is a bloody mess on the floor of a large warehouse Emiliano owns.

Then, I have his bruised wife. She was found by her cousin and a few of my men, bound and beaten after being left for dead a few miles from their home. Salazar is missing and so is my sister. Salazar is missing and his wife is deathly afraid of her own shadow after being abused by the man who swore before God to love and protect her.

Closing my eyes, I try to regain even a small semblance of rationality. I'm past angry. I'm past the stage of rage. This is a territory I've never ventured into, but welcome.

I keep trying to understand why Lourdes would do something like this. How did it get past the security I keep around them and the many employees that help run the house, and after searching for a bit, I noticed a discrepancy. Each time Salazar came for her, a friend would pick her up and then drop Lourdes off after her date, while he waited at a nearby restaurant. The owner confirmed as much.

Then, you have my sister's manipulative abuse of that same friend with a nasty cocaine habit and the willingness to do anything for a hit. Lourdes used her, something out her natural character, and I've made it so she gets the helps she needs. She's been shipped to a convent and will spend some time there getting clean and finding her faith.

My sister purposely hid this from me. Everyone.

My sister slept with a married man, not caring about who she'd hurt in the process.

And while I'm still furious, that anger has ebbed a bit after listening to the recording the day she disappeared. My fury, which has been unleashed on everyone that's had a small role in helping her hide this, has simmered into a manageable state where I think before pulling the trigger.

She threatened him with me, and he forced her to leave in fear of retaliation…

My wrath, or that of Quintero.

Salazar has made a mess of things and the clock is ticking —unforgiving.

My eyes shift across the room and land on the two men bound with their hands up and in an "X" position. They stand on the tip of their toes, and with each shift of their weight to alleviate pressure on their joints, the handcuffs clang against the metal bars.

I walk forward after passing my brother the offered drink without a word and flick open a small pocketknife. The blade is small in comparison to my other toys but is as sharp as a scalpel, and when I stop in front of the older of the two and lift his chin, his eyes widen.

His fear is palpable.

His urine stains the floor below.

"Do you remember now?"

"Patron, this is a mistake. We'd never do anything against your family." Not once does he meet my eyes. Instead, they remain on the blade as I bring it closer to his chin. The cold steel makes him flinch on contact, and a pathetic whimper passes through his lips. "Chiquito—"

"Has a lot to explain, but at the moment, I want to hear from you. Jimmy, where is she?" He's trembling, sweat rolling down the side of his face, but get no reply. "I won't ask again. Where is my sister?"

Closing my eyes, I begin to count. At the five mark, my hand shoots out and the blade embeds itself deep into his right side. Two more seconds and I twist, enjoying the way his flesh tears and blood pours from the wound.

"Please stop," Salazar's brother says low from the floor, body writhing in pain. "We don't know where they are."

"So Lourdes *is* with him." Not a question as we both know the truth. I have video surveillance from my mother's home the night he took her. It's clear as day. Undeniable. "Where?"

"He took her—"

"Cállese, hijueputa!" The man beside Jimmy, the quieter of the three yells out, and I smile. The action causes him to shrink back when I turn from his friend to him. "Let us go, Mr. Lucas."

"I'm sorry, I couldn't make out what you said beneath the rattle of your teeth." Turning my head, I meet my mother's stare and then Emiliano's. "Did you two get that?"

"No, Hijo."

"No, brother. Not a word."

"Daniel?"

"No, Patron. Unintelligible."

I turn back with a raised brow. "Repeat. No one here speaks bull-shit mumbles."

"This is false imprisonment and is punishable by time in jail."

Four distinct laughs reverberate throughout the warehouse, but it's my mom's that sticks out. It's also coming closer, from right beside me now, and I don't stop her when she throws her arm back and forward, breaking the glass of water she'd been drinking from in Juan's face.

Multiple gashes appear at once. Some small and some deep, but I don't pay the rivulets rolling from each any mind and take her hand in mine, inspecting it.

I won't fault her for wanting to hurt these three sons of bitches, but getting injured while doing so isn't allowed.

"Close and open your hand, please."

"I'm fine. Promise."

"Humor me." With a huff, she does as I ask, and her movement seems fine. There's also no sign of pain, and when Mom sees I'm satisfied, she rolls her eyes. "You still have two cuts I want looked at."

"Superficial."

"No arguing."

"You're a good son. Both of you." Emiliano, who is now on the other side of me, reaches over to squeeze her hand before we turn our attention back to our guests. Ire pours from our veins and patience is running thin, each one addressing a wounded man.

Blood stains the floor below as blows are landed, cuts are made, and stab wounds are added to the list of injuries. However, it's as I bring the wooden handle down across Jimmy's nose, shattering the bone and opening a gash over the bridge, that the little brother decides to speak.

"He's taking her out of the country, Mr. Lucas."

"Where, kid?"

"To Venezuela, with the help of the Cortez family and the president." Emiliano's hold on the back of his neck is tight as he holds him up, carrying most of his weight as Edwin's bruised body sags from lack of strength. He's the most innocent of the three, but his hands are dirty, and this will be his atonement. "Chiquito will have immunity in exchange for your capture."

"Thank you, Edwin. I appreciate the cooperation in this—"

"He's lying!" Juan's a bloody mess with over thirty cuts varying in sizes adorning his flesh. "Let us go and I'll tell you the truth. Who's really involved."

"You're a piece of shit, and your mother will be ashamed," Mom spits out after delivering a shallow slice across his neck. "Rot in hell."

After leaving her request with that action, she retakes her seat on the other side of Chiquito's soon-to-be widow, entwining their fingers together in support while Daniel waits patiently. He's been silent and following my orders to stand back, but his moment is coming.

The two bullets in my 1911 are a gift.

"Tell me, parce. Win me over with your bountiful knowledge."
As I say this, Daniel presses a few buttons on the remote control I'd
placed in his hand earlier today. The whirling of mechanical parts
moving fills the room as does the voice of Salazar from Mom's property as the screen lowers and flashes—the scene now playing
matching the words coming from the soon-to-be-a-dead-man's
mouth.

*"We need to leave, Lourdes. That son of a bitch brother of yours
will be on us soon enough."*

"Did you leave her?" Lourdes's *voice is angry, her body
language tense.* "Are you getting a divorce like you swore you would
that first night?"

"Mi amor, don't be like that." He tugs her against his chest, a
move she tries to fight, but she gives in when he pecks her lips. "You
know where my heart lies."

"Quit your lies. Quit hurting her." Her face is pinched with
anger while trying to pull away. "When a relationship is over, mutu-
ally you break things off. There's no taking your time or a few months
of planning a separation down the road. Over means done. No
more."

"Now you care about my wife?"

*"I won't deny making some bad choices and owing her more than
an apology. We should've never been, and I see that now."*

"You don't mean that." His tone is tinged with anger at her
words. *"You love me."*

"Love and hate walk a very fine line."

"She means nothing to me, Lulu. You know that."

"Answer the question, Chiquito. Are you or—"

"Enough. No more questions." His hold becomes tight and my
sister whimpers, yelps to be let go. *"Shut the fuck up before someone
comes looking, Lulu. You don't want your mother or sister-in-law to
end up in a body bag because their curiosity will kill the cat."*

"Let me go, and leave. I never want to see you again."

He barks out a laugh, sardonic and cocky. "No one is taking you from me."

"I'm not yours," Lourdes sneers, but you can hear the fear. See it in the way she shakes.

"That's where you're wrong, you stupid little cunt." Salazar brings his lips to hers once more, biting the bottom one and when he pulls back, there's blood there. "After I turn Alejandro in to the Quintero family, no one can save you. I'll make sure Emiliano, Daniel, and every last brown-nosing soldier under his command will die with the help of Signio Cortez before the sun comes up."

The recording stops and everyone remains quiet. My guests are breathing hard, and poor little Edwin is whispering the Lord's prayer.

"Daniel."

"Yes, Patron."

"These two are yours," I say, pointing at the two tired and bloody bodies bound to the metal. "He walks."

Flicking my eyes to Salazar's brother, I nod, and Emiliano pulls him toward one of the chairs. And it's when he's close that Mariana makes a sound. The first in hours.

It's part whimper, part sob, and the room takes in how she hugs him tight and he apologizes. No malice. No fear. They were forced to do things or accept the cards my ex right-hand dished out.

"Why did you help him?" The question comes from Daniel right before pulling the trigger twice. Both heads bounce back, slamming into the pole as blood sprays out. They sag against their hold, and horror-filled, vacant eyes stare at us. "You're not a bad kid, Edwin. I know you."

After a moment, he pulls back from his sister-in-law's embrace and swallows hard. "He threatened to kill my mother."

Same father, different mother.

"You could've come to me. I would have—"

"He shot her in the leg that night in warning, and I... I couldn't take the chance. I'm sorry, but I had to protect her and Mariana. It was the only way to get close and try to help her escape. Both girls if it came to that."

"If?" I ask, taking my Cabot back and placing it in the holster.

"I was hoping he'd chicken out. He's terrified of you."

"Good to know, and you're forgiven." Walking over to Mom, I bend at the waist and kiss her forehead before doing the same with Mariana. The men will be coming with me as we have another meeting to attend, but Edwin will be staying here for the time being. "I'll be transferring your brother's pension to your name, and I hope to never cross paths this way again. Go to school and make me proud."

"Yes, Patron." He's wincing, and the swelling on his face is becoming grotesque.

"Mom, get him checked out and in bed to rest. I'll be back."

"Already called, and the doctor will be here shortly."

"Thank you." With that, I exit the warehouse while pulling out my phone. I press the number five on my cell, and the call is picked up on the second ring. "Give me an update."

"All accounts have been emptied and your message delivered."

"Thank you. I'll be in contact and don't leave the city."

27

ALEJANDRO

"SHE'S BEEN SPOTTED, Patron." Geronimo rushes through the entrance that leads to the outdoor dining area in my mother's home twenty-four hours later. I've been here since Lourdes disappeared—searching every inch of this country for the past few days—and have no intention of leaving until she's been found. Solimar understands this and supports my decision while waiting for my return, making herself at home where I plan to retire with her someday.

"Where? When?" I ask, placing my coffee cup down and sitting back.

"Lourdes was seen thirty minutes ago walking alone near the southern border to Venezuela. The informant owns a small eatery nearby and recognized her, calling us once back at her locale. About fifteen ago, and after getting confirmed visual, I came to you."

"Who confirmed?"

"The woman's son, who owns a smartphone. He managed to take a picture undetected and promised to stay close and report back."

"Thank you." I take his phone and go through the series of frames taken. There's no mistaking my sister in them, but it's the last one that makes me pause. "Who are these two?"

"She's being watched by two armed men in a truck keeping their distance, completely unaware, but no Chiquito near the vicinity."

My mom's cry of relief and Emiliano's curse in the background reaffirm my earlier thoughts; this is too easy. Too much of a coincidence that she's been left to wander and the culicagados keeping track are a sad excuse for a trap.

Our president is either scared or overconfident.

My money is on the latter.

But I've expected as much and have a few back-up plans in place.

"Load up the car and gather eight men. We leave in ten." I'm already standing from my seat when Mom's hand shoots out and grabs my wrist, halting my moves. "Something wrong?"

"I'm happy, Mijo...thrilled, but worry is filling my heart. I want everyone back safe and sound." Those eyes hold so much sadness— fear. I've seen this same expression on her face before, and it boils my blood with ire. It's the same helplessness from the day Jose Quintero began this war.

"Always three steps ahead..." I trail off and raise a brow, wanting her to finish for me.

"And no witnesses left behind," she adds with a nod and a small smile. It's her job to fret, but I'm a man who looks at problems from all angles. Truth be told, it doesn't take a genius to see who's behind Chiquito's actions and how they conned him into becoming my Judas.

If Quintero wants a distraction, I'll play along. Emiliano and I know what's coming, and we're counting on his idiocy. It's why he's staying behind, and my mother will wait inside the special bunker along with my sister-in-law until it's safe to move, and then we'll convene at my hacienda.

They want to kill me and capture him to display as a trophy.

A plan destined to fail, but I'll humor him. For now.

"We're ready, and two armored SUVs are waiting. I took the liberty of moving men to the front to await orders."

Laying a kiss on my mother's forehead, I walk toward him and clasp his shoulder, squeezing it. "We need to speak about your promotion when this is all said and done, Viejo. You've earned it."

"Thank you, sir."

"You're a good man." With that, I turn my head and give my brother a look to set the rest in motion. Carlos and another of Solimar's guards confirmed Matias plans right before they removed her from the presidential home.

Quintero is too cocky. He likes to hear himself talk—paying no mind and looking down upon those who work for him—which they resent.

It creates hostility. Anger.

They hold no qualms in selling him out, which I appreciate.

We're out the door and speeding toward the nearest highway heading south in less than five minutes. Traffic is light in these parts, the seclusion of the mountains and various farms keep it so only those who reside here use these streets.

Geronimo merges without looking and those traveling with us pass our vehicle while we get off two exits later. There, I house a private helicopter on a small landing strip which is already set in motion when we arrive.

It'll take a few hours by car to reach my sister, but I'll be there sooner. Watching over her. Killing those who stand in my way.

Geronimo's nephew is there when the car swerves to a stop right in front of the aircraft; he's holding our headphones and a few essentials Lourdes might need. "Patron, we can leave as soon as you wish. It's refueled and ready."

"Gracias, parce." I take the headgear and climb into the pilot's side. Once they follow, I check the gages and our communication line. "Strap in, and keep your weapons drawn, men. I expect blood will be shed."

WE'RE INSIDE of an unmarked vehicle a few parking spaces behind the men following Lourdes, watching, and taking account of everyone that comes within distance of their car. So far, there have been two other oversized hijueputas with AKs in their grip. They come, say something, and leave.

Not once do they survey their surroundings.

Not once do they turn down a free grope from a local whore.

"Ten minutes on the dot," I muse, scratching my jaw as once again they do their rounds. My sister walked inside of an old hostel-looking building not far from here, her exhaustion palpable, and disappeared behind a closed door after hearing my call.

A sound we've made since kids that resembles a croaking rooster, but I saw her shoulders sag with relief.

"Looks like they're delivering food and beers." Geronimo's right. All four stand outside and clinks bottles, placing their weapons on the hood of the vehicle without a care or worry. They're eating and laughing—making lewd gestures at anything that walks by in a skirt.

"How far are the men out now?"

"Thirty minutes."

"Tell them to start cleanup the moment they arrive." The last word hasn't left my lips when Lino slips into the car, his lips thin and his eyes narrowed. "Report."

"They're on Cortez's payroll and he paid the guards on patrol tonight a million pesos each to look the other way. Unfortunately for him, those two were sent home with food poisoning, and the substitutes were amenable to our request for half the price."

"Good." My 1911 Sacromonte glints under the streetlight right above our vehicle. I check the magazine and the other two men follow with their Glocks. "Any extra bodies to look out for?"

"Two more in a small bar not far from here. They're on a rotation system." As he says this, the group of men laughs at something and the one on the left fires a single shot into the sky.

"Drunk?"

"Yes, Patron."

"Head there and end it. I want two dead bodies by the time you come back."

"It's a privilege."

"Hagale, Mijo." Geronimo looks on with pride as his nephew exits again without drawing attention, not that the drunk fucks take notice of anything other than a set of tits.

"Thank you for accepting him, Alejandro. It means a lot to me."

"He's a good kid and impresses me on merit, not familial ties." Geronimo nods and we turn back to watch the idiots. The next ten minutes come and go with the men now passing a bottle of Aguardiente between them, and it's when the first one drops his gun and it goes off, hitting a nearby parked car, that we exit.

Our doors open but don't close, and before they notice our presence, two drop to the ground with bullet holes to the center of their chests. There's a scream that follows; a woman walking the streets in a neon green outfit stumbles away and her face becomes ashen when it's my face her eyes land on.

I bring a finger to my lips, and she nods, scurrying away without another word.

"What the fuck! Show yourself, hijueputa!" the shorter of the two left standing screams, his stumbling form waving the gun in the air as if it were a sparkler. He's too shitfaced to realize I'm but a few feet away, his friend all but frozen in his spot while Geronimo delivers a single gunshot to the head of each man struggling on the ground.

"You have five seconds to drop to your knees, asshole," I grit out, my aim on his knees. This one I'll be taking back alive; his bravado is amusing. "Three."

"You'll pay for…motherfucking son of a bitch!" he howls, dropping like dead weight to the asphalt when a bullet lodges itself into his right kneecap, then the left. He's bleeding and crying, the gun and swagger long gone.

"What was that?"

"Lucas." It leaves him in a faint voice and his hand trembles, the gun slipping from his fingers when the fear kicks in. He's like a deer caught in the headlights and when fight or flight kicks in, his flesh scrapes against the jagged ground to flee. Three small movements, the trail behind him bright red, and he gives up. *Theatrical and a waste of time.* "I'm sorry."

"I know."

"I'll tell you anything—"

"In exchange for your life?"

His head bobs in affirmative and his bottom lip trembles. "I'm just a paid Sicario with no affiliation. It's just a contract."

"Geronimo, please attend to our dear friend who pissed himself. I'll need your help with this one."

"Si, Patron."

"Hagale." Three cars come to a screeching stop and doors open a second after Geronimo empties his magazine in the body of my *friend,* the Sicario's compadre. Each bullet ricochets off the ground and empty businesses behind us as blood splatters, becoming a light mist surrounding us. And as the body drops and his chest no longer expands with a ragged breath, the rest of my men begin to dispose of the scene. "Get him into a car and delivered to my home. We have much to discuss and at the moment, understandably, he's gone into shock."

"Of course. Consider it done—"

"Tombos!" Lino yells out, coming around the corner and limping. There's a bloodstain growing on his right side, his teeth are gritted from pain, but I'm more focused on the hand he's holding. In the handprint across her cheek. "Three squad cars just pulled into the bar and we had to take the long route. I don't know how long it'll take for them to come this way or if anyone mentions hearing something."

"What the fuck happened?"

"He saved me, brother. That man...he," Lourdes breaks out into a sob, her body shaking so hard, and I pull her into my chest. What she's been through will leave a mark, and it'll take years for her to recover. "The one they call Chucky broke into my room and he...he almost!"

"I shot him in the dick, then shoved my gun down his throat and pulled the trigger." Lino finishes, but his story leaves more questions than answers. His eyes are not on me, though, and I watch him take her in. Not with lust but with respect. With a mixture of admiration and guilt.

I clear my throat and his eyes meet mine. "Thank you, Lino. I owe you one."

"No thanks needed." He tilts her head in Lourdes's direction and cups one hand over her ears. There are things he doesn't want her to hear, and I take the hint. "Both are dead, and I only followed the tracks his friend left toward the asshole in her room—boasting about it in the men's bathroom—before I blew his brains."

"Explain later." At my command he nods, the wound on his side making him stumble when he turns toward his uncle, who's watching with concern. I give them both a head shake that all is fine. "Get him in the car and jump behind the wheel. These two need a doctor and fast."

"We'll be back to the copter in ten, sir. I'll call ahead and have medical aid waiting."

"Hagale. Let's get out of here."

"Q'HUBO, cousin. How are the States treating you?" I say as soon as he picks up. He'd left me a voicemail earlier in the day for me to reach out but it's been impossible until now, especially as I'm transporting a wounded soldier and my sister back home and the news of Emiliano's arrest along with two guards have dominated all forms of domestic media.

Quintero's preening like a peacock one second and dodging questions on the disappearance of his family the next.

"Can't complain," Javier chuckles, the sound of a door opening and closing coming through the line. "Been a few busy months, but things are beginning to calm down now."

"You good?"

"I am. Getting engaged soon."

"Is that so?" A chuckle escapes me and I close my eyes while Geronimo drives us back to my home where my Preciosa and the others wait for me. "You sure Mariah won't run? Spending her life with your ugly mug isn't a prize."

"Fuck you, asshole." His amusement ceases almost as soon as it appears. "We'll catch up on that later because you will be attending, but I don't have much time and I need you to call someone in Miami. He has what you're looking for."

"And what's that?"

"Guns and targets."

"How many and what kind?" I'm already calculating the slight change in the course. I can stay here and search for Salazar while Daniel goes to Florida with a few of my men. My priority is here, but bulk purchases like these are necessary for what's to come. "My men can—"

"You have to attend, primo. It's impolite otherwise as this is a business associate of Mr. Asher."

"Javier, my sister and Solimar come first." My eyes flick behind me where a sleeping Lourdes snores lowly. She's tired and bruised— alive, and that's all that matters.

"Just trust me."

"Hagale." I rub my jaw, scratching the five o'clock shadow there and for a brief moment, I remember the pretty way my little flower whimpers when she feels the stubble between her thighs. "Send me the information and I'll make the arrangements."

"It'll be in your email shortly." Javier disconnects the call before I can thank him, but I don't take offense. Not in our way of life. Calls are only made through encrypted lines and kept short and to the point; anything longer and the DEA could pinpoint your location or discover dealings.

"Everything okay, Patron?" Geronimo asks, meeting my stare through the rearview mirror.

"Yes." Looking down at my screen, I bring up Solimar's phone number and type out a quick *I'm coming home* before pocketing the device and staring ahead. "Just a slight change of plan, my friend."

"Whatever you need."

"We're taking a family trip to Miami soon."

28

Solimar

I WAKE TO a pair of lips on my skin and a scent that fills me with calm.

He's here and smiling against my skin when a small sound of need leaves my lips. And yet, I don't move or touch him or disturb this quiet moment between us.

His skin on mine feels like heaven, and more so when each movement is followed by a kiss or nip. By the feel of his cock, hard and thick, skimming up my thigh and settling on my hip as he lays behind me and wraps me in his arms.

I don't know how long we lie like this with soft touches and silence, letting our contentment speak for itself.

There's no need at the moment for screams of pleasure or words of love; I know how he feels.

Can feel it with each rumble that builds in his chest and leaves his lips while he lavishes any inch of skin he can reach with kisses.

Then, there's the way his hardness slips between my thighs and lightly touches my entrance—a gentle rhythm of kisses that makes me tremble in his hold.

"I've missed you, Preciosa."

"Missed you…oh, God!" A buck of his hips and he's inside, stretching me to the point of pain, and it's a delicious torture. Pleasure overtakes my senses while a sense of home makes me feel light.

I'm his, and he is mine.

I found my person.

"*Fuck*, little flower. You feel so good," he grits out while grabbing my thigh and pushing it slightly back and over his leg. I'm open for him like this. His to take and own. "Motherfucking tight, wet heat choking my cock. You're perfection, Solimar. Made for me."

"Yours. All yours." I cry out when his hips tilt and Alejandro presses against the little spot inside that makes my muscles clench and eyes roll back. "Please, Papi. I'm close."

"Then come on me, Preciosa. Bathe my cock." Picking up speed, he rides me harder—pinning me in place while pressing a single finger against my clit. He rubs me in time with each thrust, and on the third pump, I shatter.

My orgasm slams into me and my lips part, a silent scream catching in my chest as he grunts behind me. Now he's using me for his pleasure, and I fist his sheets, needing to hold on to something as the world around me dissolves into a chaotic bliss.

Someone's crying in the background, and it takes me a moment to realize that it's me.

I've lost myself to him.

Willingly gave my life. My body.

"I'm going to spend the rest of my life worshipping you, beautiful." Alejandro bottoms out and holds still; I feel him throbbing inside me, and the sensation is enough to throw me into another orgasm. The intensity leaves me breathless and after a few minutes, that euphoric rush turns into exhaustion that lulls me while his velvety voice croons in my ear.

There are words of love, of devotion, but the last thing I remember before the world faded...

Marry me.

THE NEXT TIME I come to, I'm alone and the sound of voices laughing carries up the stairs. It pulls me from the haven of Alejandro's room after getting dressed in a simple light blue romper, and after following it toward the back terrace, I'm greeted with a few faces I know, and some I don't.

Nerves overtake me and I stare at my mother, not knowing how to act.

Did I pretend to be perfect? A part of me so deeply ingrained it's hard to shake. A safety net.

Or do I allow myself to let go and be me? To enjoy meeting the women in his life.

"She's beautiful, Mijo! Look at that face," his mother gushes and stands, taking the choice from me while making her way over and pulling me in for a hug. And it's not just any hug. No. This one's loving and full of acceptance, not cold or full of pretenses.

It's the kind that leaves you warm and makes you feel welcomed.

"It's a pleasure to meet you, Mrs. Lucas," I say after she steps back and I regain a bit of composure. Her easy acceptance has caught me off-guard and so have the smiling faces watching the exchange. Even my mother, who's been a worrying ball of nerves, seems at ease and happiness.

And yet, it's her son's I notice and linger on.

Yes, meeting his family makes me feel special, but nothing compares to the love showing in his eyes.

To the outside world, he might seem serious and unaffected, but the small crinkles at the corner of his eyes tell me otherwise. They smile at me. Show me his true emotions.

"Call me Sara, Solimar. We're family, and formalities don't exist in this nucleus."

"Gracias." I blush and duck my head a bit, feeling a little over-whelmed by how easily she adds me to the list of people she calls hers. "That means a lot."

"No need to blush, sweetheart."

"She's been doing so all her life," my mother interjects, giggling into her cup of coffee. "No matter what we did or she tried, it's uncontrollable."

What we did means my father hated it and berated me every chance he got. That he paid a lot of money to "experts" to rid me of this habit, and when they all failed, I got punished for being an inso-lent child.

This is the same man that hasn't called since we left. Not Mom. Not Carlos. Not me.

"I wouldn't want her to change a single hair on her head." At Alejandro's voice, another breakfast companion giggles, and my eyes turn toward the other young woman in his life: his baby sister. Lourdes Lucas is beautiful, bruised up, and safe where she belongs.

I'm happy to see her.

I also don't overthink my next move and go with what feels natural, walking over and pulling her into a hug that rivals the one her mother gave me. She trembles a bit in my hold, pulling me in just as hard, and when we pull back silently, there are tears in our eyes.

"I'm so happy to see you," I whisper low so only she hears. "We've all been praying for your safe return."

"Thank you. It means a lot, and I hope you don't think badly of…" Lourdes trails off as a sob catches in her chest, and just like I would be in her position, embarrassment floods her posture and she stiffens.

Chairs scrape on the terracotta flooring but I pay them no mind and pull us toward the inside of the home. The only person I take a moment to let know all is okay is Alejandro, and with a simple shake of my head, he holds a hand for everyone else to stand down.

Once inside, I make a beeline for Alejandro's office and close the door behind us. For a few minutes we stand awkwardly, but I make the first move and take one of the two seats across from where my love sits. "When you're ready, I'll listen without judgment."

"I'm fine." She doesn't look me in the eye but fidgets where she stands, wringing her hands and shifting her weight from foot to foot.

"You're a terrible liar, and that's not a compliment. As a president's daughter, I can spot bullshit a mile away." I keep my expression neutral; she doesn't need someone to hover or push, but wait. Listen. Do what no one did for me, and that's allow me to live my life.

Until her brother showed up.

He gave me my identity back, and I'm returning the favor. Lourdes needs someone in her corner, someone to be there, and even though we're strangers, I'll step up to fill that void.

"Is that why you're engaged to Signio Cortez? Same guy your cousin is screwing?"

"Not by choice. Not anymore."

There's a bite to my tone, and immediately her eyes become glazed and lips tremble. "I'm sorry."

"Don't apologize. I don't need you to."

"Why are you being nice to me? Is it because of Alejandro? You can't buy—"

"You're in a tough situation, Lourdes..." I point to the seat beside me "...taken advantage of. Those are two things I'm pretty familiar with, and as someone who's had her life changed to fit someone else's narrative until your brother showed up, I understand. It's why I'm not going to judge you. Why I'll listen and wait and help where I can."

"Everything's so messed up." She finally takes the chair beside mine and slumps, wiping the tears that continue to fall without pause. "There are things that no one knows, and I'm afraid. If they find out—"

"You're pregnant, Lourdes. Aren't you?"

"Christ. How?"

"Loose clothing only hides so much, but close contact can't."

Lourdes nods, patting the barely visible bump there. "My family is going to kill him."

"And that bothers you?"

"No. I want him to die for his crimes."

"Did he force—"

"No. Not with me." Self-recrimination is heavy and so is her guilt. "His wife took the brunt during our trip through the country-side. He promised me forever and I fell for it, believing I was what he wanted and loved when in reality, I was the final piece in his sick love triangle. I'm the obsession he couldn't control, and I let myself get dragged down after hearing a few sweet words."

"You've made some mistakes, sweetie. We all do at some point in life."

"I willingly slept with a married man. I'm a whore."

"You're not," I hiss out, taking her hands in mine and squeeze. "Yes, it wasn't your best judgment and I won't deny it, but this is where you change the course and make amends. Where you grow up and face things head-on."

"Thank you." She sniffles and then gives a watery, sad smile. "I'm sorry our first meeting is like this. Please give me the chance to show you I'm not an—"

"Cut it out, Lourdes. He's a sick man who deserved whatever karma throws his way."

"And I'm the asshole who'll collect on the damage, Lourdes." We pause at Alejandro's steely voice, the anger in it. "I promise you this."

"How much did you hear?" his sister asks, face now pale.

"That I'll be an uncle soon."

"Are you mad?"

My eyes cut to his, and the look I send dares him to make her feels worse than she already does. He sees and gives me a minute shake and smile, something she misses, and I relax in my seat.

"I'm angry you've been hurt. That you didn't come to me when he approached to verify his bullshit." At his words, Lourdes jumps from her seat and into his arms. She's sobbing again, nodding, while he speaks lowly in her ear and rubs her back in a soothing manner.

This is something she needs. To know her family won't abandon her after the mess she involved herself in.

Knowing they need a few minutes before she comes clean to her mother, I walk past them and to the door, pausing with my hand on the knob. I look back, and our eyes meet. There's so much gratitude in his, and mine have to show the pure unadulterated love I'm drowning in.

I love you, he mouths over the top of her head and I nod, saying the words back.

There are things we need to discuss—his lowly spoken marriage proposal—plans to make, but for now, this is where our focus will remain. She's not alone.

Her family is and will be there.

All of them. New and old.

29

ALEJANDRO

I'M IN MIAMI BEACH two weeks later, having set up an exchange with a supplier that comes highly recommended. Malcolm Asher doesn't do business with just anyone, and being this is a personal friend, I made the trip instead of continuing my search.

Just like he promised, Javier had the contact information in my email within seconds of hanging up, the note attached urging me to call. To trust that it would be worth my while.

Moreover, Thiago Rivera promises a unique experience and while killing Chiquito remains a priority, I'm intrigued by this. By the kind of artillery he traffics.

"You'll be okay while I'm gone?" I ask Solimar, tucking a stray piece of hair behind her ear. She's placed the luscious black strand high atop her head in a ponytail, the ends curled and swishing from side to side when she moves.

It's tempting to wrap the strands around my hand and bend her forward. To fuck her like the depraved animal I am.

"We're going shopping, Mr. Lucas. What's the worst that could happen? I chip a nail on a rack?" Her mock annoyance is cute, and I'm tempted to bite her. To take her with me and shield her innocent mind from the world.

Solimar can be naïve, and I love her just like this. Want her to feel safe and never look over her shoulder in fear.

She doesn't see the bad in people, such as her cousin, who I don't trust.

Laura called her yesterday while we were out, pretentious and full of it, but I stood back while they spoke briefly. Solimar kept it short while we waited for our lunch to arrive in an outdoor café, and not once did Laura ask her how she was or felt, but instead, filled the five-minute and thirty-second conversation with Signio and his poor, bruised body.

I was more than proud when my little flower hung up and turned off her phone after promising to catch up later.

"A lot of things can go wrong, sweetheart. This is not our native country, and here you're a tourist with money." I wrap a curl around my finger and give a small tug. She comes closer, pressing against my chest. "Corruption and crimes are global pandemics. Don't go out with that vacation mindset that gets others in trouble. Go out, have fun, but be aware and never stray from your guards. Understood?"

"Yes." It's breathy and I feel the movement of her chest rising rapidly—her hard little nipples against me. Rubbing. My mouth waters and I groan, causing her to giggle. "Something funny?"

"I love you being all protective and caring."

"That's because you're my heart, Preciosa. My life."

Rising on the tips of her toes, she pecks my lips and pulls back. Her eyes are a bit teary-eyed. "One day I'm going to marry you, Mr. Lucas."

"That, my beautiful little flower, was never in question." I knew she heard me that night but needed to verify I wasn't running or shying away. I didn't take it back, nor did my affection for her diminish while playing aloof. "And I'm not waiting a lifetime, either. I want you to take my name, be mine in this life and every single one that follows. My love. My wife."

"I do."

"Good girl." Bending my head, I lay a small kiss on her lips, nose, and finally her forehead before stepping back. "I'll see you later today."

"Where are we meeting again?"

Her sassy grin pulls a smirk from me. "I never said, but I'll always find you. Always."

THE WORDS *SPECIAL News Bulletin* blink across the screen of my phone as I study the latest headline. It's another story on my brother, the monstrous sibling of empresario Alejandro Lucas, who's been linked to the destruction of a federal building not too long ago.

Funny enough, I've never been arrested or so much as questioned regarding the incident.

No text. No call. No citation to appear before the justice department of Colombia.

And yet, reporters are salivating at the chance to scandalize and draw in viewers by feeding them incorrect bullshit. If they had the facts it would be one thing, but you can't prove what doesn't have tracks.

Clicking the link, I skim down the regurgitated and lacking glob of journalism. It's the same as every other story that broke out, and claims that Emiliano's in custody and already serving time on what could be a thirty-year sentence.

Little do they know, the tombos at the state penitentiary work for me, and my brother comes and goes as he pleases. That asshole is having a vacation and avoiding a *honey-do* list a mile long.

He owes me.

"Patron, we're here."

"Gracias." Pocketing my cell, I take in the area we're in. The warehouse is a little out of the way from our hotel as Hialeah is a neighboring city with a heavily Cuban demographic and heritage. It's residential meets industrial with 49th street being its central focus.

It travels from the east side and through the west, connecting you to shopping, restaurants, and multiple mom-and-pop shops, providing anything and everything you could need.

Thiago's warehouse sits surrounded by empty lots that in their prime responded to the heavily growing demand of textiles globally. Now, though, they're owned by one family: Rivera De Leon.

To an outsider, this would appear to be an average scrap yard, but looks can be deceiving.

Geronimo pulls into the private parking lot along the right side of the building—I get out and my men follow.

They're armed to the teeth with heavy artillery. Our weapons were ignored by a customs agent for a special one-time donation to her retirement fund and a bag of my personal blend of coffee.

I don't travel without it. Never have.

Geronimo stands slightly behind me and gives the command to open the large metal doors. They clang against the concrete walls— bouncing hard—as I walk through them and spot Mr. De Leon immediately.

He's a muscular man with tattoos and whose presence is meant to intimidate. And yet, I'm the focus of attention when his men all stop and stare. They're waiting. Hands moving toward the guns on their bodies.

It's a mistake, and he's quick to correct them with a simple shake of the head. They relax when he doesn't respond, and I admire his command over his workforce.

I'm not alone, though, and he doesn't show any signs of surprise when my heavily-armed soldiers wearing their camouflage follow me inside a few seconds later.

Their expressions are emotionless and body language robotic. They are trained to fight and kill on command, no matter who the target is.

I walk over, stopping two steps from him, and extend a hand. "Nice to finally meet you, Thiago. I appreciate you meeting me personally and on such short notice."

Thiago takes my hand, grip firm. "I make it a habit to meet all potential buyers."

"That is a smart thing to do. A lot of criminals out there." My men raise their weapons, pointing at him. He might be a friend of Malcolm, and Javier vouches for him, but I'll never do business with someone that shows fear. Too much can go wrong while dealing with an individual unable to control impulses or pull a trigger if need be. I'm impressed when he chuckles, not so much as a flinch, but I keep my expression even. "Something funny, De Leon?"

"Extremely."

A quick glance at a man standing close by, his cousin, and forty of his men show themselves—they're scattered throughout the room and holding the kind of weapons I'm here to buy.

Anything and everything; M1911, M-10, AR-15, Uzi, and the last and most amazing is the military-grade tanker with a functioning missile ready to fire if need be.

At once, my smile grows and then I'm laughing, full on and deep from my gut as I release his hand. "You are one crazy son of a bitch!"

He shrugs. "So I've been told."

"It's a quality I admire in those I do business with." My soldiers lower their guns and stand in place, posture rigid and body alert. My eyes shift over to the large case still open with a Mac-10 inside, silently asking if I can take a closer look. He nods. "As you can imagine, a man in my position needs to surround himself with people unafraid to make difficult decisions." "Understandable." He takes a step back and his men part like the sea of Moses. "Now, shoot it."

"Do you have somewhere in mind?" I test the weight of the piece in my hand. "Is there a range on the premises?"

"Depends on you, Alejandro." At my perplexed expression, he gives another signal. There's a door on the far back wall and from that entrance, a man is dragged inside beside a movable target they put in place rather quickly. The paper has ducks on it and is humorous in a place like this. "Human or—"

"Let me go!" *Malparido hijueputa.* That's what that pathetic asshole meant right before I slit his throat.

"Where is he?" I hiss out, shoving a hot metal rod through the bullet hole in my guest's knee. He's no longer drunk and belligerent —now he's scared—puked himself when the reality that I am every-thing people say about me sunk in. "Tell me, and I'll end your suffer-ing. Where is Salazar?"

"I don't know." He's a blubbering mess, barely understandable after I kicked his teeth in. Only the first few broke, and I withheld my full force because a broken jaw doesn't answer questions.

As for other body parts...

His body convulses as another blazing poker is forced into his body. This time, through his underwear and cauterizing a testicle.

The man screams and cries; a snotty mess of regret, and yet remains quiet on my old friend's whereabouts. Motherfucking idiotic.

"Final chance, Kiko." Geronimo hands me a butchering knife, and I run it down his flesh from Adam's apple to pelvis. "Where?"

"He's where sunshine is more than a nickname."

Chiquito struggles; he's dirty and a little beaten—the same stupid son of a bitch that impregnated my little sister and traumatized his wife. I know the full story now. I know she was spared from the worst, but I'll never forgive his betrayal.

My right-hand man beat and raped his wife while my sister cried to be let go from another room. While one screamed in pain, the other broke her hand fighting to help and escape.

Nothing will ever be enough to erase their horrors, but I'll help in whatever they may need. They'll live their lives without fear because he'll be rotting somewhere in Colombia where maggots will feast on whatever remains of Chiquito Salazar.

I don't blink. I don't think twice.

I'm no longer a rational man, and with every ounce of emotion—the raw rage on my face—I whistle loudly. The sound reverberates throughout the large building and his head snaps up, giving me the perfect opening. All color drains from his face and he mouths my name a second before I pull the trigger.

One bullet and Chiquito Salazar is dead, his head thrown back as fragments of his brain and skull spread behind him.

I'll see you in hell one day.

I look over at Thiago and smile. "I'll take them all. Everything you have."

"You know the price."

At this, Geronimo's steps forward with two briefcases in his hands. They're placed atop a cargo box and then opened. "There's two million dollars there and eight more if we can triple this order within the month. There's a radical movement growing, and I sit at the helm of this war. My men will need the best to fight."

"Done."

We shake hands, but I pull him in for a man hug. "I don't know how you knew about him or why he was here, but that son of a bitch has been avoiding my wrath for the last month. This goes way back —weeks of watching him fuck up—this was coming either way, but he decided for me when he hurt my family."

"An unforgivable act."

"Thank you for this kind gesture." Pulling back, I clasp his shoulder and look over at the merchandise being prepped for shipping and the efficiency in which his men handle everything. "I appreciate this, De Leon. You've won my loyalty."

"You're very welcome."

30

Solimar

"SO, WHERE ARE we heading to first? I'm kind of starving," Lourdes says from the front seat of the rental SUV beside Carlos, who's in charge of our safety. Two more armed guards are accompanying us, a man and a woman, but they're following in a nondescript car two spots behind us as to not draw attention. "That omelet this morning left me kind of blah."

"What are you in the mood for, Mija? It's almost lunchtime anyways." Sara's tone is gentle next to me, but beneath the surface, she's angry and hurt—feels betrayed by her daughter—and I wouldn't be surprised if at some point on this trip, they have it out.

It's been simmering since they found out she's pregnant.

Everyone's genuinely happy about the baby, but you can feel the disapproval of how it came to be. As a woman, it's something I struggle with as well because being the other woman is never acceptable. I feel for his soon-to-be widow—my heart breaks for her and the hard position this has placed Alejandro in with their family.

A family that I've come to respect after they took in the Lucas family after his father's arrest.

Some are pissed. Daniel is torn. The wife is begging for someone to end it all.

It's another reason why I admire Alejandro. How he's taken charge and promised to deliver Salazar's body in a casket to help soften what his sister has done.

Will it magically disappear by doing this? No. Not really, but the effort and support he's given shows his heart.

Looking out the window, I take in the city and all its traffic. For a weekday and in the middle of work hours, every lane is full of passing cars flying at higher speeds than the signs along the streets suggest. They zoom and cut and honk; I've seen four people get cursed out within thirty minutes and oddly, the craziness has some charm. It reminds me of our busy highways and the way people react to that one driver that refuses to go over thirty in a sixty-five lane.

It also makes me think of my cousin; she's an angry driver. Behind the wheel, she's a menace and I've prayed to more than one God the few times Carlos let her drive after nagging him half to death.

There's a pang in my chest at thoughts of her. She's changed. She's not the same girl who used to come over and spend hours playing dress-up while complaining about how much she hated math. Or how unfair it was that birthdays only came once a year.

And when this is the longest we've been without the other, all she cares about is Signio. Him. His body. His injuries that I have no clue about.

I regret answering that call yesterday. I should've turned my phone off like Mom did the moment we stepped outside the presidential grounds.

"…what about you, Solimar?"

My head turns in her direction and I give her a sheepish look. "I'm sorry, Sara. What did you say?"

"Food, kiddo? Are you hungry, too?" Mom interjects, snickering from the last row, and my cheeks heat up a bit. "Anything that you might want to try while we're here?"

"I'd like to try Cuban food while we're here, but if you guys want—"

"That sounds amazing. Can we?" Lourdes asks her mom, giving her a small smile from over her shoulder. "There's a place I wanted to visit later tonight for dinner, but now will be even better."

"That's fine with me." Mom pulls out her phone, typing something, and a few seconds later another phone pings within the car. Carlos coughs and she looks anywhere but at me when I stare back with narrowed eyes.

I'll admit to enjoying it when her cheeks pink a bit, too.

"Carlos, can you put this address into the GPS? It's not that far from where we are now, I believe."

"Of course, Ms. Lucas." A red light comes up within a few minutes and he does as she asked, putting in the address she rattles off. It doesn't take long for the signal to turn green, and immediately after merging into the turning lane a few feet away that leads into a strip mall, my guard makes a U-turn.

He follows the signs toward Collins Avenue and turns right three lights down. Then, it's a straight shot and we arrive right before the lunchtime rush begins. There are a few people already waiting outside, waiting for the sign to be switched and the door unlocked, and we're lucky to be the third in line to be seated.

A place has to be good if you have a small line before opening for the day.

There's a small booth near the back and Sara asks for it, ensuring we're near an emergency exit and out of the way of others. The only problem is the bathroom's on the other side of the restaurant and between two unused dining rooms at the moment.

"Hi, welcome to Mi Palacio. My name is Nayda, and I'll be your server this evening." There's a round of *holas* from the group while each takes an offered menu. "Can I start you off with a drink or appetizer?"

"A glass of water," comes from Alejandro's mom, and mine.

"A Coke," is Lourdes's choice.

"Jupiña," I say after perusing their choices. There's something so delicious about a cold pineapple soda. "And an antojito platter for us to start."

"Perfect. Let me start on this and I'll be back in a few minutes to take your order." As soon as she's gone, I turn to Mom and give her a sheepish look.

"Let me guess. You need to go?"

"Yeah. It's cold in here."

"All right, let's go. I'm just as bad as you are." She slips out of the booth first, and when I join her, we notice the other two giving us identical *what are you two going on about* expressions. "We're just going to the bathroom."

"Okay." Sara looks lost, while her daughter can't stop looking toward the kitchen entrance to see if our appetizer is ready. "Are you feeling okay? I can call my son and—"

"I'm fine. I swear." A small snicker escapes. "We both have the bad luck of entering a cold room and needing to use the facilities. It never fails, and always when our food arrives. This is a preemptive strike against our bladders."

"You are adorable, Miss Quintero. No wonder my son is so taken with you."

"Thank you." Mom and I turn to leave, my smile wide, and I pause just a step or two from the table. Something is compelling me to say what's on my chest—to let her know how much I already feel for them. So, I take in a deep breath and let it out slow. My nerves have kicked in for some reason and they take notice, but I don't shy away. "You have no idea how much it means to me that everyone has been so welcoming...loving, toward the granddaughter of the man that's caused you so much pain. I'm so sorry for what he did to you.

What my father is trying to accomplish on the back of a lie to further his political career. I'm ashamed to be related to them and I promise to help your son, a man I love with all my heart, right this wrong."

There are tears in their eyes and a soft smile on each face when I turn to leave again. Mom doesn't say anything when we head toward the bathroom and enter, but I catch the look of pride on her face a second before it becomes utter horror.

"Hello, wife…daughter." That voice sends a shudder down my spine. He sounds neutral and calm, but when I turn my head in his direction and take in my father standing a few feet from me, I see the hatred in his eyes. The ire exuding from his body infiltrates every inch of the small alcove that holds the women's bathroom.

The door is but a few feet from us. The front entry is a quick run in the opposite direction, but the glint of metal at his hip and the two men that appear behind us destroy any notion of escape.

Matias Quintero is here to force us back home.

"No words for me?" He's being condescending, and I know better than to speak. Instead, I send a silent prayer that somebody comes looking for us. That our guards outside stop him from whatever he has planned. "For your dear old father who's been worried sick."

"Matias, leave her alone. I'm the one—"

"Shut the fuck up before I strangle you and leave the body behind for your lover to find."

"Lover? What are you—"

"Stupid is not a good color on the first lady." Dad pulls something from his pocket, a bundle of pictures, and tosses them at her feet. Photos after photo of her laughing, smiling, touching Carlos's arm while doing mundane things. They're innocent, nothing sexual, but to him and his ego, they're ridiculing him. "Look at the last one. That's a personal favorite of mine."

Mom bends down and with a shaky hand, picks up the photograph he's talking about. A gasp leaves her, her frame shaking, and a sob of *no* passes through her trembling lips.

There's no doubt that the man in the picture is Carlos, and it's the SUV Alejandro rented for our excursion while here. The front window is blown out and the man slumping with a bullet hole to his chest is my guard of many years.

My tears flow and I bring a hand up to my mouth, horrified that he'd go this far. "Why?"

"Because that hijueputa made a deal with the devil, Solimar," he growls out, taking the few steps between us and gripping my arm so tightly I know they'll be bruises. Dad bends his head and puts us at eye level. His smirk can only be described as evil. "He betrayed me, kid. Just like your mother. Just like you."

I swallow hard, my knees shaking. "Are you here to kill us?"

"That's up to you." Dad lets go of my arm and brings both hands to my shoulders, digging in his fingertips to the point of pain, and turns me around to face my scared mother. She's crying and shaking —watching on helplessly with no idea how to react. "Come with me willingly, and I'll let this puta walk out of here without repercussions. She can keep my son and I'll even donate a few dollars a month for his expenses, but you will serve your purpose."

"What purpose?" I ask brokenly, knowing I'll do whatever is needed to keep my family safe.

"That's something we'll discuss at home." He steps around me and holds a hand out. "Now, are you coming?"

"You'll never come for them again?"

"You have my word."

"And you'll leave the Lucas family alone?"

"That'll cost you a little extra, daughter of mine, but consider it done if you agree."

A sob rips itself from my chest and I nod my head, placing my hand in his, and silently let him lead me out. I keep my head down and refuse to make eye contact with the whispering patrons all around us as we cross the front dining room and then exit the restaurant.

No words are said.

Not so much as a look, but when the door of the vehicle closes behind me and I turn to sit forward, there's a prick in my arm and the world around me becomes hazy fast.

Everything blurs and voices meld together as a hand pushes my hair back and whispers their hello.

31

Solimar

"**A**BOUT TIME YOU grace us with your presence, Solimar. It's been a long time since I've had the pleasure of spending time with my granddaughter, the national whore from what I hear." My grandfather Jose is sitting in the corner of my room back in Colombia, and I don't remember getting here nor falling asleep. I'm still wearing the same clothes, and the pin I used to give my ponytail more height scratches at my scalp.

It's uncomfortable and I grimace, in part due to the tenderness, and the other the horrible taste that lingers in my suddenly dry mouth.

What did they do to me?

"Hola, Abuelo. It has been a long time." I'm not going to give him the pleasure of seeing how much his words hurt or the fear that grows because if he knows, so does my father. His beady eyes look at me with amusement, and when he stands to come closer, I can't stop myself from moving over to the opposite edge. "What brings you here? Are you on vacation?"

"Something like that." He ignores my obvious distrust and takes a seat at the edge of the bed, his older frame slightly hunching forward, but that doesn't make him any less intimidating. If anything, my distrust grows. This man has never sought me out or cared past the photo-op staged by his people. "Now, tell me. How did you meet Alejandro Lucas?" His tone is harsh, and the clench of his fist over the handle of his cane worries me."

"How do you—"

"Answer the fucking question, Sol."

"Leave my room," I say. My voice is low but the sardonic laugh that escapes him is proof that he heard. "I came back to keep my mother and brother away from this darkness, and while it was of my own volition, answering questions wasn't part of the deal."

"At least you've grown a little backbone in the last few months." His eyes travel around the room and settle on an old photograph of Laura and me. "I always thought you were a mousy thing that wouldn't bring anything to a marriage table. No sass. No smart mouth." When his harsh stare meets mine again, I see amusement in it. As if he's privy to something I'm not. "A docile woman is nice, but killing her spirit and will make for a pleasurable experience."

"Why are you here? Really?" I'm not close to the room's door, but if I need to flee, the bathroom is a few steps away and has a window big enough for me to climb out of. "This is the most time we've ever spent together without it being an obligation. Just say what you need to and leave. I don't care about the rest."

"As you wish." The last word hasn't passed through his lips when the cane in his hand is swung up and comes down across my knee faster than I can move. It hurts. God, it hurts, but I bite my lip to keep the cry behind my teeth. "Where is my money, granddaughter? Where did that fucking hijueputa put the fortune I spent my entire life accumulating?"

"What are you...*fuck*!" I cry out, holding my shin where the second blow lands before jumping off the bed. I'm a bit unstable and my legs buckle a bit when I put my full weight on them, but I get out of the way and across the room before he could strike again. "Get out. Get out, and don't come back."

"Where is my money, kid? I'm not going to ask—" The door is swung open and in walks my father and Signio; I refuse to call him my fiancé. "Ah! And here comes my good-for-nothing son who let the perfect presidency go to waste."

"I told you to let me handle everything, Papa. What did you do?" Dad's talking to him but looking at me. More accurately, at the two red spots on my leg and the small welts there.

"Just had a lovely conversation with the traitor. Nothing more."

"Get him out," I hiss through clenched teeth, my body shaking with a mixture of rage and pain.

"You heard the lady, Viejo. Up you go." There's a veiled threat in my father's words and Signio jumps into action, helping the older Quintero male out of the room, but not before giving me a look full of hunger and contempt. Of hate-filled desire.

Signio mouths the word *later* and sends me a wink that makes me shudder.

The door clicks closed behind them, and then it's just my father and me. It doesn't make me feel any more comfortable, and I move closer to the bathroom door, an action he takes notice of and shakes his head.

"I'm not going to lay a hand on you, Mija. Relax."

"And yet you want to sell me to the highest bidder?" My voice betrays me, the hurt palpable. "Why? How could you ever do this to your own flesh and blood?"

"I could ask you the same, don't you think?" He mimics my pose on the opposite wall, arms crossed over his chest and face unreadable. "Why sleep with the enemy of your father? Why help him destroy those who've always been there for you?"

"When have you ever been selflessly there?" Tears gather at the corner of my eyes and I blink rapidly, fighting to not let him see how much hurt he's caused over the years. "Tell me, Dad. Give me a single example where you were, when it didn't benefit you in one way or another."

"This is silly. I don't need to prove—"

"Because you can't. It's that simple." Wiping my face, I let out a sarcastic chuckle. "But then again, I doubt you care if I'm upset or disappointed that I'll never have any kind of daughter/father relationship with you."

"That statement is a bit melodramatic, Solimar. Grow up and act your age."

"You mean, do as you say?"

Pushing himself off the wall, he stalks across the room and grabs my face in his hands—his grip's tight, and my jaw hurts from the strength he's exerting. "You're walking a fine line with all this talking back. Don't test my patience."

"If you care about me at all, please let me go."

"The wedding is this Saturday. Make peace with it." Then he's gone, and I crumble into a heap of nothing on the ground. Saturday is only three days away, and I pray that Alejandro comes for me.

"Hello, dear cousin," comes from the door, and I shift my eyes in her direction. Laura's standing there and she's not alone; Signio's with her and holding a possessive hand over her stomach. She's pregnant, the small bump showcased by her tight top, and the daddy is the man my family is forcing me to marry.

This is so messed up. Why would they do this?

"What can I do for you, Laura?" It's lifeless—you can hear the exhaustion in my tone, and yet she invites herself to have a seat across from me. I don't say anything and neither does she, but after a few minutes, it's the jerk beside her that breaks the ice.

"How's your mother, Sol? Will she be back in time for the wedding?"

His idiocy pisses me off and my eyes narrow. "That's a stupid question to ask. Why would she ever come back to this hellhole?"

"Don't be rude. He's just trying to—"

"Why are you here, Laura? What could you possibly want?" The less I've been around her, the more I notice how selfish she is. Self-absorbed. Only a selfish person would get involved with a man engaged to her cousin, of all people, and then ask said cousin to cover for her while sleeping with him.

She never kept it a secret. She never asked me how I felt or thanked me for sticking my neck out.

Laura used me over and over without a single crap given.

"What the hell has gotten into you?" she snaps, having the nerve to look offended. "Why are you being so hostile when we drove here to visit you and explain a few things."

"Get on with it."

"I'm going to ignore your bad mood for the time being." My response to that is to twirl a finger in the air in a *whoop-de-doo* motion. "I swear you were never so obnoxious before. That man sure did a number on you."

The way she says "that man" grates on my nerves and I stand from my seat, walking across the room and opening the door for them. "Leave."

"Quit being so prissy, prima. No sense in getting stuck in your feelings, when it's a lost cause."

"Get. Out."

"Watch your tone with the mother of my child," Signio hisses, moving to stand quickly and then groans in pain. He's suddenly spasming and cursing Alejandro's name. *How brave when the man in question isn't here.*

"Look at what that animal did to him." Laura goes from flapping her arms to being in my face within seconds, her pointer finger digging into my right breast. She's furious and looking at me as if I were scum beneath her shoes. "How could you let it happen?"

"I'm going to suggest you remove your finger and remember you're pregnant."

"I hate you," she sneers while removing her hand, only to attempt to slap me. Before her hand can connect, though, I grab her wrist and push it back none too gently. "You fucking—"

"It's nice to finally see the truth after all this time. You're jealous." I'm laughing again, and it's not a sound I'd call pleasant. My heart is breaking all over again, and all I can do is laugh with them like they've been doing at my expense for years.

I'm the butt of the joke. The naïve, stupid girl who'd gone to bat for her when in reality, my flesh and blood could care less about me.

"Of you? Never." Signio is watching the exchange from the floor and not complaining about being in pain. Now, he's smirking and when catching my stare—winks. "I have everything you will never have. He loves me and not you. Will never want you."

"The feeling is mutual."

"Liar."

"Christ, you're blind." Shaking my head sadly, I step back and once again motion them toward the door. "But for once, it's not my problem. You'll figure it out one day."

"I'd be bitter too if I were in your position."

"Out."

"Have you asked yourself yet how Uncle Matias found you in Miami? Living it up on South Beach?" In that moment, the ground beneath my feet becomes unstable and I use the wall closest to me for support. *How could she give me away? How could she put my family's life at risk?* There's so much I want to say—the urge to knock her teeth in is overwhelming—but nothing comes out. I'm lost inside the pain her betrayal causes. "I recognized the area during our call, Solimar. I've been to that same eatery with girlfriends in the past."

"Why?" That's all I can manage. My throat feels raw.

"Because having him on my side means I can keep Signio. We've worked out a deal that appeases both sides, and all I had to bargain with was your location."

"Leave before I forget you're pregnant, Laura." The anger in my voice catches her off-guard and she takes a step back. "Now."

"You wouldn't—"

"There's a lot of thing you don't know about me." I take a menacing step forward, fist clenched at my sides. "Get the fuck out of my room. Last chance."

With a huff, she leaves the room while dragging Signio behind her. I don't look at either of them as they cross the threshold, but I do slam the door closed and then sink to the ground. My breathing is choppy and tears are threatening to spill, but I won't give them—any of them—the satisfaction of breaking me.

If my time with Alejandro taught me anything, it's to not show weakness and fight back.

When the times comes and if I have no choice, I'll marry the jackass. I'll sign my name on the dotted line and play pretend while building a false sense of control.

I'll bide my time.

I'll wait to get my revenge.

It'll be me who walks away a widow.

I'm not giving up on my happiness with Alejandro, and I'll do whatever I have to for it.

He's coming for you. I know he is, and he'll be proud his Preciosa didn't bow down.

32

ALEJANDRO

"**W**HERE IS SHE?" I ask the two guards eyeing the gun in my hand and shaking in their seats, while my mother and sister cry a few steps away.

Three hours.

Three motherfucking hours since my little flower disappeared without a trace, and the nonexistent security feed at the restaurant is partially responsible.

Because I'd be the dumbest motherfucker on this planet if I buy the coincidence claim. She disappeared when their cameras were turned off for scheduled maintenance by their provider.

"Patron, we parked as Carlos requested, near the back exit, and didn't see anything." The male of the two shifts his eyes toward his coworker nervously. "No one came in our out from our end."

"Is that so?"

"Yes...*shit*!" My hand is wrapped around his neck now, lifting him from his seat while the other guard whimpers in fear. "Please, we did—"

"I have a critically wounded guard and a missing fiancé." Mom gasps—says my name lowly, but I pay her no mind. Not now. Not until Solimar is back in my arms. "So, I'll ask once more. Where. Is. She?"

"And my mom, Mr. Lucas? Can you search for her too?" *Christ,* I'd forgotten her baby brother is here. He's too young for any of life's cruel reality to touch him, and I loosen my grip—the man crumbles to the floor, but young Matias shakes his head. "I've seen worse. Just, please...please find them."

His unshed tears—eyes so much like hers—cause my chest to ache and I nod. "You have my word. I'll bring her back."

"Thank—" The door to the penthouse our family's sharing is thrown open, and in the doorway stands a disheveled-looking Mrs. Quintero.

Sweaty, eyes bloodshot, and with her hands stained in blood.

"Veronica." I say, and those wild eyes settle on mine, crumbling into a painful wail as her son rushes forward. He doesn't care about her state or the red markings on her body. Instead, he hugs her hard and whispers something that's almost too low to hear.

But I do. I catch it.

"Was it him? Is he here?"

"Si, Mijo." Veronica begins to shake, the shock of whatever tran- spired hitting her. "Now, please go to the room and bring me the small red cosmetic bag on the vanity."

"Okay." No arguing. No questions asked.

Once he's out of earshot, her focus turns to me. On unsteady legs, she walks over and grips my arm tight. "Matias took her back to Colombia, Alejandro. He threatened to kill me where I stood after showing us pictures of my Carlos, shot and left for dead." A broken sob passes through trembling lips. "My little girl sacrificed herself for me while I stood frozen and in shock. I blanked, and it wasn't until they'd left that I came to. I rushed out of the restaurant, searched for any sign of our guards, and all I could find was Carlos fighting to climb out of the SUV. He's the one that told me to run when I rushed to help him. He warned me that this asshole shot him and since we didn't know who else was working with my husband, I needed to get out and not lead anyone back here.

That son of a bitch just signed his death warrant.

"Thank you, Veronica. I apologize for this...for what my—"

"No." She's shaking her head vehemently, clutching my arm tighter. "This is on him. He's a power-hungry asshole and if it weren't for my kids, I'd curse the day we met."

I'm nodding, my fury growing with each beat of my heart. My veins throb and muscles are coiling tight. "How long will it take your son to find the bag?"

"It's our cue for him to exit and wait elsewhere."

Very smart. "Close your eyes."

"I trust you." Veronica does as I ask, blocking one of her senses a few seconds before I pull the trigger. The male guard is dead within seconds, the bullet to his neck causing him to drown in his own blood.

"Thank you. Now, I'm going to turn you around, and you three will pack up and be ready to leave within the hour."

"And the cleanup?" Lourdes asks while Mom steps in and takes Veronica's hand, pulling her out of the room. "Do we need to wait?"

Geronimo, who's been standing off to the side, pockets his phone. "Already taken care of, courtesy of Thiago, Patron. I sent his cousin a text inquiring about organic composting."

I nod in appreciation. I'm going to owe him a hefty bonus when all is said and done.

He's more than earned it.

"Gracias, Geronimo. Have the plane ready to go in one hour; anyone who's not ready then will stay."

"Consider it done."

IN LESS THAN TWENTY-FOUR HOURS, I'm back in Bogota and staying at a hotel less than half a mile away from Casa de Nariño. I can see the presidential palace from here. Count how many guards are at the gate, and through my eyes on the ground, I'm aware of every second of Solimar's stay.

These are men that know Carlos—close friends—and have heard from him as recently as a few hours ago.

They know Matias Quintero paid for his assassination outside of a Cuban restaurant in Miami. They know I'm coming to burn this place to the ground and everyone in it that stands in my way.

All ten on watch tonight will work through the morning when another group is set to relieve them. They'll never make it inside for the switch. The platica I've given each man is more money than they make in the accumulation of six months. It's enough for them to spoil their families a little bit and still save for any rainy day ahead, something that most citizens around the world can't afford to do.

"Where is he now?" I ask through the walkie, the message going to the earpiece of the guard outside Sol's door. He doesn't answer right away but does turn his end on so I can listen in. At first it's low, but that changes after a few seconds.

Are we sure he's still in Miami?" The voice coming through the walkie-talkie is older and speaks gravely, as if the owner smoked a few packs of cigarettes a day for more than ten years. *"I want that hijueputa's head on a spike to decorate the front lawn, Matias. Make it happen, and find my motherfucking money."*

"I'm working on it." Another male speaks, and I can deduce its Matias talking to his good-for-nothing sperm donor. *"He's been spotted on South Beach by Angela who's still with him. Seems he's looking for Solimar in Florida, not here."*

That's because, in exchange for her life, Angela is serving a higher purpose. Lying comes naturally, and she's agreed to feed false information to save her hide.

"And did you find who made the hack?" Ice clinks in a glass before they call out for the guard I'm listening through to refill their

glasses. *"Because that man isn't smart enough to do it himself. Once an ignorant farmer, always an ignorant farmer. Alejandro is just like his father: a dreamer with mediocre hopes for more."*

I chuckle at this.

Never underestimate your enemy. They've never understood this but will soon learn.

I am the devil's son, and I'm here to collect my pound of flesh.

"No. Nothing yet." There's a tinge of annoyance to the president's tone. Of exasperation. *"Whoever cleaned out your accounts is more than likely long gone, Father. Besides, they are not our focus. Solimar needs to marry Signio or the deal with the Russians is off. Cortez wants this union and will hide behind the charity work we present her with. A few stolen women here or there won't draw too much attention, and much less at the innocent woman helping to feed the poor."*

Jose chuckles. *"That's quite a deal you have going for yourself."*

"Harvested organs go for a high price on the black market. I'm nothing more than a supplier."

"And you think your daughter is going to help you? Can you keep her under control?"

There's a beat of silence and then a hum. *"She doesn't have much of a choice. I hold no qualms in slicing up Veronica, my wife or not, and my daughter knows this. And if she wants her mother to stay alive, complete obedience is the only way."*

Chairs scrape against the flooring and their voices begin to drift. They're not saying anything of importance, but I make up enough. The wedding is tomorrow at ten a.m. with four hundred of their closests attending.

Signio Cortez will never make it down the aisle.

"Where is she now?"

"In her room. I delivered her dinner before being called to serve their drinks."

"And is Cortez in the building?"

"No, Patron." The sound of a door opening and closing comes

through the line. It's quieter where he is. "Those two are at Codicia for the bachelorette party, and her cousin Laura is at home."

"Gracias, parce. Keep a good eye on her." I wave a finger in the air and Geronimo stands, keys in his hand, and already walking toward the door. "I'll add a little something extra for all your troubles."

"You've been more than generous. Just save her. She's too good for these monsters."

CODICIA IS CLOSED to the general public when I arrive, but no one dares to deny me entry when I arrive. Instead, the same woman from the night I met my little flower is at the hostess stand and this time avoids all eye contact.

"Welcome to Codicia, Mr. Lucas. Tonight we have three floors of debauchery: voyeur, audience participation, and an open orgy. What's your poison?"

I ignore the gasps behind me from Laura and offer a smile to the poor employee. "I'd like to start at the orgy and end up in voyeur, if you don't mind."

"Excellent choice, sir. Please present your wrists." There are ten men with me tonight and with Laura as my special guest, that makes twelve. One by one we get stamped with a special dye only to be seen under a fluorescent light until we get to the petulant princess who tries to refuse.

"I don't want to be here, Mr. Lucas. Please take me back home." There's an ever-present tinge of snootiness in her voice that grates on my nerves, but I ignore it for my Sol. Because hurting this idiot would only serve to hurt the one I love, so I'll be going a more unconventional route.

I'm going to do her the favor of opening her eyes to the reality she neglects.

That asshole loves no one but himself and the flavor of cock.

"Don't test my patience. I give no fucks when it comes to your comfort."

"Solimar would never—" She shuts up at the click of a gun and extends her wrist.

"Smart girl." My praise is condescending, and she bristles but remains quiet.

We enter the establishment, and it's clear that tonight's theme is sex. A free-for-all and Laura's face shows signs of worry as she pulls in closer to my side.

Men look at her as we pass. A few pause their solo exploration and leer.

"Do you wish to explore or find your boyfriend?"

"Please." Her voice is just shy of panic as a group of naked men and women pass a little too close for her comfort, and more so when two of the women wink at her while I chuckle.

"Elevator." Geronimo takes his place beside her while the others make a path toward the elevator bank where one holds it open and then closes the latch when we pass. "Third floor near."

"Yes, sir," they answer in unison, and all you hear between grunts and moan is the heavy footfalls of my soldiers.

The old-school elevator whirls to life after Geronimo pulls the lever, and we ascend in silence. You can tell she wants to ask questions—that she's curious but doesn't have the courage or time to do so as we arrive at the same rooftop terrace where I met my beautiful girl.

And if she thought the first floor was scary, she's just entered her worst nightmare.

Not because sex is something to be ashamed of, but because we didn't need to search hard for the man we came to see. Her sob is loud, and yet it's drowned out by the moans and slapping of skin. He's surrounded by men and women and services both.

Hands and mouth and ass. He's open for the taking and loving every single moment of being dominated.

Signio's head is thrown back and a look of ecstasy is spread across his features.

"Is that the man you love?" I ask her, holding back a chuckle as Signio turns his face and kisses a woman who a few seconds ago had another man's cock in her mouth. "Is that the man you hurt your cousin over? Who you chose over flesh and blood?"

"He swore I was all he wanted."

"You think he lied? Used you?"

"But why?" Her watery eyes meet mine and no, I don't feel a single ounce of remorse for hurting her this way. A broken heart is nothing compared to the humiliation Solimar suffered in silence while she paraded around town with him. When she embarrassed her in front of friends and family—the entire country. Those pathetic tears will never be enough for me. "We're having a baby. We're going to get married after he annulled his marriage to *her* and move to Spain where we could be free to love one another."

"That *her* has a name," I say, lip curling over my teeth as I fight to keep my temper in check. To not show her how fucked up I can be when provoked. "She's more of a woman than you'll ever be."

"Why are you defending her? Her father and grand—"

"I love her." That snaps her lips shut, and whatever rebuttal sat on the tip of her tongue is dead. But more importantly, a second later Signio comes, and his guttural growl breaks her heart and shatters her world. "A real man doesn't cheat or pit family members against each other with lies and games. Solimar has never cared for him. Has never sought him out. He used you because for a man like him, you're an easy target who takes care of his man-child needs. This is not love, Laura."

"Why are you helping me see the truth?"

"Solimar is the only reason you are still standing and breathing. This is for her. Not you."

She continues to cry as I give the signal for her removal. Almost needs to be carried out while I turn to face the man of the hour.

My gait is slow as I cross the room and stop a few inches from him, my soldiers behind me with their weapons drawn. Slowly, people take notice and they begin to exit the room via the stairwell. Not that he notices, as Signio's lost to the pleasure: touching and licking and swallowing come.

And it isn't until his lovers take notice and scream that he looks up and our eyes meet.

All color drains from his face. The men and women lying with him run out of the room.

"Celebrating your last night?"

He swallows hard, hands covering his nakedness. "What are you doing in Colombia? I thought—"

"Patron, we found this one trying to get away." A guard drags over the older Cortez, tossing him right beside his son. "He tried to blend in with a group overcrowding the elevator."

"Thank you, Jonny."

"At your service, Patron."

He stands back, and I focus on the two on the floor. The floor is empty at this point, and the rest of the establishment is being evacuated. Codicia is the double-edged sword he thought to be a haven for his depravity, but when you serve entertainment to the criminals of this country and abroad, you must understand that the tombos who patrol the area will never come to your aid.

Delinquents see but never tell.

"Get up, gentlemen. It's time we go for a ride."

33

ALEJANDRO

P *resent...*

I WALK THROUGH the door of the presidential palace like I own the place. Staff members are bounding every corner, looking busy while ignoring the criminal making his way toward the backyard where I know Solimar is sitting.

She's watering the gardenias this late in the day to avoid running into her father, spending her time in the one area of the house the asshole never ventures and which she's found solace in.

I can smell her delicate scent the closer I am. It surrounds me and I groan—my need for her is a consuming time bomb waiting to erupt, and I won't hold back.

Not when I've slept without her in my arms for days.

Not when I've watched from afar to keep her safe until all my ducks were in a row.

She's right where Jonny told me she'd be, and the moment I cross into the garden, there's a shift in me and I notice how her shoulders stiffen and head tilts back. We're in tune with one another. Sense the other's presence.

"My beautiful little flower," I croon low, and she turns. Those expressive grey eyes show gratitude with a hint of anger, and I'll take it all. The good and the bad. Her sweetness and fury. "I've missed you, Solimar."

"Where have you been? I thought—"

Before her next intake of breath, I'm caging her in my arms and holding tight, filling my lungs with her scent. "I've been less than half a mile away and keeping watch from within these walls. Trust me when I tell you I've always been here."

"Then why not come and get me?" There's some bite to her tone, but that doesn't stop her from nuzzling my neck and dropping a single kiss to my chin. "I've missed you so much. I hate it here...it's so cold and empty."

"And you'll never live that way again." I take a step back and bring both my hands up to cage her face. My lips hover over hers, skimming back and forth slowly. "I wasn't kidding or testing the waters when I said *marry me*, Solimar. That was a declaration of my wants and needs. Of how I want to spend the next seventy years of my life."

Those gorgeous grey eyes sparkle in the moonlight, but the soft smile breaking across her face steals the very air from my lungs. I'll always remember her at this moment as the years pass us by...

Soft. Sweet. Mine.

"I want to be your wife."

"I'm your husband." Her skin is soft beneath my roughened fingertips—yielding—almost melting against me as I pull her in closer. Chest to chest. Lips hovering. She's like the finest of silks; a motherfucking delicacy that's been awaiting my arrival and only yearns to please her owner.

Because she's given herself to me.

Every sigh. Every moan. Every inch of her has always been meant for this brute of a man.

Solimar Quintero is my prize. A reward and coveted possession.

"Please, Alejandro. I need you." Those beautifully hooded, light grey eyes are on my cognac-colored ones, and in them, I see the same emotions reflected back at me. Hunger. Anticipation. A nearly knee-buckling yearning that makes me throb against her midsection.

"Say it, Solimar." My voice is rough, the grip on her right thigh tightening—fingers digging in as I place one leg over my hip and then the other; I have her right where she should always be...

In my arms, her heat against my cock.

The beautiful girl pinned by my body moans and the sweet sound settles on the tip of my cock, causing me to flex against her heat. It also pulls a hiss from me, my teeth gritting as I look down and take in how the short, white cotton summer dress has shimmied up and over her hips. Those supple thighs tremble, and my fingers on her right one dig in deeper, harder as I enjoy the sinful view.

Indecent perfection.

I shift my upper body back, just enough to get a better look.

She's wet; the evidence makes the almost translucent material completely see-through.

My eyes snap up when a needy whimper passes through her lips. "Answer me."

"Papi, I... *please!*"

"Answer me, Preciosa." Lower, my hand encounters her round and firm asscheek. I palm the flesh—squeeze hard enough to make her mewl before gripping the tattered remnants of her panties and tugging them off.

A single pull and she hisses, shaking in my hold when the delicate material rubs harshly over her sex. My little Solimar bites down on her bottom lip, withholding the moans that want to slip free so we —I—don't get caught, and I find the action sweet. Endearing.

Pointless, since I'm here to end it all tonight. To collect on a fifteen-year-old debt.

"Say. It."

"I belong to you, Alejandro. Only you," she moans out, lips parting just enough to see the tip of her tongue peek out. I follow how she slides it over the very edge of her Cupid's bow. How her cheeks flush and perspiration beads over her neck. "I love you."

At those words, my eyes close and I breathe in deeply. A unique scent—her sweet, sugary decadence surrounds me, and I groan. I feel her heat. Her wetness as it seeps through and caresses my cock through my slacks sans underwear.

I'm hard for her.

I'm throbbing.

I'm hers.

My hips snap forward and my dick rubs against the juncture of her thighs, finger slipping a bit deeper inside her puckered hole. There are a few *por favor* and *mas,* but I don't give in. Not yet.

Not here.

We'll be leaving soon enough.

That thought sobers me at once and after another pump, I slip from inside her tightness and right her clothing. My forehead falls to hers and my eyes snap open just as she whines, her pretty mouth set in a pout. "None of that."

"But Alejandro—"

I silence her with a quick and harsh kiss. "I love you, too."

"Baby, I—"

The click of a single gun interrupts our moment, and I shift my head minutely to catch sight of the asshole responsible. It's a man I loathe. Someone whose history with my family brought us full circle and to this moment.

"You're a dead man, Lucas," he says, and my smirk only deepens.

"Good evening, Señor Presidente."

"I'm going to enjoy every second of…" Quintero's words trail off as several high-powered rifles are cocked. His men—those that work the grounds day in and out—along with mine, surround us from all angles with their barrels pointing at an ashen man whose purpose in life should've been to take care of his family. It takes him a moment to compose himself, to hide the nervous shaking of his hands as the men come a little closer. Five steps forward and stop. "Arrest him! Have him placed—"

"They're not here for me, Quintero." His eyes shift to mine, and the expression of his face is one I've been waiting for: fifteen years' worth of patience and planning. He's scared as I face him. Intimidated as those around us make no moves to detain me. "Please remove the president and escort him to his room for the evening. He's not allowed outside under any circumstances until called upon tomorrow at ten."

"Yes, sir," multiple voices answer in unison.

"What are you doing? Get your hands off!" Jonny and another guard, both good friends of Carlos, knock the back of his legs and Matias falls to his knees. His eyes are wide while I smile and pull out my phone. The number on hold rings twice as I put it on speaker-phone so Mr. President can witness this conversation and participate. "Patron?"

"Is Emiliano there?"

"He's listening, and bags are packed. All we need is the confor-mation for release."

With a brow arched, I place the device closer to Quintero's mouth. "Now is the time to play nice with me, Matias. Let's not start this relationship off on the wrong foot."

"Fuck you," he spits out, the spittle hitting my pant leg. Disgusting. "I'll never—" Two guns are placed on opposite sides of his temple, effectively shutting him up. Solimar makes a small noise from her place beside me, not in fear but surprise, while gripping the back of my dress shirt. I try to shield her from his line of sight, but his mouth doesn't take the hint. "You're going to allow this criminal to treat your father this way while manhandling you like a whore? To abuse my right, daughter?"

It's the wrong thing for him to say.

Every person here knows that.

However, I stand my ground and let the fiery beauty beside me unleash years of pent-up anger. In a flash, Solimar's in his face with her hand poised back and high. The hatred coming off her delicate skin sears me, but the sound of her hand connecting with his flesh is therapeutic for both of us.

For her—because she releases the hurt.

For me—because I get to help her through these emotions.

She doesn't stop at one or two—five harsh smacks land across his face and a bare-knuckle punch leaves behind a broken nose and a slightly swollen hand. My Preciosa is breathing hard, towering over the man who's hurt them over and over again.

"Hate is a strong word, but nowhere near enough for how much I despise you." Tears gather at her eyes and a few spill, but still I don't jump in. I'm here if she needs me, but will always support and encourage her to face her demons. "You're a lousy husband, a pitiful father, and a waste of space on the earth. If I ever see you again, it'll be too soon."

"I'm the pathetic one?" He barks out a laugh and then spits on the floor. Blood from his nose has slipped past his lips and coats his tongue. "He doesn't love you and never will. Alejandro Lucas is using you to get to me and will drop you once I'm gone."

"Why would I leave my wife?"

"W-what?" he sputters, chest beginning to heave. "You married this son of a bitch!"

A solid kick to the chest is my rebuttal to the insult. It sends him sprawling back, and he hurts his hand as he catches his weight on it. "Not yet, but you're personally invited to the nuptials tomorrow at ten."

That sends him into a fit of rage while the guards drag him away. He's cursing. Threatening.

The staff doesn't move to help him or ask us what's going on. Instead, it's business as usual with a special event taking place the next morning.

A throat clears, and I look down at my phone. "Did you get all that?"

"That's a presidential pardon if I've ever heard one. Miss Quintero, we appreciate your clear head in handling a delicate situation while your father has fallen ill. Our thoughts and prayers are with you."

"Gracias." She shaken but not backing down. Her chin is up and head held high. Her eyes are watery but at peace. "I apologize for the mix-up and wrongful arrest of my brother-in-law."

"He'll be released right away." I can make out my brother's voice in the background asking for a cigar and shot of Aguardiente before facing his wife.

"Thank you."

"Congratulations to you both, Patrones."

34

ALEJANDRO

SOLIMAR'S WALKING TOWARD me dressed in white.

She's a timeless beauty and a sweetness so pure that I ache in her mere presence. The satin dress with Swarovski beading across the sweetheart neckline is her something new: a pretty little number her mother had in the back of a closet and never wore, but saved for her. It's tight across the bodice, molding over every delicate curve of her skin, while the bottom flares out a tiny bit ending in a miniature train.

And while not a conventional wedding dress, on her it's perfection.

My little flower looks ethereal as she makes it down the aisle inside a large ballroom on the premises. The same one I kidnapped her from, with many of the same high-ranking members of Colombia's society in attendance then and now.

They're watching us and speculating. Murmuring to themselves why the Cortez family and hers is allowing such a union.

How can Quintero run the country and control me?

How could he release Emiliano, who stands beside me as my best man, and fight the war on drugs?

How will he keep their interests on top of every agenda?

The answer is easy: he can't. Dead men don't have a voice.

Solimar's eyes shift for a brief second toward her father and...

Nothing. No pity or love. No remorse or longing for a relationship he failed to nurture.

However, when those stunning greys meet mine again, they come alive. Bright and happy, and the hint of naughtiness behind them is a delicious promise for tonight. *Later. Much later.*

Veronica and her brother are giving her away, and neither turns to look at the once patriarch of their family. Not when he calls their name. Not when their grandfather sneers a few choice words.

He does shut up a few seconds later when Geronimo takes a seat beside him. *Pussy.*

"Who gives this woman to this man?" the priest asks, nervously swallowing.

"Her mother and brother do." Veronica's voice is strong, leaving no room for the questions sitting on the God-fearing man's tongue. This isn't a normal wedding, and its ending will never be forgotten. The three of them have made peace with what's to come. They've seen the evidence I turned in to the secretary of justice early this morning. "May God always bless this union, Mija."

"Thank you, Mom." They hug, wiping away the happy tears that have fallen. "I love you both so much."

"We know." Nudging her chin in my direction, Veronica smiles warmly at me. "Protect each other, and never go a day without saying I love you."

"You have my word; she'll always be safe with me." Slim fingers entwine with mine as her mother and brother find their seats on my side of the aisle in the same pew as my kin.

I bring her hand to my lips and kiss each knuckle. "You ready?"

"I've always been yours, Alejandro."

Together, we turn to face the priest. A united front.

He begins the service by reading a passage from the Bible about love and its unselfishness. About the purity of our union, and the blessing it is to find one's soulmate.

And while he talks and leads us into a prayer, I nod at the man entering the room from behind the officiant. He's tall and quiet and gives me a nod, letting me know all is in place. No one sees him walk around and then take his place off to the side, blending in with my guards and a few members of the state's military.

Solimar knows, though. You can see the resolve in those expressive eyes and the nerves begin to take control. I mouth the word *breathe* and she nods, thighs slightly rubbing together.

She has a weapon there. A wedding gift from me.

Strapped to her thigh is an all-gold Ruger I had designed for her small hand. My first of many wedding gifts, and when I presented it to her this morning, she giggled like a little girl with excitement.

"If anyone sees any reason why these two should not be wed, let them speak now or forever hold their peace." As the priest finishes his question, Lino walks in and removes her younger brother from the scene. He's injured. The bullet wound was thankfully a clean entry/exit, but he's not cleared to participate past this role.

There's a beat of silence that follows their exit before hell descends upon the room.

Her father and grandfather both stand, shouting to the room their hatred for me and my wife. They charge toward us while the Cortez duo sits and doesn't move an inch—biding their time to see if an escape is possible.

And I'll let them. Maybe.

"This hijueputa is a criminal and disgrace to our nation. He needs to be arrested." That comes from her grandfather, an older-than-dirt man charging the altar with an undignified expression marring his features. And he almost makes it to the edge, just a few steps shy, when the federal employee steps forward with a signed indictment in his hand, courtesy of the vice president.

He'll be in charge for the next three months until election day.

He'll step in and then disappear without a trace to a quaint little villa in Tuscany.

You see, no member of government is above the law, and our current president has a laundry list of infractions, from embezzling to the murder of innocent women in Thailand to sell everything from their organs to forced sexual acts while alive. Then, you have his attempt to take over my land and poppy production/sale.

He overstepped his bounds and will now pay the price along with his father.

The mid-morning news is already running the scandal along with the news of my marriage to Solimar Quintero.

"Jose Quintero, you are under arrest for the death of Mr. Lucas Sr. and the false imprisonment/confiscation of all his belongings."

"That's a lie! His father was a—"

"You are also being charged with tax evasion, fraudulent activity in your offshore accounts, and the physical abuse suffered by your granddaughter recently." The room has grown quiet, and a few have taken out their cell phones to record this humiliating moment. "Turn around, and hands behind your back."

He's lucky I haven't broken his leg in repayment for hurting Solimar—*yet*. I'll wait to personally visit him once he's inside and sleeping in a communal room.

"Do you know who I am? I will not be treated like this by some culicagado—"

"Hands behind your back, or we will use excessive force."

"You'll pay for this." That threat is for me, but it also sets off the shocked man beside him. Matias Quintero doesn't disappoint and reaches for the gun on Geronimo's holster, who just so happens to be distracted by the arrest happening near them.

His face is red, and sweat dots his temples. His hands are shaking, and his breathing is a bit choppy while pointing the barrel at my chest. "You will never walk out of here alive."

A gun goes off, but it isn't his.

A bullet pierces flesh, but it doesn't end his target.

All eyes turn to Veronica and the small black handgun in her grip. Her shoulders are tense and eyes hard. "You'll never hurt my family again. You'll never threaten to take them from me."

Her husband's shocked expression becomes vacant a few minutes later as blood continues to pour from the wound in his chest. The stain grows and some drops litter the floor below while his father is arrested amid cries of injustice.

And while the commotion clears and witnesses are told to vacate the premises, two of the four have indeed escaped. Too bad for them, I like the chase. To not play by the book as I've done with the other two.

They can run, but I'll catch up. Today. Tomorrow.

In approximately thirty-six hours…

It doesn't matter.

My attention is on my new bride. The woman I married at the rise of dawn in a private ceremony this morning before God and our family.

She's all that matters, and while things played out in a way designed to alleviate them of any guilt, I'm at peace. Jose will rot in jail. Matias will rot beneath the earth.

"Are you okay?" I ask, stroking a finger down her face after exiting the room. We're in a gathering room with her family close by, the justice department head running them through what's to come. "Tell me what you need, and it's done."

"That man stopped being anything to me years ago."

"Being upset is normal and—"

"I love you so much, Alejandro." The emotion and honesty behind those three words cause my heart to thump harshly inside my chest. Makes me feel one hundred feet tall. "Thank you."

"No need to thank me, Preciosa. Your needs will always supersede mine." I bring my lips down to hers, nipping the bottom before soothing the sting with the tip of my tongue. "My purpose in this life is to make you happy—protect you, and if I fail at either, then I don't deserve you."

"You more than deserve me." Solimar wraps her slender arms around my neck, pressing herself closer. "And if your purpose is to make me happy, then mine is to provide pleasure."

"Is that so, little flower? It's a dangerous offer to make."

"It is." She grips the hair at the back of my neck and pulls. The slight sting feels good. "And I have something special for you to take ownership of. A tight little hole that's begging for her strong husband to take and—"

Before she can finish, I have her thrown over my shoulder and I'm striding toward the exit. "Have a good day, and don't bother knocking because we won't answer."

"But we need to discuss what happened today. This is a crime scene, Mr. Lucas."

"Tomorrow we can discuss." The government employee's mouth opens, a rebuttal sitting on the tip of his tongue, but the look in my eyes ends that. "This is your only warning. Disturb me and my wife today, and I'll shoot you myself."

EPILOGUE #1

ALEJANDRO

T *hirty-six hours later...*

I GAVE THEM a head start because it amused me.

Because while my girl will never admit it aloud, I know that the death of her father hurts. To know he'll never repent, and that things were left unsaid, would leave a sour taste in anyone's mouth, but my little flower is moving forward.

They've gone to collect the body and buried him in a private ceremony at the family mausoleum. They cried, exchanged anecdotes of the early years where his humanity was still in place, and then she came home to me.

I loved her slowly.

Whispered my love.

Promised to always be there for her.

"Good evening, gentlemen." The two in question look up from their cement boxes, expression fearful. They've been begging to be released since arriving. They've bribed my men with wealth to give them safe passage back home.

And yet, Cortez father and son are still here.

Side by side and bodies covered by the concrete box they're kneeling in, I have access to their sun-blistered faces and a hole the size of a water hose. It's plugged tight and with no drainage. They're each set up with a personal watering system meant to remove the skin clean off their bones.

"How are you, Signio? Feeling better?" No answer. No eye contact. *Maybe he's lost his tongue?*

"Don Cortez, how about yourself? How's life treating you?"

This one has more life in him, his beady eyes narrowing to the points of slits while regarding me. "Why are you doing this? You already got the little slut...*fuck*!" His scream rings loud through the trees, echoing off the nearby grove and scaring away the birds relaxing at the top. They scatter as another pump of acid drains into the concrete box housing his near-naked body, falling over his flesh and melting down the skin and breaking down the muscle beneath.

"Go ahead. Insult her again." It's a dare met by silence. By tearful eyes and the horrid stench of his pain.

"Alejandro, I never wanted this. They forced me to chase and almost marry her, but my heart has always belonged to someone else." This I know to be true, but it didn't stop his ego from seeking revenge on a harmless woman for not being attracted to him. "Please. Please, Mr. Lucas, I beg you. Let me go back to—"

"No." Another scream, this time from the younger, and he's a blubbering mess by the time the three bursts of acid finished their initial harm. Signio is almost incoherent, and the area just below his jaw is raw from his struggles—the sharp cement rubbing and tearing at the base of his neck. "Again."

Both this time. Acid pours nonstop into their forever home, and the smell of decomposing human anatomy is sour. A rancid scent that one never forgets, and more so as those pitiful eyes stare at you and beg for mercy.

From the pain. From my wrath.

"No mas." Signio has the nerve to say no more, and I laugh. Geronimo and a recuperating Lino laugh.

It's hilarious how someone could beg for the mercy they never had when the shoe was on the other foot. The problem for them, I have no mercy. No remorse.

The only part of me that's still inherently good is waiting for me with my guests back at the main house. She is light and love and innocence. She's sweet temptation and heavenly touches.

Solimar is my salvation and demise all in the same breath. Moreover, I gladly give her that power.

"Patron, Miss Quintero requested we come back at noon, and it's fifteen till," Lino says, holding out his cell phone where my sister sent him a reminder text. They've become good friends since the night he rescued Lourdes, becoming a positive influence on her. He doesn't judge past mistakes. He supports and listens.

If anything, I see a little hope bloom in her spirit, and I'm keeping an eye just close enough to make sure neither gets hurt. The kid is one of the good ones, and I plan to keep him as my personal driver while Geronimo steps into his new role as my right-hand.

"Thank you." Turning to take a closer inspection of my guests, I catch the look they give each other and click my fingers. This time, the flow won't stop until the barrels feeding the line are depleted and they're left to soak in the poisonous substance.

It fills to the brim, a little spilling over the neck opening, and it's tinged with red. Heavy amounts of red.

Much better.

Leaning over so I'm at eye level with the side-by-side screaming men, I sigh. "I gave you a chance. I warned you to stay away, and yet you ignored me." Lino steps up and shoves a thick piece of wood into each of their mouths. Both men bite down, gnawing their teeth back and forth to the point lips are torn open and one loses a tooth. Slowly, they are dying as the acid eats away who they are and will leave behind a mess not worth horse shit behind. "This is what happens to those who stand against me, gentlemen. May the good Lord have more mercy than I did."

With that I turn around and walk away, leaving them to die alone and suffocating in their pain.

The ride back to the house is fast and bumpy with my cutting it so close, but the annoyed expression melts off my Preciosa's face when I walk in with ten seconds to spare. It's a pretty full house today as we entertain business associates: old and new. As a certain buyer comes with an offer I'm intrigued by.

Malcolm Asher sits in my outdoor terrace nursing a gin and tonic while his wife London, Mariah his cousin, and my Solimar discuss decorating the interiors for the upcoming holiday season. And while they go on and on about color schemes and what's popular, I focus on the man my cousin calls his *Boss*.

"My apologies for the small delay. I had something important that required my immediate attention."

Malcolm stands from his seat with an outstretched hand, smirking at me. "Those things tend to happen from time to time. No apologies needed."

Turning from him to Javier, I pull him in for a hug. "It's been a long time, cousin. Everything okay?"

"It is."

"She said?"

"Not yet," he hisses, looking over at the women who are too engrossed to care about what we do. "Soon, parce. Soon."

"Good." Sol hands me a drink and I look up in time to catch the question in her eyes. I nod, letting her know it's done. She gives me a minute head movement and retakes her seat, leaving me with two at-ease men with a file in front of them. "So, what brings you here today? How can I be of service?"

"I've purchased three of the largest pharmaceutical companies in the US within the last six months, Mr. Lucas. All will be run solely by me without a board of members, and I'm in search of top-quality product." He sits forward and pushes the envelope toward me. "In there is my proposal for your product and legal documentation showing that you are its owner and I'm merely a vendor. Look at it and discuss it with your wife. I'm more than open to negotiations and lenient on certain clauses."

"And what's in it for you?" I'm not going to waste my time reading this. Javier knows better than to waste my time and that this is not Chicago where Mr. Asher rules. "Give me your number?"

"Seventy-five/twenty-five, and you keep the higher percentage. And two, global dominion in its entirety. Everything people eat, drink, use, or simply indulge in will go through us."

"Us who?"

"The Imperium."

"I'll agree with one adjustment—"

"You want a cut of the bigger pie."

"Always."

"I had a feeling you'd say that, Mr. Lucas. We accept."

EPILOGUE #2

ALEJANDRO

F*ifteen months later…*

"FUCK, I LOVE YOU," I murmur against her lips, hips pumping in and out of her slowly. We're riding the high of our release, pulling from each other every last shiver while the water inside the tub splashes and drips over the rim.

It's a beautiful mess in this bathroom.

The result of holiday planning and hosting.

We're lost in each other while outside our bedroom door, our families are having dinner together downstairs. It's the day before Christmas Eve, our first shared holiday after I kept her to myself last year, and I'm tired of sharing her. Of someone needing her opinion on dishes and the spices used and what napkin to use with what ring.

At this point, we could eat empanadas using paper plates while sipping Postobon and I wouldn't care.

Is it rude of me? Yes.

Do I care? Fuck and no.

Not when my beautiful, pregnant wife goes out of her way to seduce me with every breath and batting of her eyes. With the way she bites her lips and finds every excuse possible to touch me.

My arm.

My back.

My cock when no one is looking.

There's nothing more decadent than making the sweet and inno-cent—hungrily corrupt.

Her innocence drew me in, but the promise of wickedness behind those grey eyes controls me.

"God, I needed that," Solimar moans, stretching her arms high and putting those perky tits at eye level, almost skimming my lips.

"Always so needy," I murmur against a stiff peak before taking it between my teeth, biting down hard enough to sting. She loves that, though. The taste of pain and pleasure. "Was this morning not enough?"

"That was an appetizer and you know it, Mr. Lucas." Solimar is looking at me from beneath long lashes, eyes hooded and hungry. She swivels those sensuous hips, and my cock responds by thick-ening inside her.

I'm always ready for her. No matter how many times.

"Kick them out and we can spend the next three days in bed." I release her and flick the tight tip. "There's still your dance studio to christen along with the downstairs media room. There are cameras to test and soundproofing to rate."

"And you say I'm the needy one." Her voice is breathy, body shivering at the thought of filming and watching in real-time.

"*Christ.* Is that why you added the one bar against the mirrors even though ballet isn't my specialty?"

"Guilty." Lazily, I pump in and out. "Besides, your old teacher—"

"Wait!"

"Something wrong? The baby?" I'm already standing with her still impaled, her legs around my waist as we exit the large, claw-foot tub my girl fell in love with during our stay in Miami. "Are you in pain? Talk to me, Preciosa."

"I'm okay, Papi, but what you said just brought back a memory."

"Don't scare me like that." Laying her down on our bed, I cover her body with mine, mindful of the baby bump. Chest to chest. My cock nestled tightly in her heat.

"Such a good husband. Always worrying."

"You and this little one are my priority." At my words, she clenches, pulling a hiss from me. Taunting little thing wants to play, but I'm curious about her jostled memory and take her slowly. My strokes are deep, controlling as I pin her hips to the bed and love her with no hurry. "Now, you mind telling me what's on your mind?"

"Now?" It's a keening little cry as I pull out, leaving just the tip inside. "Can we discuss this after?"

"No." Fisting my cock, I run the bulbous tip through her slit and circle her clit. "Tell me?"

"So frustrating," Solimar growls out and it's the sexiest little sound. A small hand slips over mine and pushes it aside, jerking me just how I like it. "All I was wondering is how you made it to the dance studio so quickly after the Gabriel incident? What happened after I left?"

"Why does it matter now." I'm gritting my teeth hard; her hand on me is exquisite. "Answer me."

"Curiosity—"

"Killed the cat." I pump my hips twice, savoring her tight hold. The way her fingers struggle to wrap around my girth. "Does it matter?"

"Tell me, Papi, and I'll make it worth your while."

"You're dangerous."

"And all yours." Those three words always unleash something in me that I can't control. Before her next intake of breath, I take control of both hands and place them above her head, slamming in to the hilt. My thrusts are fast—almost animalistic with my insatiable need for her.

She's changed my life. Brought peace and love, and the yearning to take her over the precipice of Nirvana burns deeper with each gyration. With each pump of my hips.

"Oh, God. Alejandro, I'm—" I cut her off with a searing kiss, taking her breath as my own and feeding it back. We're slick with sweat, bodies grinding, and when I slip a hand between us and skim a nail over her bundle of nerves, Solimar pulls her lips from mine and screams.

She's tight, wet heat.

She's my heaven and hell.

"Motherfucking mine," I grit out through clenched teeth as my orgasm slams into me and she milks my come. Every rope combines with her slickness creates a scent uniquely ours and I inhale deeply, closing my eyes as the last shivers rush through us. "Fuck, *I* needed that."

"I know you did." Sol cups my face, caressing my stubbly cheek with her thumb, and I look down at her. She's sated, face flushed and breathing a little choppy, and yet her expression holds a bit of amusement. "You've been growling at everyone for the past two days."

"I'm not someone who shares." No shame; I shrug. I'm also not going to mention that her grandfather is in a hospital in Bogota with two broken legs and a mouth without teeth at the moment. It was a Christmas gift to me, from myself via the use of his cane.

Same cane he used to hurt Solimar. *Piece of shit asshole.*

"Men," she huffs a laugh before raising a brow. "So, about that studio? Gabriel?"

"That's simple." Pulling out, I sit back and lay a possessive hand over her stomach. At only four months, it's small and round and perfect. "I bought the studio shortly after meeting you. And two, I shipped him back to his country with a few broken limbs and the kind suggestion to never return."

"Jesus. That's just..."

"The truth. I've never hidden who I am."

"I know." A pinking tint spreads across her cheeks, and it's not from my previous taking. "Is it horrible that I find those actions sexy?"

"Not at all. They just solidify what I've always known."

"And what's that?" Solimar bites her lip, her legs widening once more. Always so needy. Always so beautiful.

"That you were made for me."

OUTTAKE

Solimar

Dear Solimar,

I hope this letter finds you in a better place and away from the people who've hurt you, myself included. I'm sorry, prima. So sorry that I let myself get pulled into a stupid game of unfounded jealousy over a man not worth dog shit on the ground.

But this is all on me.

I made the mistake and forgot where my loyalties lie. I forgot who I am, and what I'll never allow myself to become again.

Please know that I didn't leave because of you, but because it's the right thing to do. I need to work on myself, be a better person before this little one is born. He—because I truly feel it's a boy—doesn't deserve to live his life with a woman who's more concerned with her looks than the well-being of her child. With someone so lost in her self-importance that she failed the one person who's always been there for her.

I love you, Sol. I love you and I've hurt you, and for that, I'll never be able to forgive myself.

Please be happy and hold on to the love you've found. He's a keeper.
A good man, and one day, I hope to be able to visit and see for myself
the beautiful life I know you'll build together.
Best wishes and all my love,
Laura.

"WHAT ARE YOU reading?" Alejandro asks, coming to stand behind me inside of my old room. We've been married since early this morning, a ceremony lit by the early morning sky and barefoot in the grand garden behind the presidential home. His mother and mine were there along with our siblings, everyone happy and excited over the joining of two families that refuse to be torn apart by greedy, worthless men.

It was the perfect ceremony.

What I've always dreamed of.

"Nothing. It's nothing," I moan low when his lips settle on my neck and pepper kisses up and down the expanse, nicking my collarbones before repeating the process. Because it *is* nothing and doesn't change a thing. And maybe in time I'll feel differently, but right now the only thing that matters and deserves my attention is this man.

Not someone who threw me away for a cheap thrill.

I've been wet for him since this morning, a needy little mess due to my desire to please and thank him for his love and devotion.

Because I see it. The stormy yearning that lives within us that consumes while nourishing our souls. We've always been meant to be, and I know that now. I breathe it in each time he looks at me.

It's in our touch. Our kiss. The way we make love, demanding more from the other, and then soothing the aftershocks.

We're always perfect, but tonight I want a little more. To explore something I know he wants.

It's my wedding gift to him.

Hands skim my right side and pull the zipper down. The fabric parts and falls, catching on my hips before I shimmy and then step out. There's something he doesn't know and I'm a little nervous, but before he reaches out to grab me, I step back.

"Sit." It's a command that he follows, taking a seat on an antique chaise lounge inside of what has been my bedroom for the last few years. Alejandro is watching me through hooded eyes, pulling off his wife-beater before leaning back and patting his lap. *Not yet.*

I want to make this last for him. Give him what he needs just as the beautiful man before me gave me half an hour to calm my nerves and relax before coming to find me once more. It was the opening I needed to read the note I found this morning addressed to me and check on my little surprise, the latter of which is making me drip down my thighs.

"You have exactly five minutes before I pin you beneath me, Preciosa. Make them count." This is a scene I've pictured before, fantasized about while touching myself to thoughts of him.

Always him.

"Hands behind your head, husband." I'm crawling up his body from the foot of the furniture to his hips, straddling right over his hardness and grinding down. "Don't move."

"Little girl, you have three minutes. Do your worst and then pray for mercy at my temple."

"I'll do a little more than that." Taking in a deep breath, I push up on my knees and stand. He's beneath me, looking up, devouring every single inch of my near-naked body with only a tiny white pair of panties covering my surprise.

This little pair is held by two delicate strings on each side, and when his eyes meet mine again, I pull. One tug and they fall, exposing my slick core to his hungry mouth.

He licks his lips and my thighs tremble. The thick bulge in his slacks peaks out from the undone waist, zipper open and no underwear beneath can be seen, which gives me easier access for what I have planned.

The muscles in his arms flex, and now the countdown is almost over. Alejandro's fighting the urge to grab me, to make me scream his name, but before he can, I turn around.

There's a hiss from him that follows, his thighs bucking up of their own accord, and I take that as my cue. Throwing a quick wink over my shoulder, I bend at the waist and tease the bulbous tip of his cock while beneath me his body freezes and breathing becomes labored.

Those hands that had been behind his head are now gripping my waist while the other explores. "Fuck me, Preciosa. This is a beautiful sight."

"It's all for you," I moan, hips swiveling as he pulls and pushes the plug in and out of my ass. "I'm ready for you."

"Baby, what you're offering is—"

"I want you to fuck my ass, Alejandro." No sooner has the last syllable passed through my lips than I find myself on my back atop the chaise with a beautiful warrior hovering over me. He's toying with me, testing the strength of each thrust of each entry, while I'm nearly clawing at the sheets.

I'm wet. Swollen. And near tears of frustration within the span of a few minutes and he knows this.

No one can read me as he does. No one can bring me pleasure but him, and I'm so turned on that the lube I used earlier to prepare me is nearly useless. My juices run down from my opening to the crack and then disappear where the toy is deeply lodged after his last push of the jeweled end.

"So motherfucking beautiful and mine." It's a growl, lip curling over his teeth a second before they latch on to my nipple and pull. The tug sends a shock of pleasurable pain to my pussy and I clench, trapping the plug where it is with a scream. "You want this, don't you? Want me to break you and then put you together again."

"Please!" I cry out, clawing his shoulders in an urge to get him to move. To come closer. "I'm ready for you. No foreplay or waiting." My grey eyes meet his hooded cognac ones. "Take what's always been yours…oh, God!"

I'm not sure when he pulled the plug or when his pants disappeared, but then he's there and I'm clenching for a different reason. Alejandro pins my legs back with his body while his cock seeks out my entrance, pushing the head in and then pausing as the tight ring of muscle clenches. He's bigger than the toy I've been using, thicker, and the indulgent sting takes my breath away.

"Talk to me, Preciosa. You okay?" Concerned eyes meet my lustful ones and whatever he sees makes him chuckle, the movement sending little bursts, of pleasure through my body.

And that's just the head. He's going to feel amazing.

"More. All of you."

"Are you sure?" As he says this, his hips thrust forward and a few more inches sink in, my muscles giving way to his strength. He's not halfway in and I feel stretched and full—every processor in my body is shooting off at the same time, and an overwhelming tingle forms at the tips of my toes and begins to run up my legs.

"Yes. Papi, don't make me beg." I wiggle beneath him and free his hold on my leg, wrapping them around his waist tightly, and urge him closer with the heel of my foot. That earns me a little more, a bigger thrust, and my eyes roll back. "It feels so good. My body is vibrating and I've...*oh God*!"

A swift stroke and he bottoms out, pinning me with both hands on my hips. "You going to come for me, little flower? My cock in your ass going to make you squirt?"

"What's happening to me?" The sensation is growing, and I feel warm, almost feverish as my body coils tight and my clit throbs. From the bottom of my feet to the very last strand of hair on my head, I'm sensitive and desperate and I don't know what for. All I am aware of is my need for this man.

"That's it, Sol. Squeeze again...just like that," he hisses out, grip tight and his thrust forceful. Deeper. Alejandro's riding me hard and using me for his pleasure, taking what he wants while giving me everything in return. "Motherfuck, baby. You're my heaven. All I'll ever need."

"I love you, Alejandro. Always." My eyes roll back and breathing becomes difficult, but it's when his right hand leaves my hip and slips between us that I lose focus. I've been fighting a losing battle since walking into this room, and the thread of coherency I fought to hold onto snaps. A single pass of his finger over my trembling bundle of nerves and I explode, crying out his name as my back arches and every limb in my body feels as though it's vibrating.

There's a rush of wetness that leaves me, and his responding growl shakes us.

His curses above me are like a prayer, and when his hips snap forward a final time, I'm hit with another wave of ecstasy.

I feel him coming inside me, and it's what I consider heaven on earth.

This is how I want to spend the rest of my life. With him. Loving him.

And I'll pray every night to grow old together with the love of my life beside me.

He is mine and I am his, and let no man separate what God has brought together.

I'm home.

THE END.

Now LIVE:
Beautiful Sinner
SIN
COVET
MINE
YOURS
MY SINFUL VALENTINE
RISQUE (Pre-Order)

Elena M. Reyes is the epitome of a Floridian and if she could live in her beloved flip-flops, she would.

As a small child, she was always intrigued by all forms of art: whether it was dancing to island rhythms, or painting with any medium she could get her hands on. Her passion for reading over the years has amassed her with hours of pleasure, but it wasn't until she stumbled upon fanfiction that her thirst to write overtook her world.

She's a short and sassy Latina with an adorable pup, a kiddo that keeps her on her toes, and a husband who claims she'll cause him to go bald prematurely. Lol

Want to keep up to date with Elena's crazy book life?
   Follow here:

Newsletter Sign Up: http://bit.ly/2nHJxTI
   Email: Reyes139ff@gmail.com

Elena's Marked Girls.
Come join the naughty fun.
Link: https://www.facebook.com/groups/1710869452526025/

facebook.com/AuthorElenaMReyes

twitter.com/ElenaMReyes

instagram.com/elenar139

bookbub.com/authors/elena-m-reyes